CW00500485

To Ann
X
Love
Raymond
('Tom East')

THE GREENLAND PARTY

Tom East

Benybont Books

https://www.benybont.org/

First published 2019

This is a work of fiction. Names, characters, and incidents are the product of the author's imagination. 'Vatsaaq' and 'Eqalassaq' are fictional. Most of the other places named are real but are used fictitiously. Any resemblance to actual events is entirely coincidental.

ISBN 978-1-9164942-4-4

To Suki, Joseph, Edmund, Ping and Annabella

ACKNOWLEDGEMENTS

I am grateful to JOYCE JAMES and to the members of the former 05 Group (at the time JEAN BARRACLOUGH, JAN DAVIES, PAT FORSTER, ROWLAND HUGHES, CAROL JONES and DOMINIQUE SPEAREY) for their helpful comments and suggestions on the text.

The Greenland Party

Chapter One
The Ice Queen

Sunday, 28th August, 1994, Vatsaaq, East Greenland

'I still can't think why there should be three blocks of ice in the pool down there. The big one is far larger than anything I've seen at any season. And there's something unusual about its coloration. See there.'

Harry glanced up gingerly to see where Lars was pointing. His gaze had been fixed on the small pool during the earlier part of their descent, although when they'd reached the steepest part of the downward incline he'd been forced to give all his attention to the treacherous path. He could see the blocks were tracing out a circular motion in the pool, the other two revolving around the central one as if all were members of a frozen solar system. The largest was indeed semi-opaque. He didn't know what to expect in terms of colour, though was surprised to see it was strongly yellow-hued.

They descended more slowly from that point. The ice-block began to take on a strange rosiness as the sun's rays struck it directly. As they reached ground level they could see this was caused by an object apparently inside the ice. Before they'd half-crossed the "pasture" of pink flowers, not nearly so lush as it had appeared from a distance, they both knew what the object was. Neither wanted to put this knowledge into words.

Not until they reached the edge of the pool did Lars break the unstated pact of silence between them, unnecessarily announcing 'It's a body'.

The large block was revolving almost imperceptibly as they watched. At the same time it was drifting slowly nearer to where they stood. The body was in some odd way fixed behind the ice. Neither of them wanted to walk around the pool to see more.

They watched in fascination as the motion gradually revealed the secret of the ice. First, it became clear the person was naked. It was a woman. Then, even through the thickness and distortion of the ice, they could see the figure was extraordinarily full. Finally, the ponderous rotation brought the woman's whole form into view. Her forearms seemed actually to be locked into the ice. It was as if she were clasping it to her. The sight was grotesque.

Suddenly, a sliver of ice flaked off and the block tilted in the water, causing her head to flop sideways in a way startling to them both. Now there could be no mistaking the over-florid complexion, still pink despite the chill, nor the broad head and slightly coarse features, nor the halo of yellow hair framing the lifeless stare. Crystals of ice and unmelted snow flecked her hair in a pattern giving the grim parody of a crown.

'Essie!'

Harry's cry was involuntary. He tried to analyse his own reaction. Did it sound like a personal rather than a professional or simply human one?

Reluctant to look toward his companion, he kept his gaze fixed on the still-revolving iceberg, aware Lars had stolen a sideways glance at him. He hoped the young man would say something to break the silence hanging between them in the cold air. Lars held his peace. Harry was forced to speak again, trying to control the tremor in his voice:

'It's Mrs Smith, Lars. Essie Smith, from our party. How on Earth...? We've got to get the police. How do we do such a thing here?'

Lars still said nothing. Like Harry, he seemed to find it difficult to drag his stare away from the ice and the horror it framed. When he did turn to Harry, his expression was almost sheepish.

'I am the police.'

'You're what?'

'Not a full-time policeman. I am like the, what did you call them? – specials – you told me about in your country. I'll need to call in someone from Ammassilak or Godthåb – Nuuk – to do the full autopsy. To take over the investigation as well, most probably. They'll be sure to want to do the post-mortem in Greenland rather than Denmark , if our laboratory is ready. It was supposed to be opening this year, but I'm not sure. There's never been a need for me to think about things like this.

'Maybe, since Ms Smith was a visitor to this country they'll need to call on the Institute of Forensic Medicine in København. I don't know. These things are all mixed up in what you would call "post-imperial politics". At all events, until they fly someone into Vatsaaq, this has to be my case. I have to do what I can to investigate. If only I knew how to go about it! At the moment I can't even think why her arms should be embedded in the ice. I have to find out what I can before the evidence gets cold.'

Harry winced at his friend's careless choice of words. Looking at him, he could see Lars had not realised the darkness of what he'd said. His lips were trembling as he struggled to speak again. Harry guessed what he was going to say:

'Harry, I want you to help me. I don't know what to do. I've never been involved in any kind of major crime. A few drunks and some petty pilfering are all I've ever had to deal with. But this…' The Dane's face was pale.

'Lars, I'm not a policeman any longer. I'm retired. I want nothing more to do with any kind of police work. This isn't even my country. There must be protocols. Essie is – was – a British Citizen. I can't help. I'm sorry.'

'But Harry, you're still a detective at heart. At least you'd know a detective's ways. You will know what to do.'

Harry groaned inwardly. This was the last thing he wanted. He'd meant what he'd said about wanting nothing more to do with police work. He knew he'd never been much of a policeman, even before the drink problem took hold. And he'd had no experience of murder cases, as this one surely had to be.

'Harry –?'

Lars' voice quavered. Harry sighed. He was involved anyway, as a witness, as one of the discoverers of the body. And something about the sight of Essie's corpse clinging to the ice told him he wouldn't be able to simply walk away from this scene.

'When do you say that the police will send someone in from Ammassalik?'

'They'll fly someone in by tomorrow. Maybe even this evening'.

'OK, then, I'll help'.

'Harry!'

'On one condition. You, Lars Erikssen, are the investigating officer. You make all the decisions. I'll help and advise you, but that's all I'm going to do. Now, tell me exactly what it is you want from me.'

Immediately, Lars became more relaxed. He almost sounded confident as he spoke. 'First we must remove the body from the pool,' he said. 'The ice will not melt enough to free her arms for hours yet, but we should act before the direct sunlight falls too much on the ice or the warmer water from the underground stream starts to do its work. We will need help to get the corpse and the ice from the water. This is bigger than any ice-block I've seen here.'

'Are you sure it won't start to melt soon? ' asked Harry.

'It won't properly melt for a long time, even in water like this. This pool is one of the things I wanted to show you in this special part of our country this morning. I've found nowhere else in Greenland remotely like it. The water in the pool is not hot but nor is it cold, either. It is – what is the word?'

'Tepid?' suggested Harry.

'Yes, that is the one. The inflow of water from the undergound thermal stream is rapid. This pool would be much bigger if it didn't drain away at the bottom, somewhere near its middle. After this, the flow of the ice merges with the underground stream and then goes out to sea, though nobody knows exactly where the outflow is. My plan was to get you to put your hand into the pool, so you could feel the temperature of the water. Perhaps – ?'

Harry realised with a shudder Lars was going to suggest he went ahead and felt the water anyway. The thought filled him with revulsion. He interrupted the almost leisurely explanation.

'We need to get on with things, Lars.'

'You are right. One of us should go back to Vatsaaq to get help, while the other stays here to keep watch. It'd be best if I go back. I'd be quicker. Gudrun can break the news to the rest of your your group. Do you mind waiting here?'

'No, that's fine,' said Harry, reassured by Lars' returning confidence and readiness for positive action. 'Anything else you want me to do?'

'Well; you could look around for clues while you're waiting.'

'I think "evidence" would be the word you want. But yes, I'll have a scout around while you're gone to see if I can pick up anything to help with your investigation.

"Your investigation", I said, Lars. And don't worry, I'll take care not to disturb any evidence'.

'Thank you, Harry. Here; you'd better take this.'

Lars pulled out his whisky flask from a deep side pocket and handed it to Harry. Then, without another word, he turned and ran off lightly toward the path leading to the escarpment, retracing their steps of a short while before. When he reached the incline, Lars started to make the ascent almost at jogging pace. Not for the first time that morning, Harry smiled with rueful envy at the energy of the young.

Then he looked back towards the corpse. The smile quickly faded from his lips.

This holiday had been a nightmare. In Iceland, in the pool in Selfoss, things had started to go wrong between himself and Vonnie. Then he'd made things so much worse by his drunken behaviour last night. Now this. The crime was going to be more demanding than anything he'd had to deal with in working life, even if Lars had assured him his involvement would be brief.

The others had amused themselves by christening last night with the name they'd previously given themselves as a tour group, "The Greenland Party". Party! For Harry it had been a frenetic drinking bout, with himself demolishing whisky and goodness knew what else as if he'd been tring to set a world record.

Well, no more of it. He pushed Lars' half-full flask into his own side pocket, resolving to leave it there unopened as a silent talisman.

Chapter Two

The Greenland Party

Saturday, 13th August, 1994, Keflavik Airport, Iceland

Keflavik Airport, Iceland, midnight and rain. The skies still showed traces of grey daylight but were heavy with low cloud. It was not the sort of welcome promised in the glossy pages of the 1994 brochure from Icesperience. The people on the minibus were growing restless with their gloomy wait.

'So why the exra delay then? Bad enough to have a late flight. We should have been in't rooms by now.' The overweight man with the thick bottle-top glasses voiced the collective thought of the waiting passengers in a broad Lancashire accent.

'It seems there's a problem with someone's luggage. It must be that tall chappie from Reading and his wife. I'm Doris Clatworthy, by the way.'

The opportunity presented by the neatly-dressed elderly lady to open up a conversation was not taken up by any of the other people on the bus. Nothing dismayed, she tried again, standing up and raising herself to her full five feet and one inch to make sure everyone could hear what she said:

'Doris Clatworthy. I live in Norwich. I'm a retired college lecturer. Everyone calls me Dainty. Can't think why that should be.' The quick smile she cast in the direction of the man sitting nearest to her obliged him to make some response from his seat, although he plainly resented the intrusion into his glum silence:

'Melvyn Walters. From Great Malvern in Worcestershire. That's where my wife and I live now. This is Maggie.'

'I can speak fer mesel' Mel.' Mel Walters companion was an energetic and confident-sounding young woman. She was at least ten or fifteen years younger than her husband. She rose from her seat to speak. 'Maggie

Walters. Pleased to meet yàll. Ye'll guess I'm from North of your Border. Aberdeen – that's well North o' the Border as ye'll know. Me and Mel were in Edinburgh before we moved to Great Malvern.'

'All right Maggie,' said Melvyn Walters. 'You don't have to give everyone a full biography.'

'An' I'm a runner,' continued Maggie Walters in defiance of her husband. 'I plan to do loads of running while we're in Iceland and Greenland.'

The rules of the game had been set. One by one they made their introductions. It all sounded a bit stiff and formal, but the ice was slowly starting to melt between the holidaymakers, even though, if anything, the skies were now heavier than they'd been a few minutes before.

'Anthony Ferris. From Flint. In North Wales. I work in pharmaceuticals. ' The obligatory information duly delivered, the awkward, sharp-featured man shrank back into his seat. He was clearly anxious for the spotlight to fall on someone else.

'Jeremy Smith, from Essex; Chelmsford to be exact. I work in one of our local banks. I'm the manager, as it happens.' The speaker was the man who'd been sitting closest to the driver's seat. He had almost film-star good looks but his expression was serious. He even seemed a little embarrassed as he spoke, blushing slightly. 'And this –'

'What is it with you men? We women can speak for ourselves, you know. I'm Essie, Essie Smith from Chelmsford.' Essie Smith was plumpish with a florid complexion topped off by a striking mane of yellow hair. She was about forty, but there was something much younger about her manner. This at least was the impression anyone on the bus could see she was trying hard to give.

'Aye, I've always wanted to meet an Essex Girl,' said the thick-set man who'd first spoken. He paused to wait for Essie Smith's mock-girlish laughter. This arrived on cue, to his obvious satisfaction. 'What I don't understand,' he continued. 'Is why we couldn't all get on't other bus. There were plenty o' seats free. Freddie Tanner I am, by the way. Living in Hastings down on't South Coast, these days. But I've lived in lots o' places, me. Some of 'em you wouldn't want to know about.' He winked broadly as he said these words. At this seeming sharing of a confidence, Essie Smith laughed shrilly. Everyone else remained impassive and the company lapsed back into an awkward silence.

'I'll tell you about 'em one day, Lass,' said Freddie Tanner, leaning forward, addressing the blonde woman directly.

'I think, young man, that the reason we're all on this bus has something to do with the particular trip we've all booked'. Doris, or Dainty, Clatworthy was ready with another explanation. 'The other people who flew from Heathrow with us are staying for two weeks in Iceland. We're with them for the first week. Then we're the ones who'll be off to Greenland for another three weeks. I believe I'm right in saying that.'

'Aye, seven of us for Greenland, then. Doesn't seem many, Dainty girl.'

'Nine, actually.' She didn't seem perturbed by Freddie Tanner's familiarity. 'You're forgetting the two still in the terminal building. Mr. Lanier and his wife from Reading. I was talking to them on the way over in the aeroplane,' she added, obviously feeling the need to justify the source of her knowledge. 'They seem a very pleasant couple indeed.'

'Ee, you're a mine of information, lass. Mebbe you can tell us what's holding them up all this time?'

'Well, no, but I know a man who can,' she replied, smiling. 'Or a woman, at any rate. That courier lady is coming out of the terminal building now.'

All eyes turned right and watched the brisk approach of the woman from Icesperience. They could see there were tiny beads of rain in her frizzy hair, but the moisture hadn't dampened her enthusiasm in any way. She bounded onto the minibus and started to speak almost without a pause for breath, her pale grey eyes flickering over the passengers' faces.

'Good evening, ladies and gentlemen. I am Gudrun Jonsdottir. Please to call me Gudrun. I am sorry that you are waiting still. But I have news that your fellow-travellers will soon be able to join us. Meanwhile, on behalf of The Icesperience Travel Company, I would wish you welcome to our country of Iceland. I will now remind you again of your itinerary.

'You will be staying just ouside the town of Selfoss, not so far from here, for four nights. We will see many special things: Geysir and Strokkur; Thingvellir; Thórsmörk; beautiful waterfalls like Gullfoss and Dettifoss. Tomorrow we will visit Grindavik fishing village, also to bathe in the thermal pool at Selfoss. The next day we will be visiting the famous Blue Lagoon. Towards the end of our stay in Iceland we spend some time, two days, at Lake Myvatn in the north before you come back for your last day in Reykjavík.'

She waited, more to let the others take in some breath than to do so herself. Then she resumed her accelerated speech.

'You will wish to be staying for the whole month in our Iceland. It is so beautiful a country. Everybody says this. But do not worry, I shall be coming with all of you in one week's time to Greenland to look after you there. We will have two days in the capital, Nuuk, and four at Aasiaat for you to see the famous Disko Bay. Then, before you go further North to Ittoqqoortormiit to perhaps try some dog-sledding – we will be sure to find plenty of snow for you even at this time of year – you have a real adventure for ten days in Eastern Greenland, in a little settlement called Vatsaaq.'

'Sounds exciting,' giggled Essie. 'Any polar bears?'

Gudrun looked in her direction and raised a single eyebrow.

'You will be unlikely to see bears except on the ice-floes still drifting down the east coast at this time of year. All of the wild animals stay away from people if they can. Seals, musk-oxen, yes; arctic hares and foxes you might see at this time of year also. If you are lucky you may even be seeing a herd of reindeer. But the real adventure is that you will be staying in a Greenlandic village, with Greenlanders. Yours will be the first tourist group to visit this new holiday place. I myself have never before visited Vatsaaq.'

'I thought you were supposed to be our guide. How can you expect to guide us if you don't even know the place?'

Melvyn Waters spoke with unnecessary gruffness, and the other members of the group looked around awkwardly. Gudrun herself was quite unruffled and answered sweetly.

'In Greenland you will have a local guide as well as myself. He is Lars Erikssen, a Danish man who has lived in Greenland for many years. He will meet us in Nuuk. His home is now in Vatsaaq, so you could have no better guide. You will all like Lars. I met him in Nuuk when we were setting up this new tour. And now,' she said, looking triumphantly toward the terminal building. 'Here I think come the other two members of your party.'

Everyone watched expectantly as the newcomers crossed the wet tarmac and mounted the steps of the bus. The man was tall and broad, and the minibus seemed cramped with four of the five men now on it being large-framed. Like the men already seated, the first newcomer was dark-haired, though of a more distinguished appearance. No one would have said that he approached the good looks of Jeremy, the youngest man, however. He was about fifty, a little above the average age of those present, taking into account Gudrun's youth and Dainty's advanced years. Following him was a woman of around the same age. She was petite, cheerful-looking and quick of movement.

'Is everything well now, Mr. Lanier?'

The man's expression showed he thought everything was far from being well, but Gudrun's smile disarmed him and he answered gently enough.

'Not really. Seems one of our suitcases has somehow found its way to Gothenburg. Gothenburg! We won't get it back here before Monday at the earliest. And my swimming-trunks are in that case. It's a bit of a nuisance – we're going to that Lagoon place tomorrow, aren't we?'

'Tomorrow we will be visiting the thermal pool in Selfoss. On Monday we are due to see the Blue Lagoon. The shops in Selfoss are closed on Sunday, Mr. Lanier, I am sorry to tell you. But, if you do not mind wearing borrowed trunks, I am sure that something can be done for tomorrow.'

'It's all right by me. Thank you. Well, we'd better get this show on the road.' He looked around apologetically. 'I'm sorry folks. We didn't mean to keep you all waiting.'

'Play it by the rules then, lad,'.

Harry Lanier looked at Freddie Tanner in surprise. 'I'm sorry?'

'You're supposed to tell us your name. Then you tell us what town you come from. Then you start to introduce your wife, but she interrupts you and does it herself. It's a kind of game.'

'I see.' Harry looked quizzically at Freddie Tanner. Then he relaxed and allowed himself a smile. 'I'm Harry Lanier. Swansea is where I was born, but my family moved to Tilehurst when I was just a nipper. Now I live in Reading itself. And this is is –' he gestured extravagantly towards the woman standing behind him.

'Yvonne Lanier. Everybody calls me Vonnie. I'm from Southend originally.'

'Ee,' said Freddie Tanner. 'Another Essex Girl. Welcome to the Greenland Party, Lass.'

Chapter Three
Nanoq

Sunday, 28th August, 1994, Vatsaaq, East Greenland

Harry sat on a rock by the side of the pool, awaiting the return of Lars. Qooroqilulissat was its name, as well as that of this whole area, it seemed. Despite the nausea he was still feeling, he couldn't help whispering the word to himself through dry lips. He took pride at the beginning of his comfort with the language. Greenlandic words looked jaw-wrenching on paper, but had a mellifluous quality. They rolled off the tongue without too much trouble if you could be bothered to attempt the necessary tricks with your lips and to make an effort of memory.

It seemed an age since this morning when he and Lars had been crunching along the black sand of the small cove off Vatsaaq Bay, before climbing the escarpment. Lars was no talker but, when he had something worth saying, he could be as eloquent as the next man. His eyes would take on a dreamy expression when he was talking about the sights and smells of his adopted country. The Dane was carrying on a love affair with Greenland.

Harry could understand this. There was an other-worldly beauty wherever you looked. Still, the bluish cast to the atmosphere given by the short wavelength of the light could be a bit disconcerting until you became used to it – assuming you ever could, that was. Now, sitting here alone, his senses numbed into a milder version of the pulverised feeling they'd known earlier, everything had been changed by the horror they'd found floating in the pool.

Anyone would have agreed it made sense for Lars to have been the one to go back to Vatsaaq for help. This was the only choice they could make. Lars would have been able to run back much more quickly than Harry could plod. He knew this.

All the same, Harry wished the Dane hadn't had to leave him here alone for quite so long by the side of the pool under the pale sky. He loved the vast silences of this country almost more than anything else about it but, at this moment, he could have done with some living human companionship.

It wasn't that he was unused to corpses; he'd seen more than his share of them in his time with the Traffic Division. Many were in a far worse condition than Essie. In fact, the quick inspection he'd tried to make of the body as it gently floated by had told him there were few blemishes on her body save for some ugly bruising around the throat. That cursory examination was all he'd been able to manage. Now, he was trying to steel himself to glance around once more.

The expression on her face was the worst thing. This still burned in his mind. The anger frozen onto her features told its own story of her last moments. He was now uncomfortably aware of Essie sightlessly glaring at his back. He imagined he could feel her gaze boring into him. This discomfiting knowledge, rather than any real desire to look for evidence, at last made him make the effort to rise from his seat on the rock.

A weariness had descended upon him and seeped into his bones. He would have given anything to rest for a few moments longer. After all, Lars and whoever else he'd be bringing to the valley could as easily look around for themselves.

When at last he did manage to scramble to his feet, something – he couldn't have said exactly what it was – did make him look around at the body again. The slow rotation of what he couldn't help thinking of as an iceberg had altered the position of the corpse. Essie stared fixedly, and her large mouth was slightly open, as if she were about to say something.

Harry couldn't help letting his glance rest on her extraordinarily full, shapely breasts, just beneath the water's surface. Doing this made him feel like the worst kind of voyeur and he looked guiltily around him, even though no-one was there to see the shame on his face. The thought that he was doing something contrary to nature was enhanced by the clarity and crispness of the Greenland sky and by the absolute peace and quiet about him.

He tore his gaze away from this tableau, forcing himself to search for what he could find on the ground. There appeared to be nothing unusual; not even the tyre-tracks and footprints that should have been visible if the body had been brought here in a vehicle. It surely must have been. He could see nothing beyond the few light impressions left by Lars and himself this morning.

Then, as he followed further back along the path of the finger-glacier, Harry was able to find a set of deep tyre-tracks coming to a halt about thirty metres away. From this point a heavy set of footprints was clearly visible. They led to and from the side of the glacier-like object – Lars had insisted it wasn't a real glacier, only a strange miniature of one, perhaps a lost finger formation from the massive one visible in the distance.

It didn't take him long to work out what must have happened. Someone, a large or at least broad-footed man by the look of the prints, had brought Essie's body here in a vehicle. Then, whoever it was had carried the corpse to the ice-formation and clambered up its side. From the spot where this unknown person had disposed of it, the body must have been swept down into the pool. It didn't entirely make sense, but this had surely taken place much sooner than the man – it could only have been a strong man – had intended.

A faint engine-noise sounded at some distance behind him and he looked around to see a solitary Land Rover approaching. As it drew nearer, Harry could distinguish no-one except the outline of the driver of the vehicle. Then he could make out Lars sitting behind the wheel. He was alone. How on Earth was he expecting to remove Essie's body from the pool?

*

'Harry! I am sorry to leave you here by yourself for so long,' shouted Lars, slamming the door of the Land Rover. He walked quickly over. 'It was a long way to run, all the way back to Vatsaaq. And once there I decided to have a look around. But my time in the settlement was useful. Already I have been able to find out much.'

'You've come on your own with only the Land Rover?' said Harry. 'How are we possibly going to –' For a moment Harry had nightmare visions of the two of them driving back to Vatsaaq with the corpse in its block of ice somehow wedged into the back seat behind them.

'Olaf has taken one of the transporters to pick up Silumi and Ikateq so they can perform the necessary tasks under my instruction. He will have to walk part of the way to reach the spot where they are working so we won't see them for an hour yet. Now tell me; what you have been able to discover while I have been away?'

Harry, struggling to control his gurgling innards, managed to speak in a clear way. He tried to answer Lars as if he were a policeman giving an informal report to a senior officer.

'It looks to me as though Essie – Mrs Smith – was brought here in a heavy vehicle. The driver, or at any rate the only person of whom I have been able to find any trace of in this valley beside ourselves, parked the vehicle back there where the trail ends and manhandled the body, presumably to the top of the glacier – it is easier for me to call it that, Lars. Then, later, it would have been swept down by some natural force. This would surely be the stream you told me of that runs into the thermal pool. Whoever carried the body must have been a strong man. Essie Smith is – was – no lightweight.'

Lars nodded to Harry.

'One of the goods vehicles we have in the settlement was used last night. There is no forensic evidence to be lost, do not be concerned.'

He continued.

'I told you I did some investigation on my own account. There are only four vehicles in the settlement. These are my own Land Rover and the three larger vehicles. I reasoned one of the transporters would have been used. The fourth vehicle is of a more luxurious design with seating. It is primarily, or or is intended to be, for tourists.

'The newer goods vehicle – the one you will shortly see Olaf driving – the passenger transporter, and my Land Rover all have steering-locks fitted and the keys are kept locked in my safe. A brief look at the fourth vehicle told me it had been parked in a different position, and more carelessly, than when I had driven it myself yesterday. I'd left the ignition keys in it. We often do this. Silumi, Ikateq and occasionally some of the other Inuit often use this transport in their own duties or for their own odd-jobs. Also, I was able to find a few specks of blood on the older vehicle. Do not worry; I have seen to it they are protected for later analysis. But they will have come from our victim, I am sure of this.

Lars' expression grew more serious.

'We are hardly equipped for such things here, but I did a crude – what do you call it? – scenes of crime investigation. There were clear signs of a struggle about three-quarters of the way between the tourist cabins and the old Inuit settlement. I'd assume a rock – there are a great many of them littering the ground at this point – was used on the poor woman's head. This must be what caused the small amount of bleeding, I'm sure. I think this may be the only wound on the body, besides the bruising around the throat. Were you able to see any other injuries?'

'No.' Harry was telling the truth. He hadn't been able to look closely. He didn't even know there was a head injury as well as the bruising around the throat.

'I don't think we'll be able to find the rock that caused the fatal blow. There are so many in that area. The killer may even have disposed of the one he used. All the same, I'll get Silumi and Ikateq to make a systematic search later. Knud Holm – this is the name of the full-time detective who'll come from Ammassalik – will want to be assured we've done as much as we can. He can be a little – what is your word? – pedantic in his ways.

'There were also a few specks of blood on the ground, so I took some photographs and have protected the area. We can't check the blood type ourselves, although I'm sure we'd find the group will match that of Ms Smith. I'm afraid my forensic investigation has been limited to those few things. I don't have the equipment or knowledge to do much more.'

Harry was impressed by what Lars had achieved in a short space of time. And after running all the way back to Vatsaaq.

'There wasn't much more you could have done, Lars. The footprints I found back there were well-defined,' said Harry, indicating the edge of the glacier. 'It was clear enough they were made by a large man. From the depth of the prints, he must have been burdened with something heavy. It looks as though he somehow climbed the side of the glacier, although I'm afraid I couldn't work up the nerve go to have a look.'

'This is not something you should attempt while you are alone, so I'm glad you didn't try. But well done Harry,' said Lars. 'I'll take some photographs before we leave. Everything you have found ties in with my own enquiries.'

*

'I think you like it here, my friend, for all our bad ways,' said Lars, now relaxing while they waited for the promised help to arrive. 'I'm not sure this would be true of the others of your party.The best I could hope is they will tell me they have not yet made up their minds. What do you say? How about your wife, Madam Vonnie, for instance?'

'Vonnie? Oh, she gets along anywhere. Besides, it was her idea to come on this holiday.'

'Her idea?'

'Yes. Well, I've always made a habit of leaving the planning to her. She loves it, but honestly, I could never be bothered. This time, I didn't see things as being any different, even though it was supposed to be the special one.

'One day she said to me "Iceland; what about Iceland?" And I said, "Why not?" All the time I had the thought, at the back of my mind, that this early retirement wouldn't come off. I was sure they wouldn't really want me to go. It was only talk among the higher-ups as far as I was concerned. So I left all the details to Vonnie, as usual. Somewhere along the line Iceland became Iceland and Greenland.'

He gave a short, bitter laugh.

'Well, it seemed the Force did want me to go after all. They really did want to be rid of me. They made it plain enough. The buggers all but kicked me out, after more than thirty-five years' service without blemish. Just because... But never mind. It's history.'

Harry stopped himself from saying more. He looked over the ruggedly beautiful landscape, although this time without seeing it. Now he was thinking that never before had he spoken to anyone so directly about his reasons for leaving the police, not even Vonnie. Up until now, he'd always wrapped his bitterness in the cosy word 'retirement' and kept his true feelings to himself. Keeping feelings close to his chest was something he'd been used to doing as a copper. Strange not to have to do it any more. Strange not to be a copper any more.

Harry was grateful Lars hadn't pursued the subject of the whisky-flavoured reason for his departure from the Force. Maybe he'd tell him at another time more about the good and bad times he'd had. The young man knew how to listen.

*

'One of the other things I should do when we…'

Lars didn't get the chance of finishing what he was doing to say. Harry pointed toward a heavy six-wheeler pulling a trailer rattling into view further down the trail. Neither Harry or Lars said anything more as in silence they watched the vehicle drawing up and parking next to the Land Rover.

Three men stepped out. There was a fair-haired, moustachioed Dane Harry knew by sight and two Inuit he recognised from the drunken party last night. He had a vague idea they'd been sitting in the smaller room of the Great Hall and both had liked his whisky, but his memories of the night were hazy.

'This, Harry, is Olaf. He is my good friend as well as my assistant.'

He now remembered he'd seen the blond Dane around the settlement when they arrived. The man kept well to the background, saying nothing but smirking to himself as if he were enjoying a private joke at the world's expense. Harry hadn't taken to him. Still, he now stepped forward to shake Harry by the hand in a friendly enough way. Perhaps he'd unfairly judged him from slight acquaintance.

'And these are Silumi and Ikateq. They speak little English.'

They favoured Harry with the slightest of nods, making no attempt to step forward to shake hands. Then they turned back to Lars. He didn't address them directly, but spoke to Olaf in simple English terms. This would be for his own benefit, Harry realised, though it did tell him the other Dane was also quite at home with the English language.

'…OK, Olaf. You know what to do,' concluded Lars.

Harry had been listening to Lars' instructions and also knew too well what the three men were about to do. The man named Silumi returned to the trailer and came back with a large piece of sacking and a length of stout rope. Harry was careful to position himself facing Lars, with his back to the pool and trailer. Now he was all too aware of the emptiness in his stomach. The nauseous feeling he had known a few hours ago had returned with a vengeance.

'You do not wish to see this? And I do not blame you, Harry my friend,' said Lars.

'We will have a more detailed look at everything when we return. There is more for me to do in Vatsaaq yet. You will understand now I must talk to all the members of your tour party, so I may as well start with you. You will have had plenty of time to reflect on your own movements of last night, say from eleven o'clock until three in the morning. Can you account for those hours?'

Harry remained silent. How was he going to explain to Lars that, in his memory, the crucial time was nothing more than an alcoholic fuzz?

3.2

Harry's reaction when Lars persisted with his questions had driven a wedge between them. This made for an uncomfortable drive back to Vatsaaq. He found it simplest to maintain what he hoped was a dignified silence. All the time, he kept his attention on the trail. This at first followed the rough road running westwards parallel to the Bay. The direction of their route seemed to be taking them further from the settlement.

This, it dawned on him after a while, was to avoid the rugged terrain to the south. Earlier, they'd been able to pick their way on foot across this uneven land, but there was no way even vehicles with off-road capabilities like these two could have made the more direct journey over that sort of ground. His thinking must have been correct. After travelling for at least four miles westwards, the track suddenly hairpinned around some craggy outcrops of rock, then headed south-east, back in the direction Harry expected.

Harry looked at the young Dane anew. He'd have to get used to thinking of Lars as a policeman now. What he'd said to him was right. Of course the young man had need to ask questions of everyone. It was all a matter of simple elimination. This had to be basic police work in any country, even one as remote and strange as this.

The principles would apply even to an officer as occasional as the Dane. Harry could understand this well enough. And yet something about the directness of Lars' questioning had taken him by surprise and nettled him. His abrupt manner had made things uncomfortable between them. Perhaps even someone who was as part-time a policeman as Lars couldn't afford to have real friends.

The Dane seemed happy enough to keep his own counsel. He was giving all his attention to driving. He was keeping a carefully uniform twenty-yard distance between their Land Rover and the larger vehicle ahead of them. Thankfully, Essie's body was covered by the sacking on the trailer. Under this, Harry could imagine her in that awkward arms-forward pose. It was apparent that the ice she embraced was already starting to melt, despite the earlier assurance given by Lars. The sacking was wet; there was a constant and disturbing drip-dripping of water. Despite all the efforts he was making, Harry's eyes, now blurring occasionally from his excesses of last night, were being drawn continually back to this sight.

They were nearing Vatsaaq before Harry spoke:

'You can drop me off at my cabin, unless you have more questions for me. Vonnie will be getting worried by this time.'

'Harry, I thought you'd promised to help? The police enquiry is far from over, even though I seem to have made a reasonable start. With your help, Harry. With your help.'

'You're doing well enough without a foreign fuddy-duddy like me getting in the way. Why don't you make Olaf your official Deputy?'

'Olaf is my official Deputy as you call it, or my Assistant at least. He receives a small cheque every month from Police Headquarters in Nuuk for the privilege. But Olaf is – well, he is Olaf. No Harry, I need your help and advice, at least until the detective is able to fly in from Ammassalik. The victim is from your country. She was on your tour; you know her well. It will be best if you are with me'.

Why was Lars assuming he knew Essie well?

'I really can't see the need. The full-timer should be here later today. And I'll remind you again that I'm very much an *ex*-policeman.'

Lars cast a sideways glance at Harry. Some moments passed before he responded.

'No Harry, Knud Holm won't be with us today. Nor tomorrow will he be here, unless the weather forecast changes. I telephoned police headquarters as soon as I could when I returned to Vatsaaq. I needed to let them know how things were looking and I wanted guidance. The officer I contacted couldn't believe what I was saying. Then he had to tell me there are some very bad weather conditions at present around Ammassalik and the whole of the south of Greenland. There are sea-fogs on the coast and heavy rains a few miles out to sea. In many parts there are even storms inland. The fog might soon be reaching our own coast this far north, so they tell me. The meteorologists say no-one will be able to get a helicopter out to us before tomorrow at the earliest, even if they can do it then. I need help with what they've asked me to do. Please, Harry.'

Lars' earlier efficiency and confidence, seemed to have deserted him. He braked the Land Rover rather suddenly and turned to face Harry.

'Look, I'm sorry I spoke sharply to you back at the pool. I couldn't afford to lose face in front of Olaf and the locals. You must understand this. I was nervous and the words didn't come out in the way I'd intended. Anyway, I needed to ask the questions I did. Surely you remember your own police days? They are not so long in the past, are they? I'm asking for your help with this investigation, Harry.'

'What is it you want me to do?'

'Well, there is the examination of the body. The doctor, or the nearest we have to a doctor, from the neighbouring settlement will do the preliminary post-mortem, but I'll need to be present for the examination and to write the formal police report. I'd like you to be there to help me with this. After that I'd like to go back to Qooroqilulissat for us both to have a more careful look at the – what do you call it – scene of the crime, and then …'

'You can't say the Valley of Qooroqilulissat was the scene of the crime, Lars.'

'No, you're right. In fact we're already sure it wasn't the place where Ms Smith was killed. We're certain she met her end in Vatsaaq itself. We have a suspect, you see. There is much evidence already. But I need your experience to make proper sense of some of it. I've told you: I've only had to deal with drunken behaviour and small-time theft before today. Vatsaaq is not Chicago, nor even your Reading-shire. I really need you with me for this, Harry.'

Harry was surprised at the mention of "a suspect". It was the first he'd heard of such a thing. Hadn't Lars just made another fuss about needing his assistance? So why hadn't he told him about this suspect immediately? Harry really couldn't understand why Lars was still insisting he wanted his help. What was going on? But he said nothing.

*

'No Harry. Don't do it. Why should you get involved in a crime like this?'

'Lars needs me, Vonnie. He was almost pleading with me.'

Harry didn't like to admit this even to himself, but he was flattered by the way in which Lars had asked for his assistance. Besides, it would be one last golden opportunity to show Vonnie – to show himself for that matter – that he wasn't as useless as they'd all said on the Force. Vonnie was being less than understanding.

'Lars, Lars, Lars. That's all I hear. If Lars asked you to jump head first into a snowdrift would you do it?'

'He needs my help, Vonnie,' he repeated. It sounded very thin.

'He doesn't need your help. Don't be foolish. You're a *retired* policeman. Doesn't he know that?'

'Yes, of course he does. But I can bring some of my experience to this case. He has very little. There's not usually much call for real police work here.'

'This is young man's work, Harry. A fit young man's work. Lars can very well do what needs to be done until the proper police get here.'

'For the time being Lars is the "proper police", Vonnie.'

'Well then. All the more reason for you to stay out of things.'

This was getting him nowhere. He tried another tack.

'I can't stand by and do nothing, love.'

'Why not? We've paid quite enough for this holiday.'

'But the victim – Essie Smith – was our countrywoman. She was our fellow-traveller. I feel a responsibility to give what help I can.'

This was again the wrong thing to say. Harry knew it as soon as the words left his lips.

'Essie Smith. Lars Erikssen. What about Vonnie Lanier? Isn't she your wife, Harry? Isn't she your "fellow-traveller" too?'

'But you liked Essie Smith, Vonnie.' Even as he said this, Harry knew he'd made an even more serious tactical error. Vonnie became stony-faced, standing up straighter and crossing her arms across her chest.

'No Harry. You were the one who liked her. I thought she, oh, I'm not going to speak ill of the dead, but don't you dare go putting your likes and dislikes into my mouth.'

So it went on.

*

Harry closed the cabin door behind him, taking care not to slam it, even though this was exactly what he wanted to do.

Vonnie had visibly winced when he'd mentioned Essie's name. She'd gone tight-lipped on him again. He'd compounded his mistake by trying to justify things at greater length. Her answers had come in frosty, two- or three-word sentences amounting to "you do what you damned well like but don't expect me to say I'm happy about it".

*

The post-mortem, if it could be called that, was to be held in the "Great Hall". All the buildings in the tourist quarter were neat and shining in comparison to the down-at-heel homes in the Inuit quarters less than a mile to the north, but then these buildings were only a matter of months old.

The members of the Greenland Party were the first occupants of the new cabins. Icesperience had planned for them to be ready for occupation in June, when the "Midnight Sun" would be in the sky for most of the month. It would even be brightening the night for a week or so into July. Lars had told him that, in the event, building schedules had been delayed and the company had been barely able to squeeze in this one trip at the end of the season. The sun was still now above the horizon for over fifteen hours, although before much longer it would rapidly become much colder at this high latitude. Then the days would shorten dramatically. The sun would barely creep into the sky through much of December and January.

All along, from the first time they'd seen the brochure last winter onwards, much had been made by the company of the delights they could expect on this stage of their tour. One of the treats not mentioned had been last night's "party". In truth this had been nothing more than a ferocious group drinking bout centred on Harry's bottles of *Benromach*. The Great Hall had become associated in Harry's mind with the spectacular hangover he had known this morning. Now it was becoming altogether more sinister.

The row with Vonnie meant Harry arrived late. When he entered the small ante-room being used for the purpose of the examination, the doctor and Lars were already there, bent over Essie's corpse, speaking rapidly in what Harry could tell was an odd mixture of Danish and Greenlandic.

The body was covered to the waist with a white sheet. The remainder of the ice-block grotesquely locking her forearms had been chipped away. Harry wondered who'd performed this grisly task – the two Inuit, he suspected. Essie was now free of any trace of ice and Harry could imagine that, apart from the ugly discoloration around her throat caused by the bruising, she was sleeping peacefully on the table. At least her eyes had at last been decently closed, he gratefully noted. Although he tried not to let it, Harry's glance could not help being drawn to the sight of Essie's breasts, now flattened sideways but still disturbingly large. It was a tragedy that this woman, who'd been so proud of her unusual figure, was lying there lifeless.

'Harry,' said Lars. 'I am so glad you could make it. This is Pesut. He's from Eqalassaq, the settlement about eighty kilometres to the south. Pesut has only driven along the trail at my request to help us with the examination. The doctor from Ammassalik will carry out a more detailed investigation later. Until then, we can't simply sit back and wait for the weather to clear. We need to find out what we can without delay.'

Pesut held up his plastic-shrouded hands, smiled, and shrugged his shoulders as if in apology for not being able to shake hands.

The medical man, whom Harry recognised as being of mixed European and Inuit descent, clearly understood enough English to get at least the drift of what Lars was saying but the Dane spoke as if he'd not been in the room:

'Actually, Pesut is not a true doctor. He is what would you call a pseudo-medic.'

'You mean he's a paramedic.'

For a moment Lars appeared to be disconcerted at his rare stumble in the use of the English language, but then he quickly continued:

'Anyway, he has more than enough medical knowledge to tell us all we want to know for the time being. His preliminary idea – he is quite sure of this – is that this lady died after being struck by something heavy and smooth at the base of the skull. And, as I have told you, we are fairly this was a rock. Either it was a rock, or some heavy tool or weapon. My guess would is it would have been a rock. There are so many on the ground at that point.The wound is more severe than it looked to be at first.'

Here Pesut obligingly rolled Essie's body toward the wall, so that Harry could see the contusions. The surface damage did indeed appear to be not so very extensive. The blow, if blow it was, must have been well aimed and sharply delivered.

'Then there is the more visible bruising to the neck and windpipe,' continued Lars. 'You can see the imprints and discoloration on the flesh. They can only have come from the fingers of a large pair of hands. The bruising looks bad, but Pesut is certain it was not strangulation but the blow to the back of the head that killed her. The only other injuries we have so far found are minor abrasions to her back and legs. She probably received those when she fell – we believe in fact that she must have been pushed – into the interior of the ice formation.

'All this depends on the confirmation of a full X-ray examination, you will understand. We can't do anything as complex as this here. Still, Pesut is confident his conclusions will be borne out by the full post-mortem once we are able to carry it out. I'm happy to go along with what he says for the moment.'

Following Harry's gaze, Pesut gestured theatrically toward Essie's neck. It looked for all the world to Harry as if Pesut was giving a stage performance, with Lars taking the part of Master of Ceremonies. He shook his head, trying to clear it of such wayward thoughts, doing his best to look at the bruises around the throat with a more professional eye. In Harry's own assessment, it certainly looked as if these were the marks left by the grip of a large pair of hands.

'Yes Harry, the bruising is not good to see. But, as I say, Pesut says he's sure the strangulation was not enough to cause Ms Smith's death. It looks as if whoever committed the murder did at first did try to strangle her, but then decided to finish her off by striking her behind the head with something heavy. It was most certainly a deliberate killing. Now, Pesut is going to examine her below to determine if there has been a sexual assault.'

With a precise and delicate touch, Pesut rearranged the white cloth to cover Essie's head and upper torso, leaving her legs and abdomen exposed in a way that seemed perverse and obscene to Harry, for all his years of police experience. Then the Greenlander adjusted his gloves, flexed his fingers, and took a theatrical step toward Essie's body. Harry became strongly aware of the emptiness in his stomach. He blinked his eyes. Blackness swam before them…

*

'Harry!'

Harry kept his eyes closed, not wanting to expose his hangover too abruptly to the harsh light of day. There was a thudding pain at the back of his head and the fragments of wild and troubling dreams danced around the fringes of his consciousness.

'Harry! Are you all right?'

What was Lars doing in his room? Where was Vonnie? Was this even his cabin? Something was wrong. Slowly, he forced his eyes open. Lars was cradling his head, looking anxiously into his eyes. There was another man standing further away from him, white-masked and holding up plastic-covered hands in a vaguely threatening way.

The masked man had been part of his dream, the nightmare about a naked woman lying on the table of ice. She'd called to him, and he hadn't been able to prevent himself walking toward her even though Vonnie had, all the time, been screaming hysterically in the background. And then... but already the dream was evaporating, He was becoming conscious only of the insistent thudding in his head.

'Harry... What happened? You suddenly keeled over, giving yourself a nasty crack on the head as you fell. You've been out for ten minutes.'

'I'm OK,' Harry heard himself saying. 'Something came over me. Maybe it's everything that's happened today after all the whisky last night. And I haven't eaten all day. I'm OK really, except my head is aching and … I feel sick.'

'Best we get you out of here, so Pesut can finish his work.'

Harry allowed Lars to help him to his feet. He leaned freely on the young man, despite the differences in their builds and body weights. Lars proved to be surprisingly strong, and managed to ease him through the door without difficulty.

'I think a bit of fresh air is what you need. We'll get you to the seat outside the door. You can take it easy there.'

Minutes later, Harry found himself sitting on the rough wooden bench outside the Great Hall. He'd assured Lars he'd soon be well enough if he could have a few moments' rest. And indeed, although he ached all over and his head was still muzzy, he felt himself to be recovering speedily. Almost as quickly as his consciousness was lurching back to a reality worse than any nightmare.

He gratefully drew the Arctic air into his lungs. It was growing much colder. Looking up at the sky, he could see it was no longer blue and flecked with the feathery high clouds he'd grown so used to seeing in the last week in this vast, strange country. Now the dome was heavy and grey. A swirl of nearly black cloudlets, seemingly almost at touching distance above him, looked vaguely threatening. And, as he watched, a single watery snowflake fell on the sleeve of his parka. Harry looked down as, in a strange kind of slow motion, it melted where it lay.

*

'No, Harry. I cannot possibly allow it. I should never have asked you in the first place. It was – well, I panicked for a moment. This is the truth of things. Perhaps we can talk about it again tomorrow, if the police from Ammassalik do not arrive by then …'

'Lars, I'm quite well. My fainting fit was merely a passing thing. You asked me yourself for my help. Let me give it to you now.'

A "passing thing" was a gross understatement. The twenty minutes or so during which he'd sat in the open air had done much to restore him, but the muzziness was heavy still in his head. He was hardly feeling capable of making much in the way of physical effort. The difference now was that Harry realised there was now something within himself that wanted him to see this through. He had to know the truth, no matter what it was.

'You are my friend. I cannot be responsible for your safety. Let me take you back to your cabin. It should be straightforward for us now. Olaf can help me with the rest of the investigation, as you said yourself.'

'Lars, if you are really my friend, let me do this. Let me help you.' Harry realised the irony of the situation. Now he was the one doing the pleading.

Lars looked down at the ground for a moment, then back to Harry. The young man's lips twitched.

'I know I should not be saying yes. This is crazy. But you are my friend. Even if this is something I should not say to a friend, I say yes, if it is really so important to you.' At last Lars allowed himself a nervous smile. He quickly patted Harry's arm. Harry felt more gratitude for this brief touch than for anything else that had happened today.

'Thank you,' said Harry, impulsively rising from the seat and shaking Lars by the hand. 'Yes, it is important to me.'

'Then, as they say in your country, we are back in business. No more need be said of this episode. The next important thing for us to do is to go back to the pool at Qooroqilulissat, where you and I found the body. Before we do this I think we must get something to eat, or you will be falling down again. And maybe myself too, this time. But Harry, I must ask you for myself. Why is this suddenly so important to you? Before it was I trying to persuade you to become involved with the investigation. Now it is the other way around. What has changed?'

Harry kept a straight face, but behind the mask was a tumble of emotions. He couldn't tell Lars the truth, not the whole truth at least. He didn't yet know it himself.

'You could say it's become more personal. Now, let's go and get that something to eat before I do keel over again.'

3.3

From the passenger-seat of the Land Rover, Harry watched the snow floating gently down from above. Already it was starting to veil Qooroqilulissat under a thin cover of whiteness. The consistency, soon after the start of the snowfall, had quickly become sleet-like. Now genuine snowflakes were once again steadily settling on the ground. These were large enough to make their crystalline form visible to Harry through the windscreen. He idly wondered whether he were seeing *pirhuk*, one of the many kinds of light snow recognised by Greenlanders. It certainly wasn't *qanik*, the big ice crystals they'd told him would sometimes flake from above, rapidly blanketing the ground with a kind of compressed frost.

This would be something soon to come, Harry supposed. When it would still be mid-autumn at home, Greenland would be in the grip of winter and the days would soon become no more than a few hours in length. This strange land would then grow more mysterious still. He decided what was falling now didn't quite match the descriptions Lars had given him of either *pirhuk* or *qanik*.

The brilliant white gave the valley an altogether different appearance from the one bestowed by the predominantly brown-and-green light, tinged with unworldly blue bathing it only this morning. It didn't feel like the same place; it didn't even seem as if they could be on the same planet. And, in a way the country was entirely different. At least, he knew he'd never feel the same about it again. Neither could Lars now, surely?

*

Over their brief but filling lunch of cod – cod again, though nowhere else had Harry tasted fish so fresh and delicately-flavoured – they'd talked of anything but the crime. Instead, they'd chatted about other things. Lars told him that the valley's name meant something like "the iceberg valley". He'd delighted in explaining once more that most of the place names in the country were direct renderings of descriptions of the local physical features. Many of the individual rocks had been given a unique name.

He'd gone on to tell him that, even in these enlightened times, it was the custom for pregnant Inuit women to wear a magic amulet. In that way, they hoped to ensure their unborn child would be a boy who'd grow up to be a fine hunter. There was a trace of bitterness in his laugh when he'd added that his mother in Denmark must have worn her charm back to front.

For an interlude their friendship felt as if it were restored to the relaxed empathy they'd shared earlier but, as the meal was drawing to its close, the mood had reverted to the uneasiness that had descended on the valley this morning. Lars retreated into a silence into which Harry, at first, felt he could not intrude. Still, he was starting to think it was only right Lars should now bring him up to date with the details of this investigation. After all, Harry could hardly pretend to be helping if Lars wouldn't tell him what he'd been able to find out. The Dane had yet to disclose even so much as the name of their main suspect.

'You haven't told me what Pesut said about the rest of his medical examination,' Harry said, putting down his fork and breaking the long silence. 'In fact there are many things you have yet to tell me.'

'There is not much I can say.' Lars looked at Hary, as if in surprise at his question. 'There were some minor abrasions on the back of her thighs and calves, like those on her back. Pesut found few other injuries, apart from the bruising to Ms Smith's neck and contusions to the back of her head. These were caused by the stone or whatever it was that struck her. The only surprising things we found were compression fractures to both wrists. The X-rays should tell us more, but Pesut thinks these were impact breakages actually caused inside the ice.'

Lars' looked at him with some impatience. It was as if Harry were expected to somehow know these facts.

'You already know most of this, Harry: you have seen the wounds for yourself. The doctor from Ammassalik won't be able to tell us much more, I'm sure. Pesut may not have formal qualifications or the necessary medical training to write the official report, but he knows more about the human body than most doctors.'

'Will they be able to use X-rays here? The Ammassalik doctor will be bringing the necessary equipment with him, will he?'

'Yes, I assume he'll bring a portable machine with him. After the on-the-spot examination they'll want to fly the body out for a more thorough investigation. The only thing in doubt, to my mind at least, is where the full post-mortem should take place. This could be either in Nuuk or in København. But, wherever it is, I don't think it will give us any more information. Even sophisticated tests like the analysis of the scrapings beneath Ms Smith's fingernails may not reveal much.'

'What about the examination "below", as you and Pesut so coyly described it?'

'There is little to tell. There was no sign of injury or violation. In fact, Pesut said Ms Smith was still a virgin.'

'A virgin! She was at least forty years old. I don't believe it.'

'I can only tell you what Pesut discovered.'

This new information sent Harry's mind racing off on a number of different tracks, some of them uncomfortable. His face must have betrayed his troubled thoughts and emotions, because it seemed Lars wanted to ask him something but appeared not to know how to frame the question. Either it was this or else he was afraid of asking it.

*

Lars parked the Land Rover in silence. As they crossed the now damp and slippery ground on their return to the iceberg pool, there was an even greater degree of awkwardness between them.

Now only a single block floated in the pool. This looked to be a new one. It was smaller than the formation attached so oddly to Essie's arms when they'd found the body earlier, although larger than its two satellites. It looked as if, by this time, these had melted in the tepid water.

'Lars, are there always icebergs in this pool?'

'I keep saying; you should not call them icebergs'. He smiled to soften his rebuke, although Harry could still see the lines of tension in his face. 'You will always see these formations in the late spring, summer and early autumn. In the winter they won't be present. Then, even with the effect of the thermal stream, the water in the pool is entirely frozen over. All you'd see then is a solid mass of ice.'

'Do they vary much in size? I'd assume they do from what you've told me so far. How often does a new one fall into the pool did you say?'

'If you know the time of year and the air-temperature, you can say with confidence how big they'll be. You can also predict when, within a half-an-hour, the next is due to fall. This is to do with the timing and angle of the sun's rays striking the water and glacier, as well as the effect of the thermal stream. This one, I can tell you, is a bit larger than a typical late-August "iceberg" . He tried to paste a more friendly expression onto his features.

'Normally, a fall would not yet be expected. The pattern has been disrupted. If things are now beginning to be restored to normal, the next will be smaller in size than the one you see now. It should appear soon after midnight.

'Although, I might add, it may be larger if the weather continues to get colder. At all events, it will be nowhere near as large as the one we saw this morning. That was exceptional. It is unseasonably cold at present, so things may be a little harder than usual to predict. But I can be sure of the general points of what I'm saying.'

'What about this morning's floating ice, then? When we arrived there were three blocks: the big one, and two smaller ones. Then, while I was here alone, a smaller block fell in the pool. What does that tell you?'

Lars paused. He looked carefully at Harry before continuing.

'As I said; the normal pattern we are used to seeing has been disturbed. This could be caused by any number of things: a sudden drop or increase in the overnight temperature, an unusual flow of morraine – really anything. But we both know what disrupted things this morning, don't we?' Lars sounded impatient. This was not his normal way. 'All is usually as regular as I've described, but remember we are talking about nature. The obvious assumption would be that the corpse caused the irregularity.

But I suppose there could be some additional factor disturbing the scheme of things'.

'Like someone digging a grave in the glacier,' said Harry. 'Perhaps a bit too near the central stream? That might really throw things out, wouldn't you say?'

Lars thought before answering. Now it was his turn to be the subject of questioning. Harry couldn't help noticing the Dane seemed to be accepting this with a far greater equanimity than he himself had done earlier.

'Yes Harry. I think I see what you are getting at. But why all these speculations? It seems to me far more likely Ms Smith's body was simply thrown into a cavity in what you call the glacier. Myself, I think she was actually slid head-first down the opening. I'd say the weight of the corpse caused it to break through to the underground stream.'

Seeing Harry's doubting expression, Lars expanded on what he was saying.

'The damage to the wrists almost certainly occurred when the body hit the solid ice. If she went head- or arms-first this would explain how her wrists came to be fractured and locked in the block of ice. The impact of the soldifying ice could easily have broken the bones.'

Harry tried to imagine Essie's headlong, face-downwards descent into her frozen sarcophagus. The picture forming in his mind was a horrifying parody of a fairground ride.

'Now, if I understand correctly,' Lars spoke slowly. 'You are trying to say someone deliberately dug a grave in the ice of the glacier, but near to the course of the stream,' Lars' voice interrupted his thoughts. 'This is what you are trying to suggest is it not?'

Lars frowned at him. For a moment he appeared to be doubtful about adding more. But then he continued:

'I don't know about this complicated theory Harry. It might turn out to be one elaborate way of adding more to the explanation of the irregularity, yes. But why should anyone want to do this? It would be very hard work. There are many easier ways to dispose of the body. Better ones, too. The killer, if he had local knowledge, would have known that at some time, even without the effect of the stream, the body would be released into the pool.'

Lars kept staring at Harry, as if unsure about directly expressing his thoughts.

'No, my friend. What you're saying doesn't make sense. I'm sorry, Harry. Your idea is ingenious. But – well...' His words tried to make it sound as if he'd been taking Harry's idea seriously. The expression on his face told a different story.

'Still, I think we should be thorough and consider all this as part of the investigation, don't you?', said Harry reacting to both the spoken and unspoken messages. 'Maybe this is exactly what the killer wanted, to confuse us. Let's see what the glacier itself can tell us.'

At first Lars did his best to stay expressionless. Then slowly his face creased into a more impatient smile than the one he'd been unable to resist a moment before.

'I think, Harry, that you are forgetting the basic principles of detection. Your theory can be made to fit a number of the facts, yes. But you are ignoring the most important thing. We know, or we're almost sure, who disposed of the body. The likelihood must be that he was also the murderer. This man would have no motive for digging around the glacier. He is a simple man in his way of doing things. He would have disposed of the body in the easiest way. As I say, this was almost certainly through a cavity in the ice-formation.

'In fact I'm even surprised to find he bothered to bring the body all the way out here. But come, my friend, we will examine the top of the formation if you wish. Even if the crime is a straightforward one, we should be seen thorough in our investigation, should we not?'

'Well, aren't you even going to tell me who this prime suspect is?' Harry knew he was being humoured by Lars and spoke shortly. 'I am supposed to be your assistant, aren't I?'

'Harry, I was going to tell you all you needed to know. Be patient; you couldn't know the man personally, anyway. He is a local man from Vatsaaq. Olaf was the one who gave me the crucial information. What would have happened is clear to me. I'll give you the details later. But now, we must look at the top of the glacier to put your mind at rest before the weather changes everything. We may already be too late after the fall of snow we've seen.'

*

The snow was coming down more heavily as they climbed the finger-glacier. It definitely couldn't be called *pirhuk* now. Some of the step-like serrations Harry had noticed before had already become smooth and rounded, but were still solid and regular enough to make the ascent surprisingly easy, even for Harry in his present state of stiffness.

Still, it was with a sense of achievement he at last found himself standing on the flat top. Water could be heard roaring below through hidden bore holes in the ice beneath his feet. Explosive cracking and crunching sounds reminded him the whole mass of ice was grinding unstoppably, albeit slowly, down the Valley of Qooroqilulissat.

He continued surveying the scene around him while he struggled to get his breath back. The dull yellow, almost solid-feeling sky ensured there wasn't much to see. The solid part of the glacier – he could only think of it as a glacier, despite what Lars had said – looked to be immense and unmoving, despite the alarming sounds he could hear from below. Through the bore-holes, Harry could see from his high viewpoint that the thermal stream was steaming below.

From this height, too, the character of the unusual link with the thermal stream was beginning to become evident. The stream seemed to be narrow in the few places where it was visible through the fissures. Reluctantly, Harry was beginning to think Lars' theory of the disposal of the body, rather than his own vague idea, must be correct after all.

The Dane had told him the greater part of the stream flowed underneath and out of sight, actually within the glacier. The surface of the ice was white, as the surrounding landscape had quickly become, but large parts of it were stained with weird blue streaks below the surface. It was a strange, ethereal place to be.

Looking out from the glacier top toward the path they'd taken earlier, Harry knew the view before them now should be the mirror-image of the one he'd seen that morning, but the whiteness made it difficult to see or gauge any distance. He could make out the pool ahead of them but, looking behind him, could not make out any part of the high path they'd traversed to reach it.

'Come, we must examine this quickly, before all is covered by the snowfall,' said Lars. 'It will make our descent dangerous if we delay for long.'

Harry stepped gingerly to the front edge of the ice, feeling the crunch of thousands of tiny crystals underfoot. Then he slowly knelt down and started brushing at the thickening snow covering with both of his hands.

'Be careful, my friend. You do not want to be inside the next block of ice falling into the pool. Can I ask what it is you're looking for?'

Harry continued to brush at the snow, giving no more than a grunt in answer. Then, after a minute or two, he muttered a triumphant 'yes' to himself. He turned around, still awkwardly on all fours, toward Lars.

'Come and see this. I think you'll find it fits my theory.'

Lars moved forward and crouched down to look. There was a small crater in the ice, surrounded by a web of fine cracks.

'Yes, I see it. So? What is it you are saying?'

'Well, can't you see what might have happened? It looks like someone has struck the ice at this point with a pick-axe or something sharp. Doesn't it look to you as if they were trying to dig a pit – or a grave?'

'Harry, Harry. You are making far too much of these minor details.' Lars looked at him questioningly. 'There is certain to be a perfectly straightforward explanation for what you can see. This is nature, remember? We will need more than a random mark in the ice to prove a human hand has been at work in the way you suggest. Don't you realise how much effort it would take to dig a grave in the hard ice? And even if these really were the marks of a pick, the evidence will be in the pool below us very soon – as we will be, too, if we do not quickly remove ourselves.'

Harry was disappointed at the scornful dismissal of his suggestion but could see Lars was right about the impermanence. Soon everything would literally melt away. He was probably correct about the means of disposal of the body, too. Yet this small crater in the ice was the only tangible thing making him refuse to abandon the thought that there had to be more to it than the simple explanation Lars appeared happy to accept.

'Lars, you've still said almost nothing about your suspect, other than he's a local man. Why aren't you holding him? What's the evidence you mentioned? Tell me something, for goodness sake.'

'I intend to tell you all you want to know. But I want do it in the warmth of the Land Rover, on our journey back We do not wish to be trapped if this storm becomes worse.'

*

As they made their descent down the now treachorous and far less regular step formation, the snow was beginning to drive heavily. In the Land Rover, Harry was wet, cold and uncomfortable. They'd been drenched in the last twenty minutes.

It was all he could do to prevent himself from heeding the siren call of Lars' flask, still in his pocket. But, as the Dane had hurried back up the slope to Vatsaaq earlier, Harry had vowed that in his pocket was where it was going to stay. It was a wager he'd made with himself. He was glad Lars had not yet asked for the flask's return.

They'd been driving for at least ten minutes before Lars spoke. Even then he seemed to do so as a reluctant afterthought.

'Our prime suspect is, as I told you, a local man. His name is Nanoq. He was born here, but was orphaned at a young age and brought up by everyone in the settlement.

You might think of him as a kind of group adoptee. You'll find such things are not unusual in the smaller settlements.

'Nanoq is a strange one, let me tell you. The people of Vatsaaq like to say as a boy he was kicked in the head by a musk-ox and lost his wits. His speech is very odd but I don't think he is as weak minded as they all believe. Most certainly he is the best hunter we have. At this time of year he can be out from early morning to midnight on the East Coast ice-floes, hunting seal. He was out very early this morning. You know about the summer ice-floes here in Tanu?'

Harry relaxed and eased himself further back into the seat. Lars did now seem prepared to tell him the full story.

'You told the whole tour party about the floes,' said Harry. 'The sea-water freezes in the North, and in the summer the field-ice is brought down the East Coast by the ocean current. This brings with it seals for hunting.'

'Yes, and for Nanoq it brings the polar bear, too. He is known in all of Tanu as the great hunter of the white bear. Few would dare stalk the creature alone, as he does.'

Lars had told him that 'Tanu' in Greenlandic roughly translated as 'the back of the country'. Harry couldn't help thinking of it, 'the outback'. Even to the Inuit in the more populous western parts, the east of Greenland was seen as wild and remote. What was he doing getting mixed up in a murder investigation in such a place? But involved he was. Now he meant to see the business through, even though Lars was beginning once again to give indications of no longer wanting his help.

'So,' said Harry. 'This is why you are waiting until his return, because it would be difficult to track him down on the ice floes?'

'No, we could probably track him down if we wished. We know roughly where he is. But would you want to go after such a man in such a place? No, Harry, you would not do it if you wished to see Madam Vonnie again in this life. Nanoq hunts with a motor-boat and a powerful rifle with telescopic sights, not a kayak and a harpoon.

'A couple of months ago I forbade him to bring his rifle into Vatsaaq. He is the supreme tracker and hunter but is a hopeless shot. I am suspecting his eyesight is becoming weak. His aim is all-too-often wild and he is too fond of pulling the trigger. It would be only a matter of time before someone was killed. I insisted he kept his rifle in his boat and well away from us.

'It is our good fortune he will not be carrying a rifle when he returns to Vatsaaq later today. Do you not see it will be better for us to arrest him when he is walking contentedly into our settlement after a good day's hunting than for us to walk into his rifle-sights? He will be expecting nothing. He'd never guess Ms Smith's body has already been found. This will be a surprise to him.'

*

The snow was still falling heavily. Even at their fastest speed, the wipers could barely keep the windscreen of the Land Rover clear. It was a miserable drive back. Harry found the first glimpse of the scatter of buildings more comforting than he would have believed an hour or two before.

Lars parked the vehicle efficiently. They stepped out and stood looking at each other. Harry could see the young Dane would have liked to walk away from this now – from further conversation with him and perhaps from the events of the day, too. But there were many questions in his own mind. Some of them he wanted to put to Lars.

Actually, Harry did have slight memories of Nanoq from the drinking session of the night before. He was a sulky bear of a man – Gudrun had told him his name, or nickname, meant precisely that: 'The Bear'. It couldn't have been more appropriate. As far as Harry remembered, Nanoq had kept strictly to the non English-speaking group of Inuit, steadily drinking. How could there be a connection between this man and Essie's death? Lars still had much to tell him.

'You say it was Olaf who put the finger on this Nanoq?'

'Put the finger? A strange expression, this, Harry. But yes, it was Olaf who told me about Nanoq. Some of the story he obtained from Silumi. Olaf talks to the Inuit people far more than I do, even though we've lived in Greenland for the same length of time. He and his brother Christian came out to Vatsaaq from the west with me.'

'Lars, it is not that I doubt what Olaf has told you. But have you thought he might have reasons of his own for shifting the blame on to Nanoq?'

Harry realised his mistake. Lars' pale face flushed and his eyes flashed with unaccustomed emotion.

'I do not care to know what you suggest. But Olaf, despite his faults, is an honest man. And I know for myself he had nothing to do with the death of Ms Smith'.

'I'm sorry Lars. I wasn't trying to imply anything. But if we're to investigate this crime, we must treat any information we receive with caution. You should know this.'

Lars continued to scowl, so Harry tried to mollify him.

'The last thing I was suggesting was that Olaf had anything to do with Essie's death. But surely you have to agree it would be reasonable to see if he can account for his own movements? It is the same for any one of us.' Harry wanted to add *"I had to do it myself,"* but was uncomfortably aware he'd been unable to give more than a half-explanation of his movements at the crucial time.

Lars looked down on the ground. Harry could see he was reluctant to give any answer. He prompted him.

'Well Lars? It's a reasonable question I'm asking.'

'Olaf can account for his movements for the whole of the night,' he said, looking up after a few moments.

'How can you be so sure, Lars? Have you questioned him? And what about Christian, his brother?'

Lars slammed the door of the Land Rover shut and squarely faced Harry.

'Christian was with a family from the settlement. They have already vouched for him. There is what you'd call a relationship with the daughter.'

For a moment, the young man man looked as if he was going to walk away without answering further questions about the other Danish brother. He'd already taken a few paces away. Then he stopped and looked back towards Harry.

'As for Olaf, he can account well enough for his movements. As I can, Harry. He was with me. Olaf was with me all night.'

3.4

Vonnie looked at him from across the room. Her expression showed she found it hard to believe what she'd just heard her husband say.

'What on Earth are you thinking of, Harry? You can't just go and do this sort of thing. Have you gone mad?'

'Come on Vonnie. I'm not going to sit people down and ask them to sign statements or anything of the like. It'll be in the course of ordinary conversation.'

'Huh! You don't even bother to speak to most of the others. What's everybody going to think when you start nosing around?'

This was all going wrong. He'd meant to tell Vonnie about his intention subtly, not to have another stand-up row. This would be the second today.

'It'll be much easier for me to do it than it would for Lars.' He tried to sound as if he were being as reasonable as he could. 'After all, it should be more aceptable for me to talk to them than a part-time policeman from Denmark. If I'm going to be involved, this is surely the way I can be most useful?'

'Oh, so it's Lars' idea again, is it? I might have known you and he would cook up some such daft scheme together.'

'This wasn't Lars' doing. He doesn't even know of my plans. If I told him he probably wouldn't care for the idea at all.'

'Good for him, then. At least he'd be showing more sense than you. Surely you must realise the other members of the Greenland Party are doing no more than sharing this holiday with us? How do you think they're going to react when you start trying to behave like a policeman in their midst?'

'But Vonnie, it won't be like that. What I'm going to do is –'

'Not another word Harry. You just think about what I've said.'

*

'Well, it's five o'clock. Wasn't that the time you promised to meet your young Danish friend?'

These were the first words his wife had said to him since their row.

'You know I have to do this, Vonnie. And I won't be seeing Lars for another half-hour. Five-thirty I told him I'd be there to talk to him. He asked me to come. Said he and Olaf have some important things to tell me'

Then he fell silent. So much for trying to tell Vonnie how he felt. His explanation might have been inadequate and incomplete, but he could hardly begin to tell her everything about Essie. Without that it wasn't easy to say what he really felt. Nevertheless, he'd done his best, and now felt rebuffed. It was almost as if Vonnie didn't care.

Before trying again to explain things, Harry had spent most of the last two hours alternately dozing and fretting as to whether he really should call a halt to his involvement and leave it to the younger men. Every instinct told him that to bail out now would be the sensible thing to do. The full-time detective might arrive from Ammassalik as soon as tomorrow. Or he'd surely be able to fly in by the day after. How bad could the weather be in this country at this time of year? It was only the end of August, for goodness sake.

Essie was a citizen of the United Kingdom. There must be a need for the Greenlanders to bring in someone from the British police eventually. That would certainly be the Met in this case rather than his old Force. His involvement now, albeit semi-officially as Lars' deputy, might make for complications later but... Despite his early doubts, the case itself was starting to look as though, after all, it might be straightforward. Harry was sure Lars would be mightily relieved if he did now step aside. Yes, it would surely be better to forget it all... and yet the image of Essie embracing the block of ice kept returning to him.

'Vonnie.'

'Oh, so you've decided to talk to me again?'

Harry tried not to rise to this.

'Vonnie, I really need your help to fill in my gaps from last night.'

'You'd have a lot of bits missing, wouldn't you? I've never seen anybody trying to drink so much whisky. Then you started on the illegal local stuff. What do they call it now?'

'I don't remember,' he said flatly. This was true. Harry didn't even recall seeing the local spirit, let alone drinking any. 'Never mind about that. What time would you say we left the Great Hall ourselves?'

'I'd say it was at least two o'clock by the time I was able to drag you out. Falling about all over the place you were. It was disgraceful. You having that "breath of fresh air", as you had the nerve to call it, not long before we left, only made you worse. We were the last ones to go, soon after that Freddie Tanner. He was almost as bad as you, though at least he had the sense not to try to drink the distillery dry. And Freddie didn't touch the local fire-water.'

Harry persisted, trying to ignore Vonnie's bitter reproaches. He deserved every one of them. More, probably.

'Who left first?'

'Well the so-called "party" with the locals broke up quite early. As soon as they realised there wasn't going to be any more of your proper whisky. Some of them drifted off to the other room leaving a bottle of their local hooch with you, though I believe most of the rest simply went home. At first we tourists all stayed in the bigger place. '

Vonnie looked questioningly at Harry, as if wondering whether to continue. She did:

'After that, Dainty Clatworthy and Gudrun Wotsitsdaughter left together. That would have been before ten o'clock. It wasn't very long after when Tony Ferris went. Then Melvyn Walters and his Scots wife – she's a cheery girl; more than I can say for her grump of a husband – went not so long after him.' She paused, wrinkling her forehead. 'Oh, and Lars went quite early, too. Eleven, I'd say, or maybe a few minutes after. At any rate, he went as soon as that smirking Dane poked his blond beard around the door and called to him. He ran out like a puppy.' Vonnie sighed. 'I don't like either of them, especially the one with the beard.'

Harry ignored his wife's swipe at Olaf and Lars. He didn't like Olaf either.

'And I gather Essie Smith was in the next room until well after midnight. What about her husband, Jeremy?'

'Her husband? And you have the nerve to call yourself a detective? We all assumed that's what he was at first, but since when do husband and wife have separate cabins? He's her brother, you idiot. Most of us have known this since we were in Iceland.'

'They don't look much like each other.'

'Her brother, I said. Not her twin. Brothers and sisters don't always have to look the same. You look more as if you're from Jeremy's family yourself. '

Harry recalled Lars had made a point of calling her "Ms Smith". The Dane must have considered this to be the way to refer to single women.

'How did you find a thing like that out?'

'From Dainty. She asked one of them, of course. I'd have told you about the Smiths if you hadn't been mooning over that Essie's big bust. Don't think I didn't notice. Don't think other people didn't notice, either.'

Harry winced. This was a reminder he could have done without. But he did his best to ignore Vonnie's barb.

'So, there were three of us men in The Great Hall until fairly late on? Jeremy Smith, Freddie Tanner, and myself. All of us are strongly built with big hands, wouldn't you say?'

'Yes, the three of you are all much of the same stamp, although Tanner is carrying l lot of flab. But Jeremy left not so long after Lars. Well before midnight, anyway. He looked into the next room for his sister but she was dancing with one of the local men, so Freddie told me. At least that's what I think he was trying to tell me as far as I could make out from his drunken mumblings when you were outside getting your *fresh air*.'

Vonnie looked at him mockingly.

'Now, you won't forget the women, will you Harry? Maggie Walters, Dainty and myself? None of us has big hands, but when do we report to you for the third degree?'

'Nobody is in the clear, Vonnie. Even those of us who weren't there all the time. Any one of us could have been in collaboration with the local man who looks like being our prime suspect.'

'So it's *our* prime suspect now, is it? You're really taking this detective business seriously, aren't you? You're telling me that you and Lars have already got someone in mind as the killer? Then why should you plan to go upsetting all the members of our party in the way you said? You're not a police officer these days, Harry. And don't forget: when you were one you spent most of your time in the Traffic Division. I bet you haven't told Lars that. You're pretending – pretending to yourself as well to everyone else – that you're some sort of Sherlock Holmes. You haven't told him the truth about your police career, have you?'

'I've told him nothing but the unvarnished truth, as a matter of fact.' Harry searched his memory. He thought he could fairly say he hadn't made a secret of his less-than-glittering time with the constabulary, even if "the unvarnished truth" might be an exaggeration.

He hadn't said too much about his real reasons for leaving the Force even to Vonnie. 'These things should be done properly, Vonnie. It might be hard for you to understand but I see myself as the representative of the British police here. This is something I have to do. Anyway, it's time for me to go to see Lars now.'

'Harry. Don't do it.' Vonnie's voice softened. 'Leave the whole thing where it is. Let the locals handle it.' Gone was her sarcastic, biting tone. Now she was imploring him. 'You might find out things best left to lie where they are. I'm not saying any more, because I don't really know anything more. But I've got a nasty feeling about this business. Leave it, Harry. Please. For me.'

'I must uncover the truth, Vonnie. I've got to know the whole story. I can't begin to tell you how important it is to me.'

He tried to brush his lips against her cheek, but she turned her head aside and he felt her holding herself rigidly.

3.5

Lars had spoken to Harry earlier, saying he'd discovered some important things. He'd refused to elaborate further, though was keen to emphasise that this five-thirty meeting was purely for Harry's benefit. He'd added that he wanted him to hear Olaf's account in his own words of what he and Silumi had seen. Lars said Harry's lingering suspicions about Olaf were nothing less than doubts about himself.

When he'd protested that this wasn't the way things were, Lars had simply said, "then come at half-past-five". There was no way to counter this. So here he was, on his way to hear goodness knew what. And Vonnie would be fuming in their cabin.

Sleet had now replaced the snow. It was still falling heavily and the strong wind was driving it into him. Before Harry had taken many paces, he felt his face glowing red and stinging. Still, he wanted to put a distance between himself and his cabin before stopping to properly fasten his parka or even to pull up the hood. He was anxious to get away from Vonnie before either of them could say anything more. Another word, especially from himself, might tip things over the edge. The two of them had been teetering on the brink ever since that day in Selfoss.

When Harry arrived, Olaf was already in Lars' cabin. He was leaning against the wall in a relaxed way, smoking with studied casualness and otherwise giving the appearance of being thoroughly at home. Lars managed a nervous smile of greeting as he opened the door. All Olaf offered was a curt nod from where he was in a pose speaking of arrogance. He exhaled cheroot smoke in Harry's direction. Then he turned an insolent gaze toward Lars, as if to say it was up to him to speak.

'Perhaps, Olaf, you will outline for Mr. Lanier what it was you saw late last night,' said Lars. His tone was polite and measured, as if Olaf's rudeness had been a display of exemplary manners.

'What I have to say – what I have already said to you Lars, my friend – is simple enough,' said Olaf. 'The hunter, Nanoq, had been playing cards with Silumi and Henrik – you will know I am talking about Henrik Rasmussen, the trader. Nanoq had been drinking more than was good for him, as he sometimes does. Last night he must also have been losing more money than usual, because he suddenly threw down his cards and pushed all his coins and notes toward the other two. This is not something he would normally do. Not The Bear. Lars, you know what he is like about money.'

'How do you know this?' Harry saw immediately that his interruption was resented by Olaf, who curled his lip as he answered:

'I know because I watch them play. I do not play cards myself. It is a stupid game for people with weak minds. Also, I know the rest of the story because Silumi tells me all about it this morning, when you and Lars are off together.' He turned to Lars. 'Do you want me to say what I have to say, or is this man going to ask questions all the time? Are you going to let him do this? I thought Lars and Olaf were supposed to be the policemen here?'

Harry raised his hands as if to express regret for his breach of etiquette. Olaf remained silent, pointedly ignoring him, until Lars nodded his own assurance. Then he went on.

'So the card-game is over. Finished. Then we are all surprised to see the fat Englishwoman coming into the room. It looks like she will have had a row with somebody in the next room. One of the other English it would be.

None of us has seen this, so I can tell you nothing more, but I am saying to you this is the way it looks to us all. She sits down at a table on her own at first and drinks and sulks. We laugh when we see her stupid act. Then we ignore her.

'But, afterwards, Henrik Rasmussen realises she is on her own. He goes over to join her. You know what Henrik can be like with women. He soon has her laughing. I think, well done Henrik. You will have some good soft meat to play with tonight. You can as well go to Eqalassaq and do your trading tomorrow.'

Olaf looked from Lars' face to that of Harry, grinning and satisfying himself they were both listening. Harry resisted the urge to say anything, although Olaf was clearly trying to provoke him.

'And all the time Nanoq holds his head in his hands as if he has lost the world instead of only a few hundred kroner. He is like a baby, that one, although he is a big, strong man with a big, strong temper. Then, all at once, I see him getting up and walking towards the door. I am watching everything. It is like a free show. I think he will decide to go home; we know this morning he wants to go hunting. Or maybe he has had enough of losing money at the card-playing and wants to go back to his cabin and cry about his lost kroner.

'But I am wrong. Instead it seems he changes his crazy mind and walks to the table where the English woman is sitting with Henrik. He pulls her up to him. She is surprised at first but then she laughs like it is all some joke. But we know Nanoq doesn't know how to joke. I can see Henrik doesn't like what is happening: he was looking forward to a taste of what the woman has to give. By then we can all see she has much to give. Still, Henrik knows better than to cross Nanoq when he is in this sort of mood, so he says nothing. Henrik can only go out from the Great

Hall, muttering to himself. He will be going off on his trading tonight after all, instead of enjoying the fat woman.

'This is when I think it is also time for me to go. This is when I call to you in the other room, my friend Lars. You will remember it.'

Lars nodded. Harry could sense his embarrassment.

'So,' continued Olaf, still addressing himself directly to Lars. 'Silumi tells me, Nanoq is dancing with the big woman after I have gone. He has a stupid look on his face. No-one has ever seen The Bear dance before. I have never even seen him with a woman, so I wish now I had stayed to watch this fun. Silumi tells me it is a very special dance, the English woman's dance.' Olaf paused and smiled at both of them. This time Harry could see he was meant to ask Olaf a question.

'What kind of special dance?' Harry thought he'd have to play along with Olaf's game. He was the one making the rules.

'Like this. A special English dance.'

Olaf raised his arms and gave a fair mime of something like a waltz. But then he started to move his pelvis at first subtly and suggestively, then vigorously in a way that left nothing to the imagination. All the time he moved his hips he kept his gaze fixed firmly on Lars. Lars looked uncomfortable.

'I think we've got the point,' said Harry.

'This makes Nanoq very hot, the way the fat Englishwoman rubs herself all over him.' Olaf laughed, by now enjoying himself hugely. 'Silumi tells me it is very good to watch, though the English men in your party would not maybe think so. The two of them danced like this for a very long time, Silumi tells me. He says Nanoq doesn't know what to do next, although it is clear enough to Silumi what the woman wants him to do. It would be just like the stupid bear Nanoq not to know this. The others all left for their homes while Nanoq and the woman are dancing. Silumi leaves later, too, but goes back soon afterwards. He sees Nanoq and the woman have gone. Silumi thinks: "*at last The Bear has realised what he should do*".' Olaf leered and curled his lip.

'What time was it by then? Where did they go?' said Harry, doing his best to ignore Olaf's coarse and provocative manner.

Olaf turned to face Harry for the first time.

'You think Silumi wants to look at his watch? He does not even have a watch. It was about one o'clock perhaps; before or after I do not know. Maybe it is even after two o'clock. It is not like your England here, with everybody looking at their wrists and worrying about the hour of the clock all the time. As for myself, I see nothing; I have gone with my good friend here.' He grinned at Lars. ' I think no more about it until this morning when Lars comes back to Vatsaaq and tells me he has found the woman dead.'

Olaf leaned back in contented silence. He had finished telling this part of his story and had enjoyed himself hugely. Harry sensed he was going to say more and tried to prompt him.

'Who else saw Nanoq and Miss Smith?'

'Only Silumi saw most of what there was to see. The special dance. I have told you this. The rest of the English would not have seen anything, I think. The others from Vatsaaq went home when they see there is no more of the whisky left. Henrik has to drive south, to Eqalassaq. This is where he keeps the boat he uses for his trading. He is already late because he has wasted time on the Englishwoman and has to hurry away. He may have seen them together before he left. I do not know. But Silumi, when he comes back and finds no-one left, he went outside and looked around. He saw them both, Nanoq and the woman, after they left the Great Hall.'

'What did he see?' said Harry. This time there was no objection from Olaf to his asking a question.

'Silumi tells me he saw Nanoq pulling the woman toward his cabin. This is on the other side of the village. Nanoq has little English speaking, and Silumi, he too does not have much speaking. But he hears what Nanoq is shouting at the woman. It is an English word. A word we all know. Even Nanoq.'

Olaf paused again, his smile revealing even teeth of a surprisingly brilliant whiteness, waiting again to be prompted. Neither Harry nor Lars spoke. Olaf went on, undeterred by their failure to oblige him with a prompt.

'He is shouting at the woman, over and over again, "*Nanoq fuck Essie.*" And the woman squeals like a little pig being taken to the market. She is frightened now of feeling Nanoq inside her, that one. She should have thought of these things before she made him hot. None of it is a game for Nanoq. It is not good to play English games with The Bear.'

Olaf stood leaning against the wall for a long moment, happy with the effect his words had on Harry. Then, abruptly, he walked over to push open the door of Lars' cabin and left without another word.

*

Lars shrugged, as if to both apologise for Olaf's lewd manner, and at the same time to say 'I told you so'.

'I suppose you've checked the accuracy of this story with Henrik and Silumi?' said Harry.

'Henrik left to do his trading, as Olaf says. Eqalassaq is about eighty kilometres to the south of Vatsaaq. He never stays in any one place for long; he may already have moved off from there by this time. It is a very long way south to the next settlement, and the summer grows short. For the sake of being thorough, someone from our police service will interview the trader as soon as soon as we can locate him. But I am sure this will be purely a matter of routine. As for Silumi, I have already spoken to him, and it is all as Olaf says. You can speak to him yourself if you wish, though he has little enough English.'

Olaf's story had left Harry bemused. He looked around Lars' cabin. The room was smartly kept. In one corner the three-quarter bed was made up with the sheets neatly folded back over. The small table and desk were clear and uncluttered. There were few personal touches. It didn't look as if it had a permanent occupant, although he knew Lars had been living here for some months. It could have been a newly-turned out guest cabin but for the single black-and-white picture on the wall. The photograph showed a younger version of Lars with a woman in her middle years – his mother in Denmark, no doubt. There were a few office files stacked on a shelf in one corner and a large wooden chest underneath it, but little else.

Harry had not liked Olaf from the first. He'd wondered whether this had been more to do with his relationship with Lars than anything about Olaf himself. He knew now he'd been right the first time: Olaf was someone best avoided. All the same, Harry could only believe what the Dane had said about Nanoq and Essie. His crude story had the ring of truth to it, even though he wished it hadn't.

He turned to Lars. Now was the time to get out of this mess. What he should do was to go back to being a retired policeman; to try to salvage something from this holiday. And, before it was too late, he should also try to retrieve his marriage to Vonnie. They'd been together for well over thirty years and had been happy.

'Lars, look, I'm sorry I doubted what you and Olaf had to say. But now I really think –'

He didn't finish his sentence. There was a pounding on the door. It was Olaf.

He poured out a torrent of words in what Harry knew to be Danish, though he could only recognise the names 'Nanoq' and 'Silumi'. Lars answered him briefly in the same language, and the blond Dane sprinted away, surprising Harry with his turn of speed.

'It is Nanoq,' said Lars turning to Harry, ashen faced. 'He is returning from his hunt earlier than we expected. I had posted Silumi on the Sardaq rock with binoculars to look out for him. We will take him now, quickly. I have sent Olaf to get Christian and Ikateq.'

'But Nanoq is a dangerous man,' said Harry. 'You told me this yourself. He'll be difficult to control even if he won't be carrying his hunting rifle. Can you be sure he won't have brought it back with him this time?'

'The Bear will not be carrying a rifle. There is no reason for him to think he is in any trouble. He will have left his weapon in the boat. We will take him in his cabin, as soon as he walks through the door. It will be simple. Olaf and I will conceal ourselves in the main room. We will arrest Nanoq as soon as he steps across the doorway.

'There will be no difficulty with this. But, in case there is, you will be in the kitchen with Christian. You said you wanted to help; this is your chance. Each of you will have a gun. Silumi and Ikateq will be waiting in the next door cabin. Both will also have rifles. After the arrest they will join us to help escort Nanoq to one of the store-huts. We will lock him in until the Ammassalik police arrive. But come, we have enough time to prepare, but not time to waste.'

Lars walked to unlock and open the chest in the corner. He took out six rifles. Harry was surprised to see he could readily put his hands on so many in this tiny outpost. One of the guns he passed to Harry, who noted with satisfaction it was a light and elegant BSA Martini .22, identical with the one he used in the Rifle Club at home. He knew, if he was called upon to use this weapon, he wouldn't disgrace himself. Minutes later, he was following Lars through the door, hardly stopping to think why he was doing it.

3.6

The interior of Nanoq's cabin was, in size and general layout, not unlike the one Harry had just left but otherwise there couldn't have been a greater contrast. There were empty bottles, discarded clothes and scraps of food strewn everywhere. The uncovered and badly-stained table had been reserved for some huge slabs of roughly cut fat meat. Were these from a seal or a polar bear? They smelled sickeningly ripe.

The overpowering stench of stale fish made Harry want to retch. Already they'd been waiting for twenty minutes. The strain was starting to tell on the still-delicate state of his stomach. His one attempt to exchange a hasty word with Christian Severen, with whom he shared a posting in the tiny kitchen, had met with nothing more than a grunted reply and hissed annoyance from his brother Olaf in the main room. Harry had fallen into gloomy silence.

Now he felt faintly ridiculous holding the BSA. What were the likely consequences should he need to fire it? One of the things he did at home, and the one thing he could claim to do well, was competitive target shooting. Only here he wouldn't be aiming for a cardboard bullseye.

In Greenland he was a foreign national. If he should be forced to fire a shot in anger, Harry could foresee a police enquiry or even worse. Not that he felt secure about his status in any part of the business into which he'd been plunged. What on Earth was he was doing in this strange country holding a loaded rifle in his hands?

A sudden crunching on the gravel outside the cabin stirred Harry from this worrying train of thoughts. Something in the air told him the other three men in the cabin had also tensed. He sensed rather than heard Lars drawing himself back further into his inadequate hiding place between wall and poorly-painted steel cupboard-cum-wardrobe. Olaf would be crouching lower behind the unmade grubby bed. This looked as if it had been vacated only a few minutes before but Harry knew it had been empty all day. Christian gripped his own rifle tightly and nodded sternly to him. This was it. He was here and involved, whether he should be or not.

Then came silence from outside. Had Nanoq sensed something amiss? Lars had emphasised the man's hunter instincts. Was the Greenlander planning some kind of cunning counter-strike to leave all four of them looking foolish – or dead? Harry knew a desperate urge to evacuate his bowels. He looked towards Christian. Olaf's brother was motionless and silent. He didn't seem to share much of Harry's tension.

All at once the latch was lifted. Nanoq stepped in, carrying what looked to be the pelts of dead foxes or hares. The Inuit seemed unconcerned; his movements were casual. He wore a look of dull contentment on his face. Harry couldn't help thinking the Inuit looked like a large animal replete after a good day's hunting.

He had the crazy urge to shout "*Now*!" It was all he could do to hold his silence as Nanoq stepped forward to a position from which he could not fail to see Lars.

The Danish policeman stepped forward, calmly pointing his own BSA Martini at the Greenlander's head. Nanoq froze, taken by surprise. Then he glared angrily at Lars as he saw the gun. For a moment it looked as if he were going to stride forward to crush the young man, rifle or no rifle, but Olaf had by then risen from his own hiding place and was spitting out harsh commands in Greenlandic.

Harry was relieved to see, as Lars had assured him would be the case, that Nanoq was carrying no rifle of his own. The Inuit's expression changed and he meekly let the furs drop to his feet. Then Ikateq and Silumi pushed through the door behind Nanoq, their own rifles levelled at his back. Olaf stepped forward, quickly and efficiently handcuffing Nanoq to himself.

It was all over in seconds with no real incident. Harry followed Christian into the main room in a daze. Neither of them had played an active part in the arrest, but Christian turned to him, at last allowing himself a smile.

'It is done,' he said. 'Now we can soon go back to our proper work'.

Harry was surprised to hear clear, unaccented English from a man who had hardly spoken two words together before this moment.

Harry tried to return the smile but felt suddenly deflated. This was not because of any dissatisfaction with his own part in events. Rather, there came a strong return of the feeling that had been with him for hours: there was something wrong with all this. Exactly what it was he was unable to say. In some strange way he couldn't pinpoint the key seemed to be here in Nanoq's cabin.

Now Lars was speaking solemnly to Nanoq in Greenlandic: charging him with Essie's murder, Harry guessed. The big man at first looked impassive, then alarmed, then started to shake his head, slowly at first and then more vigorously.

'Naaga! Naaga! Naaga!'

There was something pathetic about the scene. Nanoq towered over the others. He was very tall for an Inuit, half a head taller even than Olaf and Harry, and he was powerfully built. Yet he looked like some trapped creature at bay, standing there, shaking his head.

'Naaga! Naaga! Naaga!'

Harry knew what that meant: 'No! No! No!'. He'd have known this even without his few words of Greenlandic. Through his years on the Force he'd been present at enough arrests to know incredulous denial was a common reaction from all criminals, major or minor, when they realised the law had caught up with them. It usually indicated nothing more than fear. And yet he couldn't rid himself of the thought that this time there was more to it. During all his years as a policeman, he'd never had this odd feeling with nothing to back it up.

Suddenly, Nanoq's eye-rolling look fell upon Harry. He lurched forward toward him. Despite being handcuffed now to Ikateq as well as to Olaf, he dragged both of these large men in his wake. Harry leaped back instinctively.

'Naaga! Kusanartoq Essie toquvoq! Tuluk ajorpoq!'

Nanoq clenched his fists as he railed at Harry. There was a wildness about his whole bearing. It was clear his rage was directed solely at himself.

'So, the Bear thinks he can cry out to the Great White God from England,' sneered Olaf, using all his strength to drag Nanoq backwards with the handcuffs. He balled his fist. Harry could see that Olaf, angry at being pulled about by Nanoq, wanted to strike him with his own free hand. The Dane couldn't find the courage to do it.

Nanoq continued to rant, but the fight was quickly going out of him. At first he pulled Ikateq and Olaf about like rag dolls. Then Silumi and Christian lent their own considerable weights to the struggle and he fell silent. To Harry the Inuit looked profoundly sad, like a wild beast stumbling into a snare whose intricate workings it did not understand.

'We must take Nanoq and lock him in the larger winter storeroom without delay,' said Lars with authority.

'The door is strong and locks with a padlock and chain from the outside. Silumi and Ikateq can take turns to stand guard. We cannot risk an escape before Knud Holm arrives from Ammassalik. Take him now', ordered the small man in this room of comparative giants. The arrest had gone more smoothly than Harry had dared to hope but Nanoq's reaction afterwards had left him deeply unsettled.

The group led off through the cabin door. Harry was glad to be leaving the sickening smell behind. Nanoq, with Olaf on one side and Ikateq on the other, led the way. Now he was much more subdued, but still kept glancing over his shoulder, in a way showing he thought Harry was to blame for his misfortune. Christian and Silumi walked a few paces to the rear of this group of three, their rifles trained carefully on Nanoq's back. They were taking no chances. Lars brought up the rear, next to Harry, his arms filled by the four remaining rifles. He turned to Harry with a tired expression.

'Well, my friend, there is enough of this sad business for both of us, I think. Now I can go back to being a tour guide and you can resume your holiday, although I think we will be deleting the Valley of Qooroqilulissat from our itinerary. It is a shame, but I think it must be so. What do you say?'

'It is not over, Lars.'

'Come Harry, we have done our work. You have played your own part well. I have asked you to do more than I should; I am aware of this. Olaf and the others can look after things until the full-time police can come from Ammassalik, although they have now told me on the radio phone that, because of the bad weather conditions, this might not be possible for two more days. There are still thick fogs off the coast, especially further to the south. I will write my report, then I will be pleased to go back to my proper work. I have neglected the other members of the tour party for long enough.'

'I am convinced Nanoq did not kill Essie. Are you listening to what I'm telling you Lars?'

Lars stopped where he was, signalling Olaf,Ikateq and Silumi to go ahead without him.

'How can you say this? You were a policeman yourself. You should know that, merely because a man denies a crime, it does not mean he is innocent. Where is your evidence for claiming such a thing?'

'I simply know it.' Harry was barely beginning to understand himself why he was saying these words. He could hardly blame Lars for his incredulous reaction.

Lars' eyes narrowed. His voice dropped an octave and he pointed an accusatory finger at Harry.

'Think carefully about what you are saying. Do you want people to start to believe your own part is not so innocent? Why should Nanoq turn on you in the way he did? I wondered this when he spoke. There are other things I've been wondering also,' he added darkly. 'Nanoq may be identifying you with all the tourists who have come to the settlement this year, yet there may be more in his mind.' His tone softened. For a moment Harry thought Lars was going to actually take him by the hand.

'My good friend, this is not a road that either of us will wish to go down. Look, you know I have my report to write. I will give you time to think more of your hasty words. Consider them very seriously, I beg you. Come to see me, in my room, at eight o'clock this evening. We must put an end to this, once and for all.'

3.7

'I know you always like to drink your whisky neat, my friend. You have told me this is the only way it should be served. Be careful you do not come to like it so much that you allow it to be your downfall.'

Lars had put his hand on the neck of a three-quarters full bottle as soon as Harry walked into the cabin. His eyes had been irresistibly drawn to it the moment he entered. The golden transparency of the liquid held a promise Harry knew it could never quite deliver. Tonight, the whisky looked especially inviting as it caught the rays of the sun emerging from the slowly-clearing sky. It was all he could do to prevent himself from replying *"go on then; I'll have a small one."*

One "small one" would lead to another and too soon the small one would become a larger one. And then... No, he had to try. It might be a long, hard road but it was his to follow, starting from today. Harry felt for the hard outlines of Lars' small flask, still in his side-pocket. He hoped Lars wouldn't ask for this back. It had become a talisman in the silent, private struggle on which he had embarked.

'You could say it already has been my downfall,' he said. 'So, no more whisky for me. I finally decided this morning by that pool.'

'It was your problem with the police in England? Was it this that made you lose your job? It is something that will happen to me soon, losing my job. For a different reason, I should say.'

Lars made a motion with his hand to show, in a quiet gesture of support, he wouldn't be pouring a glass of whisky for himself either. Harry wondered if he was going to ask for the return of his flask but, for some reason, he seemed to have decided against it. Lars couldn't have known the status the silver-and-leather container had now taken on for Harry. Still, he was grateful for the Dane's silence on the matter.

He even wondered whether he should bring the subject into the open and ask Lars outright if he could keep the flask. This might not be a good idea. What if he answered "no", as well he might? For all his outward friendliness, Lars seemed distant tonight. These thoughts nagged quietly at his mind as he watched the Dane walk over to sit on the edge of his bed. He indicated with a nod of his head that Harry should take the only chair.

'As I was saying, it is something the two of us will soon share,' Lars said. 'Probably as soon as next year we will be ex-policemen together. But, as I am no more than a very part-time one, this will not be such a big thing for me. There has been no need of anything more in Vatsaaq before now. I hope there never will be again.'

'I told you, I was *retired'*. Harry almost shouted, surprising himself with his vehemence. Then he relented. His shameful exit from the Force was hardly Lars' fault. He should be more honest with himself as well as with the Dane. 'But, yes, you could say I might not have been retired for a year or two yet, if the Chief Super had looked more kindly upon a little social drinking.' Harry tried to laugh off his anger, but only succeeded in making a stifled choking noise in his throat. 'He was a bit of a Puritan,' he added.

'Puritan? Did not the Puritans sail to America to make a new Church?'

'Something like that'. Harry forced a smile. 'I wish the bloody Chief Super had gone sailing to America. In a leaky boat without sails and with no paddle would be my choice. Still, I shouldn't say such things. I left the Chief no alternative, I know it. I'd have been forced to do exactly the same in his position. Maybe I'd have done it in a less kindly way. But why should you lose your job? You seem to be a pretty good policeman, part-time or not.'

'Perhaps, before today, I have not been so bad. Until last year I was a policeman in West Greenland. This was in a place called Maniitsoq. Much larger than Vatsaaq. Almost a city to us,' he laughed.

'Even then, I was no more than a part-time policeman,' he continued. 'My real job was with Icesperience. But, as they are doing with all the Danes, the Home Rule Government wanted to give my job to a Greenlander. I do not blame them. Then, this year my company had the brave idea of starting this new holiday place in Vatsaaq.

'They wanted to move me here, so flattered me by saying they needed an experienced man for the new centre. I've only been here for two months but already I love Vatsaaq Bay. When I first saw its perfection, it quickly became been my favourite place in the whole of Greenland. So, I jumped at the chance of living and working here. Olaf came along with me, together with his brother Christian. They make their living in the same way as the Inuit; what the Greenland police pay Olaf is no more than a token. We are friends, in a way you perhaps would not understand. And not only as you are thinking. Olaf and I are true friends, be sure of that.'

Harry tried to keep his features impassive.

'Anyway, when the new Greenland police force heard about my relocation with Icesperience, they asked me if I wanted to continue as a part-time policeman here, too. But only till next year, when they intend to bring in a Greenlander from Eqalassaq, the larger Inuit settlement to the south. Again, I do not really mind this. Especially now I have experienced some real police duties. You have been kind enough to say I am good at this work, Harry, but I do not like it. I do not like it at all.'

'Nobody really likes some of the things the police have to do, Lars. But, sadly, we're not here tonight to talk about our experiences with the police services of our countries, are we? We're here to talk about Essie Smith's death...'

Lars rose to his feet. His expression and whole demeanour changed.

'Harry, I must ask you to stop there. I do not wish you to tell me anything. If you need to say anything about Ms Smith, you cannot do so as my friend. You must speak to me as a policeman. Or you can say it to Knud Holm when he gets here, if this would be better for you. It would certainly be easier for me.'

Harry was surprised by this abrupt change in Lars' manner. What was he thinking now? But the Dane kept talking quickly.

'I would certainly prefer you to speak to Knud Holm. This is much too serious a business for us to talk about in ordinary conversation, especially if we do not want to test our friendship beyond the limit. There has been a murder, as you do not need me to tell you. But, please, I ask you to say nothing at all to me about Ms Smith. We can talk about other things. And maybe we…'

Harry was puzzled by Lars' new attitude. He interrupted before the young Dane had the chance to say anything further.

'I thought, Lars, I was supposed to be your assistant on this case, however unofficial this might be. You were the one who suggested we speak again this evening. How can I not say anything about Essie?'

Lars sighed, and went over to the cabinet. This time he did pour a generous measure of whisky for himself. He waved the bottle vaguely in Harry's direction. Harry shook his head more vigorously than was warranted.

'You haven't been listening to what I'm saying,' said Lars. 'You know we have Nanoq locked up in one of the winter store cabins.' His face was grave and he looked uncomfortable. 'We have the statement from Silumi to the effect that Nanoq left the party with Ms Smith. You have heard from Olaf's own lips the – er – manner in which the two of them went off towards his cabin. The stories of all the other Inuit are watertight. We will be able to get a statement from Henrik Rasmussen as soon as we have caught up with him. This is not an urgent matter; we know exactly what Henrik will have to tell us.

'Do you not see that this case is now as good as closed, Harry?The day has been a long one. There has been much to do. You know this yourself. But now it is time to bring things to an end. Maybe once again we can be…'

'Lars, you can't simply leave this all up in the air for me!' Harry interrupted.

The young man sighed theatrically before answering.

'Let me tell you I have several significant pieces of material evidence that can link the crime to Nanoq if they are used properly. They can be very telling. There is nothing left to cause you concern. Forget all this.'

'I can't simply forget it. What on Earth are you talking about? You were going to tell me something this evening, weren't you?'

Lars looked at him blankly. 'I have now spoken to Nanoq,' he said, as if this explained everything.

'And?' said Harry.

Lars looked at Harry for a long moment before speaking again.

'There is evidence that can be used to link Nanoq directly to the murder. Some of it we found in Nanoq's cabin today. We have the man. Any court in the world would judge him to be guilty of this crime when they see what we found. I repeat: we have him. Why must you persist in this? The case is closed, Harry. No-one else need be dragged into it. Olaf will say nothing. You surely cannot be worried about Nanoq's protest when he was arrested. You are aware and the judge will also know what criminals are like. Besides, he will be sure you do not even understand Greenlandic. Few people from your country do.'

Harry didn't answer at first. Lars' words were a puzzle to him. He couldn't even properly explain to himself why he wouldn't simply forget everything in the way the Dane so obviously wanted. But he had to try to work out why something would not allow him to walk away from this, as all common sense told him he should. The thoughts were still forming in his mind as he spoke.

'Do you remember interrogating me down at the Valley of Qooroqilulissat?'

'Not interrogate, Harry. I know more than enough of your English to say this is not the word you should use. I asked you a few questions. I did nothing more. It was normal police work. I couldn't ask too gently in front of Olaf. I have told you all this. Do you want me to say I am sorry for my actions? I will do it if this is what you want.'

'No, no. Of course I don't. I understood when you told me the first time. I was being stupid to be so sensitive about it. That's not what we were going to talk about tonight though, is it?' Harry drew a deep breath before continuing.

'What I wanted to say is there was a period of time I couldn't account for. You know this much yourself. I saw your eyebrows shoot up when we came to that part of the questioning. As mine would have done. As any policeman's should. I was worried about the blank in my memory, I don't mind telling you this now. When you can't even explain to yourself where you were at the time a woman was murdered, it gets to you. But tonight in Nanoq's cabin, some of it came back to me. It was the smell of stale fish that did it.'

'I think it is time for you to stop talking. We have Nanoq in custody.' Lars gulped nervously at his whisky.

'Listen, Lars. Please listen for a minute, won't you?' Harry waited until he was sure he had Lars' attention. The Dane remained silent, although he looked even more edgy as Harry continued to speak. 'What I remember – and I'm quite sure this wasn't a drunken dream – was that around about one o'clock, probably well afterwards, I went outside to see the Aurora. It's what happened. Don't look at me like that, Lars. I was too pissed to realise the sky would be much too light.'

There was an absolute silence in the cabin for a moment. Then Harry plunged further into his account. He couldn't have stopped, even if he'd wanted to.

'I was sitting there, by the door, waiting on the bench. For it to get dark or something stupid, I suppose. I closed my eyes. Maybe I even dozed off for a moment or two, I don't know. I'd shipped a hell of a lot of whisky. There's no point in me trying to deny it. I drank too much for any man. Vonnie said I drank too much for any two men. But when I opened my eyes, there was this big Inuit right in front of me, staring into my face. It was Nanoq, although I didn't know his name then.'

'You're saying he was by himself?'

'Yes. He put his hands on my shoulders and mumbled something I couldn't understand. Then he looked down at the bottle. I was still clinging to it. He took his hands from my shoulders, and made a cupping shape with them. It was the last of my *Benromach* in that bottle, not your local rot-gut. Out of my mind as I was with whisky, I realised he was asking for a drink, so I gave him one. Between us, we finished what was left. And we talked.'

'You *talked*?' Lars was incredulous. 'Nanoq barely knows a dozen words of your English, His Greenlandic speech is crazy enough.'

'We talked. OK, so it wasn't a conversation in the way any sane and sober person would have thought of one. It was mainly grunts and gestures. Still, we understood each other well enough, after a fashion. He told me about Essie, although I didn't realise he was talking about her at the time.'

'He told you? Now wait; I can understand how...' Lars paused momentarily. A look of distaste flickered across his face as he used the word with vehemence. '... two *drunks* can pass a few minutes in fellowship, but for Nanoq to *explain* – why, the man couldn't explain anything if he was sober, even in Greenlandic.

Lars looked at Harry incredulously for a few moments before going on in a low tone.

'He hasn't yet been able to give me a fully coherent account of his movements last night, though he has told me some of the important things. Enough for me to know it is time for me to close this case.'

He once more looked intently at Harry.

'I mean to question him in the morning to have all the details clear in my mind. And I will certainly be speaking to him, Harry. I will be speaking to him again. Don't forget this.'

'Gestures. He used gestures.' Harry snapped back the words. He couldn't help thinking Lars was being much too coy about the whole thing. More coarsely than he'd intended, Harry used his hands to outline a woman's shape, then to make the universal sign for a phallus. Finally, he tilted his head to show rejection and disappointment.

'Only he was funnier about it,' Harry continued. 'Or so it seemed to me at the time. And then we laughed. Somehow I ended up seeing him back to his cabin. We were singing as we went. Sort of singing, anyway. *Jingle Bells* of all the daft things. Don't look at me like that, Lars.'

Harry was starting to feel very foolish, but at the same time he was starting to feel a weight lifting from his shoulders. He continued:

'Somehow, we did make it back to his cabin. Nanoq was even more drunk than I was. I more or less had to push him inside. He fell straight across his bed. I'd have said he was out to the world. And then it hit me: the stench, the awful stink of stale fish. It was the smell of Nanoq's cabin earlier this evening that brought back these memories back to me. Anyway, I remembered, too, that last night I ran outside, wanting to be sick and muttering about the Aurora. Oddly enough, I didn't throw up. Afterwards, I must have found my way back to the party, what was left of it. I don't remember anything much after that.'

'I see,' was all Lars would say in response. Then he remained thoughtfully silent. It was too much for Harry.

'What do you mean, *you see*? Don't you understand Nanoq couldn't have had anything to do with Essie's death? He was in no fit state to drive to Qooroqilulissat. What has he told you so far? Does it fit in with what I've told you?'

'Maybe,' said Lars, infuriatingly, then narrowed his eyes at Harry. 'But what, for instance, if I told you Nanoq has said nothing about you going with him to his cabin? What if he told me only that Ms Smith had not let him – had rejected him?'

'Maybe he was too drunk to remember that part,' said Harry. 'He was more drunk than I was. I've told you this. So are we going to let Nanoq go, and look for the real killer?'

'It is not so simple, Harry. You are forgetting what Silumi has already told Olaf and me. And there are one or two things I have not told you. I was not going to bother you with them...'

'Lars! Don't bugger me about!'

Lars was unperturbed by Harry's outburst. He looked at him steadily, clearly weighing things up in his mind.

'So be it,' he said at last. 'I will tell you what evidence we have against Nanoq, though only to reassure you for the sake of our friendship. Not as one policeman to another. Things have changed. You must see this. Remember well what I am telling you.'

He paused and searched his face. Harry was still baffled but resisted the impulse to add anything else. Lars at last continued:

'In the trailer, the one used to take Ms Smith's body to the Valley of Qooroqilulissat, ‚we found something besides the blood. It was a pen. One of the pens given out by the tour company to each member of your group back in your country. At first we thought Nanoq had stolen it, or found it, and did not attach any importance to the matter. Especially since he seemed to have polished it. There'd be no fingerprints but Nanoq's own for anyone to see.'

Lars looked steadily into Harry's face.

'There is something else; an important thing. It is fortunate Olaf was not with me at the time. In Nanoq's cabin I then found a big wad of notes, including a lot of Icelandic kronur. There was more money than The Bear would have seen in five years. Where would he have got so much?'

Harry remained silent. What indeed was the Inuit doing with a large amount of foreign currency? Could he have stolen it from Essie? Something told him not to voice this thought.

'Very well, I will spell it out for you,' said Lars. 'Someone like Knud Holm might well think one of the tour party was involved in Ms. Smith's murder. I thought about it and planned against telling him anything about these finds in case this was exactly what he did think. Do you understand what I'm saying, Harry? It is a big thing, a criminal thing, I am prepared to do for you.'

Now it was Harry's turn to stop and think. Up until now he'd given all of his attention to the belief that Nanoq was innocent of the crime. He'd hardly stopped to consider who could be responsible. One of the Greenland Party? Surely not… Freddie Tanner? One of the Walters? Tony Ferris? Jeremy Smith, Essie's brother? Not old Dainty Clatworthy for heaven's sake? Impossible. What was Lars getting at?

Lars continued, speaking even more slowly now. 'Even if Knud Holm believed your story – and I do not think for one minute he would – this would not in itself prove Nanoq's innocence. It hasn't been shown he wasn't working with somebody from the tourist party. And there is another thing we should then have to take into account –'

'But I've told you where Nanoq was,' said Harry, interrupting again. 'The man was hopelessly drunk.'

'At best you would be giving him a partial cover story – a kind of alibi, as you would say.' Lars seemed to be ignoring everything Harry was trying to say. 'But it would be a poor one. To a degree it confirms what Silumi has told us, and what Henrik will surely have to confirm when we get his statement. But let me tell you that Nanoq was not as drunk as you are saying. You had too much to drink yourself to know this.'

'How can you say this? How do you know how drunk Nanoq was for goodness' sake?'

'Because,' Lars spoke in patient tones, like a teacher taking time with a slow child. 'Ms Smith was taken to Qooroqilulissat in the trailer as I have told yo. The driver was at least sober enough to drive the vehicle there and back. Only six of us have ready access to the key for it: Olaf and Christian Severen, Nanoq, Silumi, Ikateq and myself. We let The Bear drive sometimes. I've already told you that Olaf was with me all night. We know about Christian. Silumi and Ikateq have accounted for their movements. This leaves only Nanoq. And he has not tried to deny taking the body down to Qooroqilulissat.'

Harry felt cold. Lars words jabbed at him like knives.

'If he heard what you have said to me, Harry, someone like Knud Holm might well say you are not yourself in the clear. Nanoq could have killed Ms Smith together with you, or on your instructions, in which case you would try give him an alibi, would you not? Do you now see the reasons for my concern? Do you not understand why it would be better for you if we kept this case simple?'

'Lars, you can't believe I'm involved in any way!'

Lars seemed calm, in total control of the situation. He was now standing in a relaxed way by the cabinet, with his arms folded in front of him. They could have been talking about the weather.

'I am not saying anything. I am being very careful to say nothing about what I think. But, do you not see, for Knud Holm this would be a plausible explanation? It fits in with all the facts as far as we know them. All the facts I should be presenting to Knud Holm. You have told me yourself you left the party to go to Nanoq's cabin – we found a button not too far from this. It was close by the charred heap of Ms Smith's clothing: my guess is that it was torn off from her red coat during a struggle before the clothes were burned. I brought it with me tonight to show you.'

Lars dug in his pocket and held out his hand, displaying an unblemished gold-coloured button, wrapped in a crumpled packet of transparent paper. Harry recognised it immediately as being from Essie's red coat. She'd been wearing this at the ill-fated party.

'This is what I'd planned to show to Knud Holm. Not the pen or money.'

'Where exactly did you find it?'

'As I said, it was found close to Nanoq's door. Old Anvik found it and she brought it to me. After cleaning it up, of course. So there'll be no fingerprints to find on this, either.'

'OK Lars, you win. We can't rule Nanoq out of the equation. You'll need to keep him locked up.'

'And should I also lock you up, Harry?

'You can't think…'

'I have told you, Harry. It doesn't matter what I think. Nor does it matter what other people say to me. But you must realise how what you've told me would sound to Knud Holm.'

Lars stood quietly. Then he gave a grimace and started to speak again in a low, discomfited voice.

'Harry, I asked you not to say anything to me. You still insisted on doing it. What I've decided to do is treat all you have told me this evening as something said in confidence to me as a friend, and not as a policeman.'

Lars waved Harry's protests away. 'I know I shouldn't be doing this; you don't have to tell me. I am breaking the law. Soon I won't be a policeman at all, so perhaps this matters less. Tonight I choose not to be on duty. I've been having a private word with you. That is all.' Lars nodded, letting his words sink in.

'Now you must not repeat anything of what you've told me to Knud Holm when he gets here, or to anyone else. All you must say is that you had too much to drink and can't remember anything. If you have to say you went outside, you should simply say you went outside to be sick. Say nothing at all about your meeting with Nanoq. Do you promise me?'

'I won't say anything. Unless my questions to the other members of the tour party lead me to do it, that is.'

Lars looked pained. 'Harry, I want you to put no questions to the others. You cannot continue as my assistant. Surely you must realise this? Anyway, I intend to make no more enquiries except for questioning Nanoq about a few details in the morning. My investigation will then be closed until Knud Holm gets here. Then I will hand over Nanoq and tell him everything I have found out – except for what you've told me and my finding of the pen and money . You have my word this conversation will remain a private one between friends. I will not say a word to anyone.'

Lars rose and held out his hand, almost formally. Harry's mind was whirling, but he he shook the proffered hand.

'I can tell you that I spoke on the telephone to Knud Holm in Ammassalik only thirty minutes before you came. The forecast is for the bad weather off the coast to continue for two days, more at least. But my enquiries are now over and Nanoq is held securely. Remember what I've said, Harry. Remember it well.'

Harry did not trust himself to say anything more about Essie Smith's murder.

'So what's the plan for tomorrow?' he asked, in an attempt to end the awkward silence.

'Tomorrow, I become a guide again, and you once more will be a normal member of the visiting group. We must consider that I still have a tour to look after. I shall ask Gudrun to call a meeting in the Great Hall for everybody in the morning. I shall announce that Ms Smith's murderer has been caught and is safely locked up in the store cabin.

'I will tell them we have to wait for the full-time policeman to arrive, and I will need to say something about the abnormal weather conditions. They will understand; people from your country are always sympathetic when they are told about the weather, even though our weather is something beyond their experience. Then I shall give details of a revised itinerary. Something Gudrun and I will want to do is to say a few words in memory of Ms Smith. You will understand this. I will work it all out in the morning. I am too tired tonight. It has been a long day. You must be tired, too, Harry.'

'I am,' Harry admitted. He was exhausted.

'Then good night.'

*

The sky was a crystal blue as Harry emerged from Lars' cabin. The weather today was as confused as Harry's own thoughts. Looking up, he resented the long Northern summer day that stopped him seeing any sign of the glittering of the stars at this hour. When they went further north to Ittoqqoortormiit they'd be further inside the Arctic Circle, and daylight would be with them for an even longer time.

His felt restless, too, after his interview with Lars. What the Dane had said was true: things would certainly get difficult for him if anyone else listened to his story. It would be hard for anyone to believe what he was trying to say. It was all he could do to understand it himself. There were moments when he couldn't be sure of what he'd seen and done.

Why was Lars prepared, even eager, to say nothing? And wasn't it a bit too convenient that there'd be no fingerprint-evidence on both the button and the pen? But now his own doubts about what had happened were growing in strength. Was it all part of some drunken northern dream? Did he really have the encounter with

Nanoq as he'd described it? *Jingle Bells*? Even to himself, this now sounded like the crazed ravings of a madman.

Then his mind drifted back to Essie's lifeless form on Pesut's makeshift autopsy table. Despite his best efforts, the image of her body kept forming in his mind.

'Good evening'. A tall figure rounded the corner of one of the cabins and spoke, interrupting his disquieting reverie. It was Olaf, smiling an unfriendly smile that gave the lie to the politeness of his greeting.

'Evening.'

'Late for walking, Mr. Lanier?'

'I've been to see Lars.'

'In his cabin?' The façade of courtesy dropped away in an instant, to be replaced by the open hostility Harry knew had been bubbling away beneath the surface almost since he'd arrived in Vatsaaq.

'Where else would we meet?'

'I do not think this is a thing I like.'

Olaf was grinding his right fist into his left palm in a melodramatic way. Harry quickly sized up the situation. Olaf was of much the same height and build as himself, but was powerful and mean, as well as being twenty or more years younger. Harry knew he wouldn't stand a ghost of a chance in a fair fight, let alone a dirty one. He made up his mind what to do.

'That's a pity. Evening to you.'

Saying this, he stepped forward, bumping his shoulder against Olaf's as he did so. He hoped he'd judged it properly: not hard enough for it to be interpreted as a direct attack that would have to be answered, but then not so gentle as to suggest he wouldn't mean business if this was the way Olaf wanted things. For a moment he braced himself to receive a punch or a kick in the back. Then, when he'd put a few yards between himself and the bearded man, he shivered involuntarily, still in anticipation of a vicious assault from behind.

None of his fears materialised. Olaf muttered a few venomous words of Danish, then laughed, loud and long. Harry felt he'd won a small victory, although he knew this unwanted war was far from being over.

That laugh... was it a killer's laugh? *'You're being bloody stupid again, you damned fool,'* Harry told himself. There was nothing to link Olaf to Essie's death. Hadn't Lars given him an alibi? But maybe this could explain the strange conversation he'd had with Lars. Was he covering up for his fellow Dane?

Essie's death wasn't uppermost in Harry's mind at that precise moment. He knew he'd have to look out for his own safety with this threatening man around. What hold could this repulsive specimen have over someone as gentle as Lars? Harry thought again of the look on Lars' mild face when he'd told him about himself and Olaf. Then he thought of Olaf's lewd mime in Lars' cabin earlier this evening.

Why had he and Vonnie chosen to come to Vatsaaq? His mind was still seething with emotions and thoughts he didn't even want to understand. He stepped inside their cabin and closed the door. It was a relief to find Vonnie was already asleep. He wouldn't have to say anything else tonight.

Chapter Four
Unwanted Help

Monday, 29th August, 1994, Vatsaaq, East Greenland

'Ladies and gentlemen.' Gudrun's voice was as light as it had been when she'd first uttered these words. This was two weeks earlier in Iceland's Keflavik Airport. It gave the lie to the darkness of what they all knew she was going to say. She looked around the assembly in the Great Hall before continuing, satisfying herself she had the attention of each one of them.

'As you know, we are here in tragic circumstances. I've spoken to all of you individually about what has happened, so there is no need for me to dwell upon those ugly events. It is also true that you came to our countries of Iceland and Greenland to see and experience their beauty. It is my duty not to forget this.

'I have therefore been discussing the matter most carefully with Mr Lars Erikssen ' .

Gudrun gestured towards Lars, who was sitting alongside the lectern. All eyes turned towards him and he bowed his head gravely.

'More importantly,' she continued. ' I have also spoken to Mr Jeremy Smith, to see if it is possible for us to go on with our tour. I am pleased to say that, in the depths of his great sadness, Mr. Smith has suggested we should continue as normally as we can. You will all consider this very brave of him, especially since the weather conditions prevent us from arranging his own return to your homeland. And I, Gudrun Jonsdottir, and all of us at Icesperience, can only agree with you and applaud his courage.'

There was a scattered, self-conscious hand-clapping Harry felt obliged to join in, without really knowing why. He searched the faces of the others. They were mostly impassive, even that of Jeremy Smith. It was the first time he'd seen Smith since Saturday evening. Only Freddie Tanner was displaying much in the way of outward emotion. His bottom lip was quivering. It looked as if he wanted to say something, or even to blubber. Thankfully, he did neither.

'Thank you all,' Gudrun said in response. 'I hope you will shortly feel able to join with us for a brief service in memory of Ms Smith. Before we do this, it is necessary for our guide here in Greenland, Mr. Lars Erikssen, to say a few words. He wishes to speak to you as a private citizen as well as in his role as the temporary representative of the police service in Vatsaaq.'

Gudrun beckoned Lars, who rose from his chair and walked slowly to her side. Harry couldn't help thinking the woman's posture spoke of amateur dramatics. The Tour Manager made way for Lars at the small lectern. He slowly looked around the small assembly before speaking.

'You will know from Gudrun that, as well as being your guide, I am at present the representative of the police service here,' Lars began, adopting a grave tone. 'I trust the fact that the duties of my office have called upon my time since yesterday morning has not been too much of a trouble for you. I can tell you that the local man we believe to be the killer of Ms Smith has already been apprehended. He is safely confined. I am therefore able to say to you that I may now resume my duties as your guide.

'There are still a few minor police matters for me to deal with, but I will have no major questions to ask any of you, so this need not interfere with our plans. It is possible that the full-time policeman, whose name is Mr. Knud Holm, will have a few routine questions later but I'm sure this will not inconvenience you in any way. As you have been told, it will not be possible for Mr Holm to come here until tomorrow, or even the day after, because of the unusual weather conditions affecting so much of our country. And now Gudrun Jonsdottir would like to speak again.'

Lars stepped away from the lectern and Gudrun resumed her place. Reading from a sheet, she said a few words about Essie Smith. '*They're really milking this*,' Harry told himself, and then immediately regretted his harsh thought. Harry listened carefully to what she was saying, hoping to learn something new, but Gudrun's words were mainly platitudes about Essie's character, interspersed with a few religious gesturings. Surely this wasn't what she had meant by a 'short service'? At last she finished what she had to say, her words tailing off with something like embarrassment. Perhaps she was, after all, genuinely upset. After she'd stepped down, Lars once more took up a position behind the lectern. He gripped its sides until his knuckles showed white, as Harry had seen the more nervous speakers doing at police training courses.

Lars stood in silence, looking down at what Harry guessed to was a bible. The silence continued. Harry wondered what could be wrong with Lars. Why was he doing this? But, at the precise moment when the group had reached the limit of its restlessness, Lars looked up and began to speak in a clear, direct voice. Harry immediately knew he'd been wrong to compare him with any apprehensive public speaker.

'The reading is taken from the first epistle of Paul the Apostle to the Thessalonians, chapter two, verses thirteen to eighteen.'

Lars' tones were deep and resonant. He looked around him as he spoke. His eyes shone. He hardly needed to look at the page lying before him. It was as if he were speaking to each one of them individually.

'But I would not have you to be ignorant, brethren, concerning them which are asleep, that ye sorrow not, even as others, which have no hope...'

As Lars continued, Harry could see he had everyone in thrall with the rhythm of his words. They brought the archaisms of the King James' Bible to vibrant life. Harry was amazed to know that a copy of this seventeenth-century volume was here in Greenland. He was even more surprised to find Lars seemed to know at least this passage by heart. Each one of those present was clearly moved by this simple service. Even Harry, who had not seen the inside of a church since the day of his marriage, felt regret as the reading drew to its close:

'...shall be caught up with them in the clouds, to meet the Lord in the air: and so shall we ever be with the Lord. Wherefore comfort one another with these words.

'And now, I ask for one minute of silent prayer, for us all to remember Ms Smith, each in his or her own way'.

Harry closed his eyes. For a moment his mind held the image of Essie wedged behind the ice, her awkward pose mocking the life that had been hers. And then his mind's eye formed an image of her as she was in life, on that day in the thermal pool in Iceland. Selfoss... Then Lars spoke again. The young man's earlier reading lingered in the air, pushing Harry's baser thoughts aside. Harry turned Lars' words over in his mind, mentally replaying them. He knew he was not only doing this for their content. He was also doing it for their music. This had touched him in a strange and troubling way.

At that moment a loud throaty noise, almost a sob, from Freddie Tanner broke the spell. Harry opened his eyes to find Lars looking at him steadily. They each held the gaze of the other for a brief but powerful instant. Then Lars smiled. It was not the eager smile Harry had known before from his friend. For some reason he could not properly identify, it was a disturbing one.

'Thank you,' Lars said, looking around at the group again. 'Can we meet back here in thirty minutes?' The magic was over. Lars once more had become a tour guide.

*

'Didn't he speak beautifully?' Maggie Walters was walking beside him. Vonnie was just ahead of them, no doubt listening to similar praise from the lips of Maggie's husband Melvyn.

'He surprised me,' said Harry, making the understatement of his life. 'He's in the wrong career.'

'I wouldn't say so. I always knew our Lars had something about him. I'm sure he'll be a good guide for us. He's done his stuff so far. And from what the laddie says and everything I see, he's not so bad as a detective, either.'

'What do you think, Dainty?' Harry spoke to the old lady in front of him rather than Maggie. He was anxious to deflect the conversation so he could be alone with his thoughts. 'Are you another member of Lars' fan club?'

'He read his Bible well, and he's got the voice for it. The lad knows he does well enough, too, though I don't hold this against him. No, if they'd both left it at the reading, I'd have been happy enough. It was all we needed. But that girl; I remember her in Iceland.' She stopped, embarrassed. 'Oh, I shouldn't be saying this.'

'What d'you mean, Dainty?' Maggie Walters placed an arm on the old lady's shoulder. 'You've said it now. May as well get it off your chest.'

'I mean that if young Gudrun didn't have anything genuinely good to say about Miss Smith, then she shouldn't have said anything.'

'I don't think that's all you mean.' Maggie was persistent.

Dainty smiled weakly. She looked around, making sure they were out of earshot of the other members of the party. She slowed her pace to allow Melvyn Walters and Vonnie would go on a few steps further so they wouldn't hear what she was going to say. Maggie leaned forward, almost eagerly.

'Oh, I wish I hadn't said anything at all. Look, neither of you must repeat a word.'

Maggie shook her head quickly, and looked toward Harry for him to do the same. Then, behind Dainty's back, she arched her eyebrows and grinned. Harry thought this more than a little wicked given what might be the nature of what the old lady had to tell them. But he shook his own head in turn, not trusting himself to put into words a promise he might have to break later.

'Well, what I mean is, she shouldn't have said those things about Miss Smith if she didn't know her well enough to say them. I don't want to speak ill of the dead but... well, she wasn't all that she should have been, that one.'

'You mean the way she was dancing at the party?' said Harry. 'I think she may have had a drop too much to drink that night. She wasn't the only one of us who did.' '*No, I had far more to drink*,' he thought. The memory took guilty shape in his mind.

'I don't know anything about any dance. Nor I don't want to know anything, thank you very much. It wouldn't surprise me in the least, whatever you might say. It's the day at Gulfoss I was talking about, when we were in Iceland. You remember we had to wait an extra half-hour for the bus? Some of us got a bit bored with watching the falls, remember? I didn't get bored, but I was getting tired, so I walked back to the roadside to sit and wait.'

Maggie and Harry nodded their confirmation.

'I saw Essie Smith wandering off with that Freddie Tanner just in front of me,' continued Dainty. 'I believe they had the idea no one had noticed them. It wasn't that I was following or spying on them, you understand. Anyway, before long they were sitting together on a rock in this sort of a copse. It wasn't really a copse. As Gudrun told us, you don't have such things in Iceland – the trees are too short and sparse to hide anyone properly. He was there, hand right inside that red coat of hers, you know, *feeling* her. And then he tried to, well you know, get hold of her properly, and up she jumped and ran off like a little girl dancing and skipping in a playground.'

Dainty looked from one to the other.

'Then he tried to leap up after her, but was too slow and fat to catch her, not to put too fine a point on it. And that's when they saw me.'

'What did they do when they saw you?' Harry said this more to break the tension than because he really wanted to know.

'That was almost the worst part of it. At least *he* looked ashamed and tried to pretend he hadn't seen me. He skulked off back in the direction of the Falls. But she, bold as brass, looks me straight in the eye, sticks out that big fat bust of hers, and laughs out loud. Laughs! Like a naughty child, she was. A wicked girl who's been caught raiding the sweet jar.'

Maggie Walters put her palm over her face, as if to stop herself chuckling aloud. Then, as Dainty turned towards her, she shook her head sorrowfully. Harry looked at Maggie, and couldn't help thinking he'd never seen such a consummate acting performance, even on the stage.

4.2

'You mustn't go jumping to conclusions, Harry. You were a copper for most of your life. Don't forget everything you learned now.'

Vonnie was right. He had to keep reminding himself about what she was saying. At the same time he was trying to take part in a normal conversation with her as she walked by his side, her arm linked through his. Seemingly, she'd partly forgiven him from the day before.

'You know, Harry, I think we can say this is the first proper day of the holiday since we arrived in Vatsaaq. And our stay here was supposed to be the highlight of Greenland. Tell me again: what do they call the cliffs we're visiting?'

'Kemiligaq. Look, here must be where we're going to stop for our picnic. No wonder Lars chose this place. It's wonderful.'

Harry and Vonnie were bringing up the rear of their group. They were walking in a leisurely fashion, partly because Harry was carrying one of the two picnic bags; more so because he didn't feel like hurrying after the day he'd had yesterday. The others apart from Freddie, whose lunch was carried by Harry and who was waiting with the rest less than patiently, were already unpacking their lunches from the other bag by the time they caught up with them.

'It's a beautiful day. I hope Lars doesn't want us to be on our way again too soon.' Vonnie sounded happy as she said this.

It was almost warm in the shelter of the rocks. The sun shone from a cloudless sky, and the wind was no more than a pleasant breath over the ground. It was hard to believe the weather could be so bad around Ammassalik. Lars had said it was still dangerous for Helicopters to take off and land safely at Kulusuk airport.

'You're right, love. I could do with a bit of a laze in the sun. Exactly like Bournemouth, this, wouldn't you say?'

'Not quite the same,' she laughed. 'I remember the days when you used to think it was great every time we went there. It was much cheaper on the South Coast and everything was far less complicated.'

Harry refused to rise to Vonnie's not-so-subtle taunt. He'd have liked it here, if only things had been different. He still *did* like it here, despite all that had happened. But how could Vonnie so easily put a thing like Essie's death out of her mind? He took off his parka, intending to use it as a pillow. Vonnie busied herself with the salmon and black bread sandwiches, tomatoes, apples, stollen cake, yoghurt and coffee.

Recent events replayed like a dream in Harry's mind. A very bad dream. But, at this moment, he found himself more detached from the horrors of the last few days. For the first time he felt he could properly reflect on his situation in a way not possible before.

Here he was, practically kicked out of the force for – face it – too much of a fondness for drink and – this was the only word to use – incompetence. They'd spent nearly a quarter of his pension lump sum on coming to Greenland. Had he enjoyed it? Vonnie may have been insensitive to compare this holiday unfavourably with those they'd spent together in their younger days all those years before, but what she'd said was essentially right.

Most of the time he'd he'd spent sulking about the way the Constabulary had treated him. Then, for the past thirty-six hours he'd done his best to demonstrate his uselessness as an amateur detective. It might be an unkind way to look at it, but that had to be the size of things from Vonnie's perspective. Or, indeed, that of any reasonable person. And yet he was sure there was more to this case. Something had happened to him since his arrival in Greenland – and not only as a result of Essie's death.

For thirty-two years his life had been orderly. He'd married Vonnie while he was hardly out of cadetship after a courtship going back to their schooldays. Slowly, he'd progressed from uniformed constable to plain-clothes man and then, ten years ago, the big one came when he was made up to Detective-Sergeant. All right, he'd never been a very good Sergeant, especially when the drink began to tell its tale, but for most of the time he'd been a steady one.

It had been the same with his life outside the Force: the move from a terraced house to a larger semi; a son and a daughter who'd done well at university and whom they still saw fairly regularly; secretary to the local rifle club for the last nine years; steady fidelity and licit sexual intercourse with Vonnie once a week. Friday was their night. They'd missed a lot of Friday nights lately. Had that been because of Vonnie's indifference or because he was always protesting tiredness?

Now he was finding out things about himself he'd never begun to guess at. The encounter with Olaf, quite as difficult as any situation he'd faced in uniform or as a detective. The hot lust – stronger than anything in his adolescence – he'd felt for Essie. He had to acknowledge the truth. Now she was dead, murdered practically in front of his eyes. And Lars… he hardly dared admit the effect this young man had on him.

'Aren't you hungry?'

His wife was holding out a piece of black bread spread generously with salmon glinting invitingly in the afternoon sun. He blinked back to the present, smiling a little foolishly. Vonnie smiled too. Then, for no reason, they both burst out laughing. For a moment, it really was like the old days.

*

Less than half-an-hour later, Lars called to the party to be on its way. The reluctance shown by Harry to get on with the walk wasn't feigned. Within minutes, his thoughts were once again of Essie and her murderer. He turned to Vonnie:

'What do you think of that Freddie Tanner, love?'

'Freddie Tanner? Not someone I want to spend much time thinking about, thank you very much. He's pudgy and not exactly Prince Charming. He's even fatter than you're beginning to be.' She patted his stomach. Harry was still reasonably lithe for his age, but was starting to protrude around the middle. 'Now, if you'd asked me what I think about Jeremy Smith...'

She arched her eyebrows and chuckled.

'No, seriously. Don't you think Freddie's a bit – odd?'

'He's a bit of a buffoon, if that's what you mean. Nothing more. Hasn't grown up yet, I suppose. Always has something to say for himself, making up those stupid jokes. And as for that fake Lancashire accent, *well...*'

'Fake? What do you mean? He's from Lancashire, surely.'

'Of course he's not.' She sounded incredulous. 'Can't you tell? It's not even a very good fake. He's from

Lambeth. Dainty found that out. She's a clever old girl, that one. He usually goes to Blackpool for his holidays, I'll bet. Can't think why he should have come here.'

'Don't you think it's a bit suspicious, trying to pretend you're from somewhere else?'

'No Harry, I don't. It's no more than one of his strange ideas of being funny.' The good humour was starting to leave Vonnie's voice. 'Now, tell me why are you so interested in Freddie Tanner? And why should you worry even if he was acting suspiciously? This murder business is all over, remember? Weren't you listening to what your precious Lars had to say this morning?'

'It's not all over, Vonnie. Please keep to yourself what I'm saying. There's something not right. The big Inuit didn't kill Essie; I *know* he didn't. And I'm sure, despite what he says, Lars is starting to think the same way too. At least, he believes Nanoq wasn't the only one involved in the murder. Mind you, it's hard to know just what Lars is thinking sometimes. Myself, I'm sure it has to be one of our party so I'm keeping a careful eye out.'

'What you mean is, you still want to play detective. That's what you're trying to say, isn't it?'

'Vonnie...'

But she had already withdrawn her arm from his.

'Vonnie, please be patient with me. It'll be all over in a day or two. The police from Ammassalik will be here by then. That will mean I wouldn't be able to be involved any longer, even if I wanted to. But I can't simply walk away from things yet. Look, I'll make it up to you, honestly. Meanwhile, please be careful about the others… Freddie Tanner especially.'

If Vonnie heard what Harry was saying, she gave no sign. She stomped off, clearly intending to walk a dozen paces ahead of him for the rest of the hike. He ran to catch up with her and caught hold of her arm more firmly than he'd intended. She looked fiery as she turned to face him.

'You're hurting me.'

'Vonnie. Don't be angry.'

'You're ignoring everything I'm saying to you and you want me not to be angry? Who do you think I am, Harry Lanier? I'm your wife, I'll remind you. Till death us do part and all that? Surely you haven't forgotten the little church in Southend? I seem to remember both of us were there.'

Harry was getting desperate. He knew he had to say something to mollify Vonnie's bruised feelings.

'When I said, "I can't leave it now", I didn't mean I was going to be fully involved as a policeman. Lars wouldn't let me, anyway.'

'Well, bully for Lars.'

Harry tried to ignore this. Vonnie had seemed to like Lars at first, although she had noticeably cooled towards him of late.

'Look, all I meant was I can't simply forget what he and I saw yesterday morning. It was ghastly, Vonnie.'

'Are you sure that's all you meant?'

'Of course, love.'

'You make sure that's all you're going to be doing, thinking about it. Please remember you're not a policeman here. This isn't even your country. Promise me you won't do anything daft?'

'Promise.'

As they resumed their walk to Kemiligaq, there was an uneasy truce between them. Harry was uncomfortably aware he intended to do a little more than simply think about what had happened.

4.3

'I can promise you something really special here, Harry. There may be nothing much to see at the moment. But you wait half-an-hour or so, then you'll be sure to see something you'll remember for the rest of your life. Even at this time of year we are likely to spot a few polar bears on the ice-floes as they drift southwards. Have you got your binoculars at the ready? You'll soon find out why I was so keen for you to bring them along.'

Lars was beaming. Right now, he could have been the enthusiastic young guide Harry had first known. Then Harry checked himself: Lars *had* been an untroubled tour leader not much more than twenty-four hours ago. Too much had happened since, none of it good.

The coastal cliffs of Kemiligaq were high, vast and rugged. Lars had led the party to a kind of hollow in the cliffs. Here, they'd be sheltered from the worst of the weather. From the higher point he and the Danish guide had now taken up, the wind whistled eerily about them. Almost as soon as Lars had finished speaking, the noise magnified into a shriek. It was a full two minutes before Harry could respond to what the young man was saying. Even then he needed to raise his voice to make it audible.

'Never seen such a place. This wind! I'm glad you told us to put on some extra layers of clothing before we came out. And there I was thinking when we stopped back there in the sunshine we wouldn't really need them today.'

'So where is Madam Vonnie? She too will wish to see the polar bears on the ice-floes. It's a sight she'll surely not want to miss.'

Harry looked around. Vonnie was about fifty yards away, slightly downward of Lars and himself and, like the others, in a shallow depression, although above the main group. He saw she was in animated conversation with Freddie Tanner. The two seemed to be getting on well, laughing as if at some shared joke. He didn't like what he saw.

'I'll see you later, Lars,' said Harry suddenly. 'I'll be back in time to have a look at the ice-floes and polar bears, don't worry.'

Harry left a bemused Lars Erikssen in his wake as he hastened off in the direction of Vonnie and Freddie. He soon slowed his pace, now beginning to feel ridiculous. The two of them were doing nothing more than talking, after all.

But, as he drew nearer, a scene unfolded that appeared far less innocent to Harry's eyes. Neither Vonnie nor Freddie noticed his approach. Freddie moved behind Vonnie, holding his binoculars to her eyes as she peered out, scanning the sea. Unaware of Harry's approach, Freddie eased himself nearer to Vonnie, laughing and whispering what appeared to be some sort of joke in her ear. Vonnie was laughing at whatever he was saying.

Then Freddie saw Harry marching towards them. He broke away from this intimate position, guilt written on his face. Vonnie also looked in Harry's direction, though her own expression gave nothing away. She even smiled when she saw him coming.

'Showing the lass the fine ice-floes out to sea, I was. It's what we've come for, so Lars keeps telling us. But I see you've got a real pair of fieldglasses there, Harry lad. Not like these pathetic things Gudrun raked up for me this morning. What are those then? They must be twenty by fifties by the look of them.'

‘They have a seventy millimetre object lens’.

Harry was seething. He didn’t know whether to be more angry at Tanner or at Vonnie. Somehow, he regained some sort of outward control. Vonnie turned her back on both of them. Without a word, she walked off to rejoin the main party, hands thrust deep into the pockets of her heavy parka. Harry was left alone with Freddie Tanner, who looked even more embarrassed and uncomfortable.

‘What d’you think of this place,’ Tanner said. ‘No donkey rides on the beach here, eh? I haven’t even been able to find any candy-floss yet.’

Harry ignored this lame attempt at banter. ‘Any reason why you’re travelling alone Freddie? Hoping to meet plenty of women while you’re here? Is that your idea?’

It was the kind of blunt question Harry would not normally have asked of anyone except, once upon a time, as a policeman on duty. But he thought Tanner owed him something.

‘I’m on my own now. My wife died six years ago, God Bless her memory.’

‘Gives you a chance to play the field, does it?’

Tanner looked wary, as if unsure of whether to protest at this brusque manner. He had an open, rather dull face, and Harry could easily read the way his thoughts were unfolding. Right now, Freddie Tanner would be thinking Harry had his focus on the man’s over-friendliness with Vonnie. So he did, although there were other thoughts on his mind, too.

‘Not these days lad.’ Freddie tried to grin, but still looked nervous. ‘More talk than action now, that’s me. I’m no youngster, you know.’

He tried again to smile at Harry. 'I'm getting like the old man in the joke. The one about the married couple. Did you hear it? There's this old couple at home, see. He's downstairs reading the paper and she's upstairs. Suddenly she calls out, "come on upstairs and make love to me". He shouts back, "do you want me to come upstairs or make love to you? I can't do both". Ah yes, that's Freddie Tanner as you see him now. I could be that old man downstairs.'

Harry despised Freddie Tanner. He was about the same age as himself, perhaps even a year or two younger. The man looked foolish, trying to fix an anxious-to-please look on his face. In his nervousness he succeeded only in contorting his features. A bead of sweat appeared on his forehead. Harry watched him and decided this was more than embarrassment. The man was afraid. He'd seen the self-same look on the faces of people he'd stopped for questioning in his work. Harry thought he'd play the jealous husband a bit longer. It was hardly an act, anyway.

'Not from what I hear, Freddie. You've got some life in you yet, I believe. You're quite a ladies' man, aren't you? I've heard a tale or two. You had a bit of fun down by Gulfoss Falls with Essie Smith, one of the stories goes. That's how it was, wasn't it?'

'Nay, lad. You mustn't talk like that. Poor Essie. She was no more than a lively girl with a sense of fun. No one deserved what happened to her. Why, if I got my hands on that big Eskimo thug…'

'You'd run a mile, is what you'd do.'

Harry turned on his heel, satisfied to have made Freddie Tanner squirm. He felt less angry with Vonnie now. Probably what he'd seen had been more innocent than it first appeared, at least on her part. All the same, he regretted that, in seizing the chance to taunt Freddie, he'd missed the opportunity to find out more about what Tanner was up to with Essie in Gulfoss. And perhaps on the night of her death, too.

*

Vonnie was waiting for him when he returned. She looked at her husband enquiringly. Her face betrayed no kind of guilt. Harry knew then he'd over-reacted to an innocent scene, but still wanted Vonnie to keep at a safe distance from Tanner.

'Had a nice chat with our Freddie, did you Harry? He's a big kid. Don't take too much notice of him. He's not worth the bother.'

'I thought I asked you to keep well away from him? Be more careful about yourself, please. I'm only thinking of you, Vonnie, honestly.'

'If I didn't know better, I'd think right now you were a jealous man, Harry Lanier.' She sighed. 'But I do know better. That's the trouble. You really do suspect poor old Freddie, don't you? Remember what you promised me no more than an hour ago?'

'Vonnie, all I'm saying is be careful. Stay away from Freddie Tanner. Right away from him. It's not much for a man to ask of his wife, is it?'

Harry realised he was raising his voice.

'Sssh, love, the Walters are looking at us.' She caught him by the arm and leaned against him. 'Maybe you were a bit jealous, after all. There's no need, Harry, no need at all. You needn't fear any competition from Freddie Tanner. And if I had to put money on anybody but Nanoq being Essie Smith's murderer, he'd be the last one I'd say was up to it, let me tell you. He's no more than a buffoon.

Now, we're supposed to be in Greenland on holiday. Try to – look!'

Harry's gaze followed Vonnie's excitedly pointing finger. The heads of all the rest of the party turned in the same direction. Even Freddie Tanner came running, or more accurately stumbling, down the slope to rejoin the group.

An extra large ice-floe had come into view very close to the shore. On it was a big polar bear, looking yellow and dirty against the pure white of the floe and the shimmering blue of the sea. As they watched, it rose on its hind legs. It looked exactly as though it were deliberately facing them to make a salute. The animal held the same position for at least a minute. They were all entranced.

Harry held the binoculars to Vonnie's eyes, standing behind her and steadying her grip in an ironic parallel of the situation with Freddie that had so angered him. They stayed in that intimate position long after the ice-floe had carried the bear further to the south and out of sight.

*

On the return journey Vonnie seemed to be content. Most of the time, she spent talking to Dainty Clatworthy, no doubt about their good fortune to catch such a splendid sight. Harry was content to walk alone some distance behind. He was enjoying the sensation of the late afternoon sun gently warming his face. It was some time before he became aware of the figure falling into stride with him.

'Penny for them?' said Maggie Walters.

'I doubt they're worth as much as all that,' smiled Harry. 'My mind is about as empty as it's possible to be. I suppose I was thinking about the Kemiligaq cliffs. They're really something, aren't they? This is the sort of thing we came to Greenland to see. And we were very lucky to see the bear so close to the shore. Lars told me he was expecting something special today, but I'll bet he didn't think the floe would be so near. A short while ago he told me it was the closest he'd ever been to a polar bear himself.'

'Aye. A real sight it was, right enough. Even my Mel stopped his moaning for a while.' She shot a sideways glance at Harry, wrinkling her nose. He was uncomfortable with this line of talk. It wasn't the way a wife should speak about her husband to a comparative stranger. It was she who had made the choice of an older husband.

'Um,' said Harry. He said nothing further, hoping to keep this conversation short.

Maggie Walters continued walking alongside, seemingly not in the least perturbed by the mild rebuff. He began to feel more edgy about this unsought encounter. She seemed content with the silence. It was at least five minutes before she spoke again.

'You know, I can't help thinking about what Dainty Clatworthy said to us. She's not one to invent stories. It does sound the sort of thing Essie Smith would get up to.'

'Look, isn't this the kind of thing you should be talking to Mel about?'

Harry was disturbed at the way this discussion was going. To have two slanders – it sounded very much like Maggie was about to deliver the second – on a dead woman within the space of a few hours was too much. When it appeared that Maggie was going to keep talking anyway, he said nothing further. She might have something important to say.

'Mel might get the wrong idea. Besides, you heard what Dainty made us promise about not saying anything to anybody else. It was what Dainty told us that brought this thing to my mind again.'

'Go on then. It sounds as if you're going to say whatever it is anyway.'

'That's better, Harry Lanier. You should relax about things a bit more. You'd be a nice fella if only you didn't take everything so seriously all the time.'

She looked fully at him and flicked her long eyelashes . He said nothing, trying not to show any reaction.

'Anyway,' Maggie continued. 'You'll know I like to do a little early-morning jogging? Just run a few miles to earn my breakfast, kind of thing. Well, there was this morning in Selfoss I was running back from my little outing when I stumbled and fell. As luck would have it, it turned out I didn't do any permanent damage. Still, my ankle was painful and swollen for the rest of the day. It really hurt at first. So I had to walk, or limp you'd be more right t'say, for the last hundred yards or so. I could still feel the pain next morning.'

'Oh yes. I remember that day.' Harry's discomfort eased a notch or two. Maggie's story might be innocent after all. 'You were limping when we went to breakfast one day. I recall Vonnie asking you about it.'

'That's the time I'm talking about. Well,' continued Maggie. 'Essie Smith had the last cabin, so I could see into it for quite a way as I was coming back. Man, I couldn't believe what my eyes were telling me.'

'And what was that?' asked Harry. He hated the way these people made such a meal of revealing their stories.

'She was standing there in front of the mirror, as naked as the day the day she was born, admiring her own bust in a way that made me gasp. She had one hand under each of those huge breasts of hers. She was massaging them – caressing each one of them in turn, you'd have to say. That's what she was doing. At first, I expected there to be a fella in there – you could understand it if she was doing it to make a man wild – but there was no one else in the cabin. You could see she was fair thrilled with what the mirror was showing her. It was obscene to watch.'

'Well, she had a fine bust.'

Maggie snorted with derision. 'Fine? Remarkably big and fat, is more like it. You wouldn't call those monsters *fine*.' Harry tried to detect a note of envy in her voice. There didn't seem to be one. 'I think she must've been doing this massage thing for quite a while. And that's not all,' she continued

'She turned around, still with her little girl's hands under those gigantic breasts, as if she had won them at a Saturday funfair or something. I'd thought before we heard Dainty's story today she hadn't seen me at all, but I've since changed my mind. Why, I think now she was *showing them to me* like she was saying "look what I've got and you haven't". It's what I truly think she was doing.'

Harry couldn't help stealing a glance at Maggie's own bust. She was trim but full figured and shapely. She caught him looking at her, as she was bound to. She laughed, clearly delighted to have made him react in that way.

'Oh, come on. You're imagining things. Go and talk to Mel. He looks as if he could do with a story like that.' Harry quickened his pace. He wished Maggie hadn't spoken to him. And not simply because Essie's image had once more been brought to the forefront of his mind.

*

Although he'd have preferred to lurk at the rear with his own thoughts, Harry knew he'd better catch up with Vonnie and Dainty Clatworthy.

'Oh, so you've decided to speak to us again, have you?' Vonnie's eyes twinkled, belying her words. 'I didn't think we were good enough for you any longer.'

'I mustn't come between a husband and wife. I don't mind walking on my own,' said Dainty Clatworthy.

'Don't be silly, Dainty,' said Vonnie quickly. 'I was only joking. Anyway, you can have Romeo all to yourself for a while. I've got to get this stone out of my shoe. It's been bothering me for the last half-mile.'

'Sorry,' said Dainty to Harry. 'I didn't mean to get in the way.'

'She really was only joking you know, Mrs Clatworthy. Vonnie's sense of humour can be misunderstood sometimes.'

'Dainty. Everyone calls me Dainty.'

'Dainty. Now, what shall we talk about?' Harry tried to give the impression of warm friendliness, but he really did have no idea of what he was going to say to the old lady. At this moment, he didn't feel like engaging in any kind of small talk: his mind was still full of pictures of the scene Maggie Walters had described.

Had the woman made up the whole story? It sounded like she might have, even though he could recall that she had indeed been limping one morning in Iceland. Could she really have seen everything she described through a window? No, it was more likely that she'd invented the story around the true incident of spraining her ankle. But why should she want to tell him a deliberately titillating tale? He could think of only one reason. This flattered him, but at the same time left him flustered.

'Well, there was something I wanted to discuss with you.'

Dainty's words brought him back to the present with a jolt.

'Oh?' Harry was surprised but relieved he wouldn't have to search for a topic of conversation.

'Your wife told me you used to be a policeman.'

'The emphasis is on the "used to be" Mrs Clat – Dainty.'

'Well, it's only what you'd call a procedural thing. I expect that's what you officers of the law would call it, anyway.' Dainty Clatworthy had obviously been watching too many crime series on the television. 'You'd expect things to be done differently in another country, but they do things so oddly here, don't they?'

'You could say that. What's on your mind?'

'I saw Essie Smith in the early hours of yesterday morning. I may even have been the last of our group to see her alive but nobody's asked me a thing more after I mentioned it. Gudrun only told us all briefly about the murder and Mr Erikssen hasn't asked me any kind of follow up questions – that's what you call them in the police, isn't it? Should I say something more to him myself, do you think, or should I wait until the proper policeman arrives here from the south?'

'The full-timer should be with us in a day or two. If you ask me, Lars seems to have made up his mind already about what happened. I'd say it's up to you entirely, Dainty. Tell you what, though. You can tell me if you like, for the time being, if it makes you feel any better. How does that sound?'

'I'm so glad you've said that. It's what I was hoping. This'll be a weight off my mind, I can tell you. I'm very grateful. Well, on the Saturday night I'd turned in before the rest of you. I was fast asleep, when this awful racket outside woke me up. Like something in the worst parts of my town. Right outside my cabin window it was; I could hear everything. So, after I'd put my slippers on – it's so cold here in the nights, even though it's barely beginning to get anything like dark at that time – I went over to my window to peep through the curtains. I saw Essie Smith being pulled along by this tall local man away from our group's cabins. I knew it was her, because she was the only woman in our party with blonde hair. The way they were acting, well, it all seemed to be more of a game than anything else. You know what girls can be like these days, don't you?'

Harry thought that "girl" was hardly the right description for a forty-year-old woman but let it pass.

'Yes, sometimes things aren't all they should be,' he said. So Dainty seemed to be at least part way confirming the story given by Olaf and Silumi. 'Is that all you want to say about it?'

'Well, apart from two things. I could hear every word the man was saying. He was saying it over and over again. Oh, I don't ask me to repeat the word, Mr. Lanier, but he was saying very loudly *" Nanoq – you know – Essie"*. It quite upset me I can tell you. After seeing this I couldn't go back to sleep – well, you wouldn't, would you? So I tried to read with my night-light to see if I could settle.

'Then, no more than a quarter-of-an-hour later, I heard someone going past my window again, this time in the other direction and running. It was a woman, by the sound of all the snuffling and sobbing. I didn't dare look out of the window again, but I'm sure it must have been Essie Smith. Then, after that, perhaps half-an-hour or so later, I heard the big vehicle and trailer driving off. I still didn't have the nerve to pull the blinds back to have a proper look..'

'And what time was this, would you say?'

'I looked at my travelling clock, but it'd stopped before eleven o'clock, so I can't be sure. I'd forgotten to wind it up, you see. But I'm certain it must have been well after one o'clock by the time the trailer was driven off. Maybe it was even after two o'clock by then. I'm sorry, but I'm not really sure.'

'I see. Well, I think you should tell the full-time policeman the whole story just as soon as he gets here.'

Dainty smiled, relieved at having unburdened herself. Some of us will need to be very certain of where we were between one and two o'clock, Harry thought. But to Dainty he said, 'Now, don't worry about it a moment longer'.

4.4

So where was all this leading? No longer could there be any doubt Nanoq was heavily involved in the crime. Everything pointed to the Inuit being the one to have disposed of the body. From the footprints Harry and Lars had seen at Qooroqilulissat yesterday, he had probably done it single-handedly. Dainty's version of events corresponded with the one told by Silumi to Olaf and then relayed so graphically to Lars and himself.

Except, perhaps, that Essie seemed to have gone to Nanoq's cabin more willingly in Dainty's account of events. Still, this was something she'd only glimpsed through a closed window. He'd also have to make some allowance for what the old lady would, no doubt, have seen as an example of the noisy misbehaviour of the young. A ludicrous image started to form in Harry's mind: he could almost imagine Dainty, complete with lace curtains twitching, as if she were still in some respectable part of Norwich.

Yet Pesut's examination had told them Essie was still a virgin. A *virgin* at forty years of age, for goodness sake! Dainty thought she'd heard Essie coming back from Nanoq's – it could only have been Nanoq's – cabin a mere fifteen minutes or so after she'd seen them together. She'd also heard the trailer being driven away. This had to be the vehicle carrying Essie's corpse. How could he begin to put everything together?

All the facts pointed to Lars' simple version of events being the correct one. Yet Harry was convinced this couldn't be the full story. His reasons were oddly mixed up in his mind with the hazy memory of his drunken conversation with Nanoq and the foul smell of stale fish in the cabin. Or had this been no more than some wild dream? He was beginning to question his own sanity...

*

It was an almost balmy evening, perfect for walking and trying to get some sense of rationality back into his thoughts. Vonnie was safely back in their cabin, happily reading one of her novels. In fact, it had been Vonnie who'd suggested he should come out here on his own tonight. He was glad she had.

'Why not go for a walk if you're so restless?' she'd said. 'Can't imagine why you still are though, after the lovely day we had at the Kemiligaq cliffs. Weren't we lucky to see the polar bear?'

He wasn't going to tell her why he was restless, even though she'd doubtless have guessed the reason would be to do with Essie and her murder. Well, a lone walk was exactly the thing he needed. But he hadn't gone very far before he realised his evening wasn't going to be as solitary as he'd hoped.

Some distance ahead of him on the path, crouching down on the ground with his back toward him, was a man, small in stature. It could only be Anthony Ferris. All of the other male members of the tour party were as large-framed as Harry himself. This was being kind to Freddie Tanner, who was seriously running to fat. What was Ferris up to? Did it look suspicious, even?

Ferris didn't move from his hunched position. He seemed to be intently examining something on the ground. Harry thought he'd better call out.

'Hello there, Mr. Ferris. What have you found?'

Harry had meant to give gentle notice of his approach, but the effect on Ferris was electric. He toppled backwards, almost as if he'd been shot. Somehow, he managed to control his balance and save himself from falling completely. In doing so, he comically flipped the magnifying glass he was holding up into the air. Fortunately, it landed back down on a weedy plant rather than the hard ground. Ferris picked it up and examined it anxiously, before even looking in Harry's direction. He wrinkled his long nose in distaste. It was obvious to Harry he should apologise. The man was clearly vexed by the incident.

'I'm sorry, Mr. Ferris. I didn't mean to startle you.'

'That's all right. No bones or glass broken.' The demeanour of Anthony Ferris changed in an instant as he rose awkwardly from his crouch. 'My fault, I suppose.' He's actually being pleasant, Harry realised.

'I know I should be more aware of my surroundings,' Ferris continued. 'But I thought for a moment I'd found a variant from the normal trefoil specimen of this plant. It would have been a great find if I had. Still, I was coming to the disappointing conclusion that it's merely a mutant variation caused by mis-growth – there's the stump of a fourth leaf here, do you see. Sorry I reacted like an ass when you called. I'm getting too used to seeing no-one else out here at this hour. I've come to regard the late evenings as my own private time in the open air. I have no right to think any such thing, I know. Most of the early mornings, too, I selfishly look upon as my own property, although I usually catch a glance of Mrs. Walters out in her running gear at that time.'

With some awkwardness, Harry realised he'd exchanged no more than a few words with Anthony Ferris in the two weeks they'd so far shared on this tour. It wasn't that Harry had deliberately ignored him, nor did he have any wish to avoid his company. It was simply that Ferris appeared to be a man who clearly preferred to fade into the background. He was more interested in scrabbling about in the countryside looking for plant specimens or whatever else it was he found preferable to human company.

'Are you looking forward to the Puisaluk Falls walk tomorrow? They're supposed to be magnificent,' said Harry, anxious to make amends. 'Not the highest around here by any means, but Lars and Gudrun say they're a graceful shape.'

'Like a fish tail is what I've heard.'

'Yes they are, though a seal's tail might be closer to it. That's what the name of the falls means, *Puisialuk* means seal's tail; something of the kind, anyway.'

'You seem to have a way with these Greenlandic names, Mr Lanier. My tongue trips over them whenever I try to say anything. Funnily enough, I have no difficulty with Latin names. *Epilobium Angustifolium* and all that.'

Now Ferris was opening up, Harry found him to be pleasant company. There was an eager smile playing across his small, neat mouth. There was an almost boyish enthusiasm in the way he twined his long fingers together as he spoke. How badly he had misjudged him.

'It's Harry, please. And may I call you Anthony?' Ferris nodded eagerly, perhaps grateful someone was engaging him in a proper conversation at last. 'Lars gave me a few private lessons in Greenlandic. I suppose the Latin is because of your botany? What was that name you used just then?'

'*Epilobium Angustifolium*? Nothing more or less than the good old Rose Willow Herb. You see it all the time at home. I suppose I'm mentioning the plant because it was on my mind just before you spoke to me. When I tried to do my backwards somersault.' Ferris looked pleased with his attempt at wit.

'You were thinking of wild flowers while you were looking at that scrub of weed, were you Anthony?'

Harry laughed. Ferris laughed, too, a little shyly.

'I was thinking I haven't seen as many of the Rose Willow Herb flowers as I expected,' Ferris said, still smiling. They're supposed to be quite common here but I've only seen a few isolated clumps.'

'Rose Willow Herb? The tallish pink flower you see no end of in woodland and waste ground at home, you mean?'

'That's the one. It's very common at home. There are different varieties. Most count them as the same species, though.'

'It's a pity we won't now be going to the Valley of Qooroqilulissat, then. There are plenty of those flowers there.'

'Yes, I know. I've seen the place. It's the only location where I've seen as many as I expected.'

'You've been to Qooroqilulissat?'

Ferris looked surprised by the rising note of excitement in Harry's voice.

'That's right. Yesterday, soon after we arrived, Lars Erikssen told me about it. Said we'd be going there in a day or two. I couldn't wait and found my own way. I nearly got lost for my trouble.'

'You were there on our first day in Vatsaaq?'

'Yes, I've just told you. Why are you so interested?'

There was suddenly an edge to Ferris's voice. Harry knew he'd put him on his guard. He'd be unlikely to learn anything from him, unless he was very careful. But he couldn't stop the words tumbling out:

'Damn it man! That's exactly where we found Essie's body! And you were there on the same day!'

'Mr Lanier, I was there in the early evening, well before the do in the Great Hall. I've already told Lars about my visit. Ms Smith was with the rest of the group at the time, I believe. And I don't like your tone. I don't like it one little bit!'

*

Harry found himself alone again. Ferris had stalked off after the unhappy end to their brief encounter. He didn't want to go back to his own cabin yet. Vonnie would be sure to guess he'd done something wrong and badger the truth out of him. His eyes were drawn to the scatter of huts in the Inuit settlement less than a mile to the north. Lars had specifically asked all the members of the tour party not to disturb the locals. At this moment there seemed to be none around, at least as far as Harry could see. Besides, he was feeling more than a little rebellious about Lars' edicts. He walked purposefully in a northerly direction.

As he neared the huts, he could see they were smaller, shabbier versions of those in the tourist settlement. There was one important difference he hadn't registered when he went with Lars and the others to Nanoq's cabin: the roofs were turfed instead of being fabricated from steel. Each one of the huts was painted in some shade of dull green, bluish-green, or even a kind of khaki. None of the paintwork looked as if it were recent. In some cases, the paint had been battered by the winter winds until the colour could hardly be distinguished.

He looked more carefully as he approached. There still seemed to be no-one around. Surely the place couldn't be completely deserted? He'd been told that most of the Inuit led a semi-nomadic existence, sharing their time between Vatsaaq and the larger settlement of Eqalassaq some miles to the south, walking the rough trackway between the two, and hunting for seals on the coast. Many of the natives worked in the shrimp processing plant at Eqalassaq. They followed some mysterious form of rota, so Lars had told him. Still, surely there ought to be *someone* here now?

Lars had tried, unsuccessfully and on several occasions, to explain to Harry the Inuit way of life in East Greenland. It was supposed to very different from that in West Greenland. A thought struck him: maybe Lars didn't fully understand it himself? After all, he'd only come here from West Greenland a few months before. Maybe he had less knowledge than he liked to give the impression of having?

The Inuit settlement still gave every appearance of being deserted. There were some ancient-looking fish-hooks rusting on the ground, a few bits of broken harpoon looking equally aged, and unidentifiable fragments of machinery carelessly strewn about, but no sight or sound of human habitation. Yet only yesterday Harry had glimpsed some of the locals going about their business here, seemingly quite normally. What was happening this evening?

Suddenly, he became aware someone was watching him from behind. It gave him a shivery feeling, but he controlled himself enough to slowly turn around. His eyes met those of a rotund Inuit boy no more than seven or eight years of age. The child showed no sign of fear; merely kept his gaze fixed upon Harry, his expression blank.

'Hello. What's your name then, youngster?'

The boy did not respond. He kept staring at Harry, as if he were an exotic exhibit in a zoo. He tried to communicate with the boy again, with the same negative result. Although there was no-one else around as far as he could see, he had the odd feeling the whole of Greenland was looking at him to see what his next move would be.

‘I wish I had some sweets to give you.’ Should he be saying this, even here in Greenland? For a moment he felt like a dirty old man out on the prowl. Anyway, he didn’t have sweets to give.

The boy kept on staring at him through puffy eyes. Harry could detect nothing in the way of emotion. He could detect no hostility in the boy’s eyes, exactly, merely the unspoken question: *Why are you here?* Why indeed?

‘Erneq!’

The single word of command, if that was what it was, had come from the nearest hut. Hearing it, the boy allowed his eyebrows to shoot up dramatically, giving Harry an even stronger impression of the young Inuit’s quizzical regard. Then, the young adventurer favoured Harry with one last fascinated look before turning on his heel and scampering around to the back of the building, as if he had been caught doing something very wrong.

*

His evening stroll had left him more unsettled than ever, and he found himself glad to be heading back to the tourist part of the settlement. This feeling was not with him for long. He saw Olaf was standing ahead of him on the track. His arms were crossed and his feet apart. There could be no avoiding the big Dane. His gaze was fixed coolly on Harry. The shoulder-barge of the previous night was vivid in his mind. It was clear Olaf remembered it, too. One thing he knew he dared not do was repeat the tactic. Olaf would be prepared for it.

The blond Dane smiled at him as he approached, once more revealing his set of even white teeth. At first, he seemed much calmer than the night before.

'Good evening, Mr. Lanier. You've been out for a walk?'

'Yes. I've been down to the Inuit settlement. For a look around.'

Olaf grimaced.

'Lars would not like that at all. I thought he'd asked all of you visitors to stay away from there? Neither would the Inuit like a thing like this. They would like it even less, let me tell you.'

Although Olaf looked even more formidable than he had last night, Harry felt his anger rising. Who was this Dane to tell him what to do?

'And I'm telling you, I merely had a look around,' he said. 'I did no harm.'

'This might not be the way the Inuit see it. To them you have already been the cause of much harm. They know you were one of those who arrested Nanoq. Some of them know more, from what I hear, though my friend Lars will tell me nothing when I ask him what he knows. Why is this? Why will he not speak to me about this business, do you think?'

'I'm not going to play guessing games about any of your conversations with Lars or of what the Inuit know or don't know. It's nothing to do with me. But you were present at the arrest yourself. So was your brother Christian. So was Lars. And Silumi and Ikateq were there, too. They are Inuit themselves.'

'This is what I'd expect an outsider like you to say. The Inuit understand Lars and myself are the police here in Vatsaaq. All they see is us doing our job. My brother Christian often helps us in our work, so they regard him as being from the police, too, even though he is not really.

Silumi and Ikateq do what we tell them; all the Inuit know this is the way things are. But you, Mr. Lanier, are a visitor to their country. They are asking each other why should you, a stranger, be present at the arrest? They are saying many things about you.'

Why indeed? It was a fair point to make. What on earth *was* he doing in Nanoq's cabin when the arrest should have been strictly the business of the Greenland Police? What was Lars thinking when he asked him to come along? Shouldn't he have made a point of insisting he *wasn't* present?

'They are even saying you and the other English shouldn't be here in Vatsaaq at all,' continued Olaf, almost snarling now with barely-controlled rage. His previous calm veneer had quickly evaporated. 'And, from what I hear, there are many dark whisperings passing through the cracks in the door of the winter storage shed. Nanoq is saying many things about you to Silumi and Ikateq. Would you like to know what they are?'

'I must get back to my cabin now, Mr Severen.'

'Am I preventing you?'

But Olaf Severen made no attempt to stand aside to let him pass. He stood there in the same threatening stance.

There was only one thing for it. He could not repeat his tactic of last night: Olaf would be ready for Harry's shoulder-barge and brace himself for it. Harry could imagine himself on the floor. Worse, Olaf would would surely use it as the pretext for a fight in which Harry could only come off a poor second.

So he stepped forward, circling the big Dane carefully, intending to give him a wide berth. But, as he drew level with him, Olaf took a pace sideways and shoved his shoulder firmly into Harry's. Then he bent his knees, comically swaying like a circus clown who'd received a mock-heavy punch. The blow to Harry's shoulder wasn't hurtful. The blow to his pride was harder to take. The Dane had obviously tried to parallel in a snide way what Harry had done last night.

'Oops! How clumsy of me,' said Olaf. 'I am so sorry. Good night Mr. Lanier. Pleasant dreams.'

Harry tried to muster a few shreds of dignity as he continued his walk in the direction of his cabin. Physically, he hadn't been harmed, but he was badly shaken.

Round two had definitely gone to Olaf Severen.

*

'Had a good stroll this evening, did you Harry?' asked Vonnie, as he came through the door. 'See anyone about?'

He didn't want to say anything about Olaf or the Inuit boy. Both encounters had been unsettling in their different ways. But he decided he may as well acknowledge seeing Ferris.

'Anthony Ferris was out there with his magnifying glass looking for some plant or other,' he said. 'I'm afraid we didn't part on the best of terms.' He thought he'd better admit this much: Vonnie might get to hear about it elsewhere.

'Oh, Harry! I hope you weren't playing detectives again. Because if you were...'

Harry thought back quickly. No, he decided it'd be fair to say it wasn't because he was asking questions like a policeman that Ferris had been annoyed. No policeman would have been so inept.

'No, I wasn't. I said the wrong thing when we were talking about wild flowers. All my fault.'

'Well, you make sure you apologise. Do it the first chance you get.'

'Yes. I will.' Harry had already decided to try to make amends with Ferris, anyway. The upset was clearly down to him.

'What's that you're reading, Vonnie?' he asked, more to break the awkward silence than because he was interested.

'Now Harry, you really don't want to know about the book in the least, do you? The title is *Autumn Leaves by the Lake*. What you'd call a *ro*-mance,' she said, emphasising the first syllable as Harry had so often done when he'd felt the need to ridicule Vonnie's literary tastes. 'Anyway, I'll have read enough after this chapter. We walked a long way today. You must be tired, too.'

'Yes, I am. I'll sleep like a log tonight.'

But twenty minutes later, when he put his head on the pillow, Harry thrashed around, disturbing Vonnie and drawing her muttered complaints. The brief hours of Northern darkness had come and gone and the first rays of early dawn were already feeling their way into the room before he managed some fitful rest.

Chapter Five
The Welcome Breakfast

Tuesday, 30th August, 1994, Vatsaaq, East Greenland

'Ladies and Gentlemen,' announced Gudrun as they all stood outside the Great Hall. 'This morning, we are, as I promised you, going to have our special welcome breakfast. This is a day later than originally planned. We have delayed it because – events – would have made it inappropriate before.'

'And would you say it is "appropriate" now?' muttered Harry under his breath, more loudly than he'd intended. Vonnie caught some of his words, and gave him a sharp nudge in the ribs.

'Now, I have some extremely heart-warming news for you all,' continued Gudrun breezily. 'Mr Jeremy Smith has told me he will be joining us for this meal. He will not be coming to Puisialuk Falls, although he hopes to be able to join us on our expedition tomorrow. And I can tell you he also intends to be with us for the rest of the week after that, or at least until Knud Holm arrives. I am sure this news will make everyone happy.'

Vonnie looked sharply sideways at Harry, warning him not to say anything else. He wasn't about to. He thought it great to hear that Jeremy Smith was trying to resume something like normality after the shock he'd received on Sunday.

'Well, I think it's a good idea, far better than having poor Mr Smith moping in his cabin,' said Dainty from behind them in the orderly queue forming at the entrance to the Great Hall.

Lars opened the door, standing aside politely as they shuffled in one-by-one. Harry couldn't help thinking it was more like attending another memorial service than going to a special meal.

*

Once inside, his negative thoughts were dispelled. The large table was full to overflowing with fruits, three different kinds of bread, a variety of cheeses, salmon made up into imaginative parcels, yoghurts, jugs of fruit juice, muesli, hams and other meats. There were elegantly steaming pots of coffee. The brightly-polished silver jugs hadn't made their appearance at a "normal" breakfast. Harry could also see that on the table there were even a dozen or so cans of lager of the 1% proof variety, all that was available here. Well, he wouldn't be drinking any of *that*, and not because it was still only nine o'clock in the morning. His self-imposed no-alcohol rule would have to apply to weak beer, too, if it were to mean anything.

Like the others, he looked around at the boldly calligraphed place-name labels. He was anxious to find his own seat, and was relieved to see that Freddie Tanner had been allocated to the opposite side of the table, way over in the far right hand corner. At least Harry wouldn't have to speak to him. Vonnie had been placed on his left. Opposite them were Mel and Maggie Walters. Gudrun and Lars were to sit at opposite ends of the long table, Gudrun nearer to him. It was as if the two Icesperience people planned to take charge of events, like school prefects on an outing. Gudrun would like that, Harry thought.

He was much less pleased about the seating arrangements to his right. Sitting alongside him in a moment would be Anthony Ferris, with Dainty next to him. Opposite Ferris was where Jeremy Smith's name-card was placed. It was a reminder to Harry that he'd soon have some difficult small talk to make. Social chit-chat at meals had never been something he'd found himself comfortable with at the best of times. This was anything but the best of times.

There were seven empty chairs against the wall. Harry wondered where Essie would have been placed.

There was plenty of room; the table could comfortably have accommodated fourteen or even sixteen people. She'd have been between Jeremy and Freddie, most probably. Harry could imagine her sitting there...

'Harry!'

'Er – yes Vonnie?' Harry was startled out of his reverie.

'My chair! You're forgetting your manners again. It's exactly like you. Anthony did the honours for Dainty without even thinking about it. And Mel has moved the chairs for both Gudrun and Maggie already.'

'Sorry. I was forgetting.' Harry made an exaggerated display of the simple act of pulling out Vonnie's chair. Vonnie had spoken quite loudly and everybody had automatically turned to look. He detected a slightly embarrassed expression on the face of Freddie Tanner, who was probably wondering whether he'd been remiss in not helping Maggie Walters with her own chair.

'We try to make this breakfast a special one for you all,' said Gudrun. 'May I ask that we wait for a few moments until Mr. Smith arrives? He should be with us shortly.'

There was a pause, during which only Dainty spoke something like normally. Even her tones were hushed and addressed straight to Ferris who simply smiled stiffly in return. Everybody else did no more than mumble a few words to their neighbours and kept glancing toward the door. Surely, thought Harry, it would have been better if they had arranged for Smith to arrive at the same time as everyone else? After what seemed an age, although in reality was no longer than five minutes, Jeremy Smith was standing in the doorway. Each of them looked in his direction, obliging him to speak.

'I'm sorry to have kept you all waiting. I didn't mean to. It's just that ... well, this morning was harder than I expected.'

'Sit down, Mr. Smith,' said Dainty. 'If we grudged you a few minutes' delay to our breakfast it wouldn't say much for us, would it? It's lovely to see you here. Quite made our day, it has.'

There were murmurs of approval from around the table. The warmth and spontaneity of Dainty's words had broken the awkwardness. Jeremy Smith gave a half-smile of gratitude and took his place. Out of the corner of his eye Harry could see that even Mel Walters was trying to crease his features into some sort of welcome.

'There's only one thing I'd like to say, if you wouldn't mind,' said Jeremy as he took his seat. 'Although I've felt the need to hide away in my cabin since Sunday, I know I've been able to count on the support of every one of you over these last few days. Gudrun and Lars have kept me informed of developments. I know you had a good day at the sea cliffs of Kemiligaq. Lars told me all about it. I'd have loved to have seen the polar bear with you, but..,' He swallowed hard. 'I … I do hope to be out with you tomorrow. So, thanks. That's all I want to say. It's a small word but I really mean it. Thanks.'

There were sighs and nods as they began to relax and set about their breakfasts. Harry reached for the Emmental cheese and a slice of the German black bread, something for which he'd developed a taste on this holiday. With a bit of luck he'd be able to concentrate on the food, and there'd be minimal need for polite table chit-chat. After all, a special breakfast couldn't be quite the same thing as a special dinner, could it?

A sharp reminder from Vonnie's knee under the table told him it could. He wondered to whom he should speak. Mel? His smile of welcome for Jeremy had quickly evaporated and he looked even grumpier than usual this morning. Maggie? No; he'd been more disturbed yesterday by her story of Essie than he cared to admit. He'd been even more unsettled by the brazen way in which she'd told it. She definitely had an ulterior motive for speaking so provocatively. Harry was in no doubt what that motive was. He was flattered but at the same time frightened. Jeremy Smith? Harry wasn't at all sure he could handle a conversation with the bereaved brother. Ferris? Yesterday's upset had been entirely Harry's fault. Harry thought now might be the time to try to make amends.

'They say that the Puisialuk Falls are really fine, Anthony,' said Harry. 'They take their name from their shape – a seal's tail. That's fascinating, isn't it?'

'Yes, so you were saying to me yesterday, Mr. Lanier. I prefer to have new subjects of conversation, myself. Especially when we know where the old ones will lead.' Ferris turned to Dainty Clatworthy and immediately engaged her in some conviviality. As soon as he'd spoken, Harry realised he had indeed repeated the same thing from yesterday, in almost the same words. Pure nervousness on his part had made him momentarily forget their previous conversation. He felt very foolish. Still, there was no need for Ferris to have given him such a frosty reception.

'I've been doing some reading in my room, Mr. Lanier,' said Jeremy Smith. 'You know, I've had more time to myself than I really wanted these last few days and there's quite a lot of literature about Greenland in the settlement. A remarkable amount of the topography takes its name from Greenlandic words. That little island near Aasiaat, where we spent a couple of hours before coming to Vatsaaq, was called "Qeqqertak Arfeg", for instance. That means "Whale Island", I understand. The valley we visited on the island was called "Seqineq Sialuk". That means

"Sun and Rain" so far as I've been able to make out. We didn't see too much of the latter there, I'm pleased to say.' He stopped suddenly. 'Sorry. I must be boring you, wittering on like this.'

'No, no. Not at all. Quite the opposite. I've developed an interest in the local language myself.' Harry realised that Greenlandic words slipped more easily from Jeremy Smith's tongue than from his own. He had a rich, rolling way of talking that was pleasing to the ear. He was soon being listened to intently by the whole table, including Lars and Gudrun.

'One thing puzzling me,' continued Smith. 'Is that nearly all the place names seem to be based on standard Greenlandic, which I believe is essentially Western Greenlandic. It's where most of the population is, in the west of the country, so I've read. Yet East Greenlandic is most definitely the spoken language over here. I've noticed Silumi and Ikateq and the others using it all the time. That's why I'm intrigued to know why East Greenlandic isn't used as the basis of more place names. Can you throw any light on the subject Mr. Erikssen?'

Lars stopped to clear his throat before answering. He did it very loudly and everyone looked at him as he replied.

'Well, East Greenlandic is used in a few of the place names here,' said Lars. 'Though I'm afraid I can't think of any examples, offhand,' He was obviously disappointed with his memory, as was Harry. 'But I think the use of West Greenlandic may be because most of the place names are ancient,' Lars frowned. 'You must remember that much of East Greenland was explored only recently in historical terms. The Inuit name for it, "Tanu" or "the back of the country", indicates this. Most of the names were probably given by early explorers from West Greenland, with spoken East Greenlandic going its own way many years later.'

Something told Harry Lars may have been making some if not all of this up as he was speaking. He'd have liked to have asked some further questions of his own. But the table in general had quickly lost its passing interest in the subject of language. Probably only hearing Lars' peculiarly loud throat-clearing and Jeremy Smith's rich voice had caught their attention in the first place.

Lars was soon engaged in a three-cornered conversation with Ferris and Dainty on another topic; something to do with the limited vegetation in Northern lands, as far as Harry could make out. Vonnie, Gudrun and Mel Waters were discussing an obscure topic about the Malvern Hills at the other end of the table. Only Jeremy Smith and Maggie Walters seemed keen to continue with the subject of the Greenlandic languages. Harry couldn't help but notice the coquettish – no far more obvious – intended enticing looks – Maggie Walters kept casting in Smith's direction. At a time like this! Had the woman no shame?

'Well, the two of you seem to know a lot about Greenland, that's for sure,' she said. 'Is there anything you don't know?' Her words of praise might have encompassed the pair of them but her eyes were firmly on Jeremy.

'In a few days we'll be on our way to our next port of call after Vatsaaq, is that right?' Harry couldn't resist asking her this so as to give himself the opportunity to show off. 'Ittoqqoortormiit is the name of it,' he said, pronouncing each syllable as carefully as he could. 'It's where we're going to try a little dog-sledding, I believe.' Harry's throat went dry after the verbal effort.

'Itik what?' laughed Maggie. 'That's a word to get your mouth around.'

'I'm afraid I won't be going with you to Ittoqqoortormiit,' said Jeremy Smith. 'I hope to go back to Ammassalik with Knud Holm. From there, I'll be flying on to Nuuk. Knud Holm might be going there himself, as I understand it. From there I hope to get home to Chelmsford as soon as I can. There'll be some formalities to attend to, naturally, but I hope they'll keep these reasonably brief and let me come back for the trial later. Then there's the funeral – I don't suppose that will be for weeks or even months. It's all very distressing'

'Yes, I'm sure you'll be able to fly home for a while. Why, you'll probably be back well before we are,' said Maggie. 'I'm sorry. We know it's been a hell of a week for you. Don't think we've forgotten that, Jeremy'.

Harry found himself on the fringe of a conversation in which Maggie Walters was expressing exactly the right level of sympathy towards Jeremy Smith, without giving too many reminders of the fate that had befallen his sister. Before long, Vonnie joined in with Maggie and soon other members of the party were also engaging Smith in conversation. Harry was able to turn his attention more fully to the black bread, but wished he were as at ease as the others. He found himself grateful when Gudrun rose to her feet again.

'Ladies and gentlemen,' she announced. 'I think we can say our special breakfast has been a success, no? We will be departing for our walk to Puisialuk Falls in exactly one hour. I hope this will give you plenty of time to do whatever you need to do before your departure.'

They led out from the Great Hall in the same orderly fashion. Mel Walters and Harry were the last to leave

'Plenty of time for us to pack our sandwiches and get an apple for the teacher, eh?' Mel Walters whispered to

Harry as they were going through the door. 'And we'd better not forget to use our potties before we come out.'

So, beneath the gruffness, Mel Waters had some sort of sense of humour, even if a slightly odd one.

*

'Mr. Lanier? Or Harry, I should say.' Dainty put her hand on his arm. Mel Waters waved his hand vaguely at Harry and wandered off, leaving the two of them to speak more privately.

'Yes?'

'All I wanted to do was to thank you so much for listening to what this nosey old woman had to say for herself yesterday. But what I saw on Saturday night did upset me. I hope you'll forgive me.'

'No one thinks of you as a nosey old woman, Dainty. I was glad to listen. It's the least anyone could have done.'

'Well, it was a great relief when you let me speak to you in confidence, I can tell you.'

'Have you decided what to do now? Whether to tell Lars about what you saw or to wait until Knud Holm gets here?'

'I think I'll wait for Mr Holm. Mr Erikssen doesn't seem to be very interested, somehow. I'm sure you're right in thinking he's already made up his mind about what happened.'

Lars certainly has decided, thought Harry. 'Well, I think you're doing the right thing,' he said to Dainty. 'Wait for the full-time expert. It'll be for the best.'

'I thought Anthony Ferris was very rude to you then. Giving you the cold shoulder as he did, I mean.'

'Well, we did have a few words last night.' Harry wished Dainty hadn't raised this subject.

'Even more reason then. He should have seen you were offering him an olive branch at the breakfast table, if such a thing makes any sense. I would have tried to answer you myself, only all this Greenlandic language talk was way over my head. I'm glad that nice Mr. Smith stepped in and came to the rescue in the way he did. Such a *Gentle*man, if you know what I mean. Clever, too.'

'Yes he is. I didn't expect him to gallop to the rescue on his white charger but I'm grateful he did.'

Dainty Clatworthy fell silent. She made no move to leave Harry. Instead her eyes searched his face.

'You want to say something else, Dainty?'

'Oh – you know very well I do. It's the story I told you and Mrs Walters about Freddie Tanner and Essie Smith about that day at the Gulfoss Falls in Iceland. I shouldn't have said anything at all. It's been worrying me ever since.'

'You mean it's not true?'

'Of course it's true!' She looked indignant. 'Every word of it is true. How could I forget seeing such an awful thing? It's just – well, you shouldn't speak ill of the dead, should you? I felt even more awful this morning, seeing that lovely polite brother of hers at the breakfast able.'

'Don't worry, Dainty. Really, don't fret about it.'

'Well, I mean to say something to Mrs Walters as soon as I can. To ask her not to say anything, either. I know I was speaking out of turn yesterday.'

'Look, I wouldn't say anything to Mrs Walters if I were you. I'll speak to her if you like.'

'If you're sure?'

'Yes. Don't think anything of it.'

As he made the offer, Harry knew this was the last thing for the subject of a conversation with Maggie Walters.

5.2

Vonnie was waiting outside the door of their cabin.

'You took your time about getting back, I must say. You were supposed to do your socialising at the breakfast table, not outside the Great Hall afterwards.' Her words were sharp but she smiled as she said them showing she'd forgiven, to some extent at least, his transgressions of the last few days.

'I'll be going off to pack the lunch now,' she continued. 'We won't be setting off for the best part of an hour. You may as well have a stroll around, Harry. See if you can chase some of the restlessness out of yourself, for goodness sake. Don't be late back at the cabin, though.'

'And don't you forget to pack an apple for the teacher,' Harry couldn't resist repeating what Mel had said.

'What?'

'Never mind.'

'You've got a strange sense of humour, you have, my lad.'

Saying this, Vonnie opened the door of their cabin. From there she'd be going to what they termed "the kitchen", the small cabin used for preparing packed lunches. The other members of the party had dispersed quickly. A pity, because Harry would have liked to have asked Lars a few more questions about the Greenlandic language. Or should that properly be "the Greenlandic languages"? Everyone had gone. Even Mel Walters had dutifully toddled off in the direction of his own cabin.

Somehow, although it was drier than yestersday, the sharp wind made it feel colder. A brisk stroll might have been a better idea, but Harry decided to have a quiet ten minutes on the old wooden bench. This was about thirty yards from the Great Hall to the south, in the opposite direction from the rest of the buildings of the tourist settlement. He'd never sat there before, but something about its rustic look appealed to him now. This morning was the time for some serious thinking.

The seat may have been no more than a short distance away, but when he reached it he felt as if he were the only person in the world. There were none of the usual guillemots, gyrfalcons or ptarmignans to be seen. These often ventured close to their cabins. Harry scanned the sky for signs of an approaching storm – they'd been promised one would soon reach Vatsaaq from the south – but he azure dome was even clearer than usual.

He settled back, thinking of the other members of the Greenland Party. It seemed that few of them, even none of them, could have had anything to do with Essie's death. What grounds would they have had? He enumerated each in his mind, thinking of them in their seating positions at breakfast.

Mel Walters? He was a bit of a grouch, true enough, but this hardly made him a killer. Besides, hadn't Vonnie said that he and Maggie had left the Great Hall early on Saturday night? What about Maggie herself? She obviously disliked Essie. As for the tale about her displaying and admiring her own breasts... Maggie had surely made that up. Harry wondered again about her motives for doing so. Could it really have been for his benefit? There may have been a slender factual foundation to the incident that she'd then elaborated wildly. But, no, even if she'd invented the whole story, this should hardly make her a suspect for murder.

Jeremy, Essie's brother? Harry hadn't talked much to him before this morning. He'd been impressed by the quiet dignity he displayed today. The way he'd tried to control his distress was admirable and surely genuine. No, Harry couldn't believe he'd have had any reason to kill his sister. Anyway, hadn't Vonnie told him that he too had left the Great Hall quite early?

Freddie Tanner? Why should the man try to disguise his accent? A Londoner pretending to be a Northerner in such a stupid music-hall way? Harry felt foolish about being taken in by the act. The man had said he was a widower, but was he really? Was his name even Tanner?

Vonnie had confirmed he'd been in the Great Hall until late. Then there was Dainty's story of Tanner and Essie at Gulfoss Falls, while they were all still in Iceland. So it wasn't merely because he disliked the man that Tanner had to stay near the top of the list.

Dainty? A ridiculous idea. Ferris? He was always skulking about the place, supposedly in search of plant species. Vonnie had told him that Ferris had left the Great Hall early on Saturday. This didn't necessarily mean he went straight back to his cabin. He was alone. Hadn't he told Harry himself he treated the evenings as his own time in the outdoors? And there would have been sufficient light at one o'clock, or even as late as two o'clock. Ferris also had to remain high on the list.

Harry tried to fight off the uncomfortable thought that there were two other members of the Party who hadn't been the subject of his deliberations – he and Vonnie . He couldn't remember enough to give himself an alibi, let alone Vonnie.

'Shouldn't you be helping your lady wife with the lunch?' A voice came from behind the seat, startling him.

'Er – what?' Harry spun around, startled to see Maggie Walters standing next to the bench, arms folded. 'I suppose I should be asking you the same sort of question,' he managed to say.

'Ah, well, my lady wife Mel packs a fine lunch. He's been doing it every day since we landed in Iceland. Why should I want to interfere? Anyway, Melvyn Walters has to be good for something.'

With no invitation, Maggie flopped down on the seat next to him. She sat nearer than Harry would have liked.

'What do you think of the country, Mrs Walters?' Harry reasoned that to keep a polite distance in this conversation would be the best way.

'It's Mrs Walters now, is it? Not so long ago you were calling me Maggie. Come on with you, Harry. Be a friend.'

'Sorry. What do you think of the country then, Maggie?'

'That's better. The country's great. I'm pleased to do my running as well as can be in this climate. And there're some fine landscapes to do it in, for sure. Holiday's not bad at all, except for the upset we've had of course. But, to tell you the truth, I did expect there to be more of us in the group.'

'The brochure said there'd be a maximum of sixteen for the Greenland leg of the holiday.'

'Aye, and there's half that number here now. There were more than thirty in the group when we were in Iceland.'

There should have been nine of us here, thought Harry sadly.

'Well, the fewer the better for me,' he said. 'It gives Lars and Gudrun the chance to give we tourists more individual attention.'

'Mr Lars Erikssen seems to give you plenty of attention, right enough. They'll be talking about the two of you if you don't watch out. But that wasn't what I meant. I thought there might be someone to run along with me.'

'Dainty? Come on. And my wife Vonnie isn't at all keen on that sort of thing. And poor Essie of course is –'

'Essie?' Maggie laughed, clearly highly amused at the thought of their top-heavy companion running. 'To tell, you the truth, I was thinking of a nice young man, or even a not so young man, to do my jogging with.'

'Perhaps if you asked Mel –?

'Mel! You've got a sense of fun, have you? Don't make me laugh! Mel would faint at the very idea. Anyway, my husband's happy for me to take my own amusement wherever I can, if you get my meaning.'

Harry didn't want to get her meaning. But Maggie continued:

'Mel! Huh! Last Valentine's Day I sent myself a couple of cards, just to see what he'd say. One of them was a cartoon of this really sexy piece. I wrote on it, disguising my handwriting, "just like you, Maggie". What would you have said, Harry?'

She waited for an answer, but didn't get one.

'The other I sent, to balance things up sort of thing, had the caption, "a woman's age is like her bust measurement. She's not interesting until she's over forty." You know what Mel did? He completely ignored the first card and picked up the second. Then he said to me, serious as you like, "you're not forty until your next birthday, are you?" Well! I'm only thirty-seven.' She looked at him teasingly. 'Both ways.'

'I'd better see how Vonnie is getting on with the lunch,' said Harry.

'No need to rush off. I'm not so bad, am I?' She rested her hand lightly on Harry's thigh. 'To tell you the truth,' she continued. 'I was hoping Jeremy Smith would have been the one to run with me in the mornings. But he was always following that Essie around like a lapdog. I didn't really like the fella so much once I got talking to him, anyway.' Harry thought this hadn't been in evidence at the breakfast table. 'And now – well. So Maggie's been looking around to see what she can see. Now you, Harry, you're a bit of a shy one, but well set up and –'

'I'm not much of a runner. I'd –'

'You wouldn't have to run for such a long way. Only far enough to take us out of everybody's sight. You know what I'm saying to you now, do you, Harry? I'm not one for wasting time playing games. You don't need me to draw pictures on the ground for that Anthony Ferris to find with his bloody magnifying glass?'

Harry surely knew what she was saying. There was no subtlety at all about her. Here was a woman, of striking appearance, fifteen years or so his junior, making a clear and unmistakable proposition to him.

'I've got to go,' said Harry, standing up quickly. 'I promised Vonnie I'd be in to help her with the lunch.'

'Well,' laughed Maggie. 'Make sure you pack some extra yoghurt. You'll need to be fit tomorrow morning. For all the exercise you'll be getting, I mean. Bright and early at seven o'clock?'

Harry turned around to face Maggie. She looked brazenly desirable sitting there. He was tempted. And very nervous.

'Seven o'clock's a bit early for me.' His resolve was crumbling fast.

'We'll need at least an hour to ourselves, Harry. We don't want to rush things, do we?'

'I – I'm not sure.'

'Ah, come on now, Harry. Don't pretend.'

'Maybe a bit of early-morning air would be a good thing.' What was he saying?

'That's better. Relax a bit more, why don't you?'

*

As he slowly walked back towards the cabins, leaving Maggie sitting on the bench, Harry was almost trembling with mixed fear and anticipation. This would be his first infidelity in nearly forty years. He was excited, but also afraid. And there was Vonnie, dutifully preparing their meal...

'Ow!'

'Don't be late tomorrow, Harry!'

So intent had he been on his thoughts that Maggie was able to jog right past him, chuckling all the time. As she did so, she'd delivered a sharp pinch to his buttock.

He stood and watched her all the way into her cabin. The one to which Mel would soon be bringing back their own packed lunch. Maybe he'd already done it and was now waiting in the cabin for his wife. Harry wondered how he could think of being unfaithful. To Maggie, it would be nothing more than a light diversion, a morning exercise not so different from the jogging she loved so much. But to

Harry... The closed green door of the Walters' cabin seemed to mock him.

Suddenly, it opened. Mel, about whom he'd been thinking with something like pity, stepped out of the doorway and hurried towards him. Had he seen them together on the bench? Had he seen the way Maggie rested her hand on the top of his thigh? Had he seen his wife cheekily pinching another man's behind? More than one member of their party who'd happened to look out of their window at the right moment could have seen the same things. Mel was a big man, as large-framed as he was. Harry could look after himself, but the last thing he wanted was an undignified brawl with a fellow-member of the group. How on Earth would he begin to explain it to Vonnie afterwards?

'Harry,' called Mel. He didn't seem to be angry. 'Maggie told me I'd find you out here by yourself. Stay there. I'd like a private word if I could. I'm coming right over.'

Here it comes... Harry tensed himself. But Mel seemed quite placid.

'I wanted to tell you what I saw on Saturday night,' he said, as he approached the spot where Harry awkwardly stood.

'You should tell Lars.' Harry drew a relieved breath.

'I have told Lars. But he didn't act as though it mattered. It seemed important enough to me, though. So I'd like to tell you. I'm told you used to be in the police.'

'What did you see?' This was getting ridiculous. First Dainty Clatworthy and now Mel Walters. What was he supposed to be – some sort of Father Confessor?

Mel stepped close to him and, without preamble, started to tell his story.

'It was after two o'clock on Sunday morning, although still not quite dark. Maggie hadn't yet returned from her run.' Mel sighed. 'You know how light it is here. I don't sleep well, even at home in Great Malvern. I happened to be close to the window, and I saw this man. A big man he was. I'd guess he was a local from the way he was dressed, but I couldn't be sure. Anyway, he was next to one of the parked trailers. Without my glasses that's a bit too far for me to be certain of everything I see, and I could only make out some of what was going on because of the angle of the window.'

'Look,' said Harry, impatiently. 'This really sounds like something you should be talking to Lars or Knud Holm about. But go on. Say your piece. Even if you have to repeat it all to them later.'

'The man was carrying something large,' Mel continued doggedly. 'Something heavy by the look of it. You could see it was weighty by the way he was walking, even though he was clearly a strong man. Well, whatever it was he had was wrapped in some sort of matting or sacking. Then he loaded it on to the back of the trailer and tied a rope around it, roughly and quickly. After that he went around to the six-wheeler to which the trailer was hitched and drove off. I thought it was a bit of an odd thing to do at that hour of the morning, but I didn't give it too much in the way of further thought until the next day when Lars told us about Essie Smith. Then I realised it could only be...'

'You assumed it was Essie's body on the trailer?'

'Well, yes, of course, afterwards I put two and two together. Wouldn't you? And then when I told Lars about it he seemed not to pay much attention. Nor do you seem to be very interested now, if you don't mind me saying so.'

'I'm sorry Mel. I don't mean to be rude. It only confirms the things we both already know. And, it seems, what Lars already knew soon after he came back to Vatsaaq on the Sunday morning. That was why he didn't treat it as new information.'

'Oh, I see.' Mel looked crestfallen and clearly puzzled.

'Did you see anything or anyone else?' asked Harry. 'One of our party out there, perhaps?

'No, there was no-one else I could see through the window. Not that I expected there to be anyone. It was later than two o'clock in the morning, after all.'

'Thanks then, Mel. This is still something you should tell the mysterious Mr Knud Holm when he gets here. It *is* important.'

'There was something else I wanted to say, Harry.'

Mel shuffled nearer to him.

'Yes?'

'Maggie tells me you're going jogging with her tomorrow morning. That's really good of you. Maggie's running is so important to her these days.'

'Well, yes, it's nothing, really. I could do with losing a few pounds around the waistline myself,' Harry managed to stutter in reply.

'You make sure she doesn't exercise you into the ground. She's a bundle of energy, my Maggie. Why, at home she goes out jogging on the Malvern Hills every morning, summer and winter. Never misses a day. She's got a veritable team of young men who take it in turns to run with her. They almost queue up for the pleasure. She's got quite a reputation locally. Some of them say things to me like "couldn't keep up with her this morning, Mr Walters" and "she was too much for me today". Regular ball of fire, my Maggie is. She's very popular with all these athletic young men. Terry, Jonno and the one they call Nobby are the regulars.'

Nobby? Harry nearly choked when Mel said this. Was he stupid, or simply blind to Maggie's sexual adventures? Or did he not want to see?

'It hasn't always been that way. Look, I'm going to tell you something privately.'

'There's no need to say anything else, Mel, no need at all.' He wished Mel would stop but the man seemed to be in a verbal frenzy

'But I want to tell you, Harry. You seem a really decent sort. You'll know how important a morning jog is to Maggie. That's why I'm so grateful to you. Exercise and me aren't the best of friends at any time. All this walking we've had to do in Iceland and Greenland is as much as I can cope with.'

Harry wanted Mel to say no more. Pictures were forming in his head of Maggie's "morning jogs". But Mel only leaned forward until his face was inches from his own. He dropped his tone.

'Today, the thirtieth of August, marks exactly ten years since Maggie and I met,' said Mel. 'It's a kind of anniversary. This is why we're on this expensive holiday. Ten years ago I was the Finance Director of a fair-sized firm in Edinburgh. Maggie was one of the typists. At the time I was going through a pretty messy divorce. Not to be too delicate about it, my first wife was trying to screw me for every penny she could get. And she was the "guilty party". That's the thing that still galls me.' His face tightened. 'It was one of the office juniors she was carrying on with. One day I'd sent him to my house with a parcel. It must have all started from there.'

Harry felt miserable. But he tried to keep an understanding expression on his face and gave what he hoped was a sympathetic nod to Mel. He didn't trust himself to speak.

'All of this is behind me now. History. And it's thanks to Maggie. She listened to all my cares and woes without one word of complaint. She was understanding itself. She was so sweet you wouldn't believe.'

Harry must have let a look of disbelief pass across his face, because Mel nodded and gave a half-smile.

'Oh, I know what you're thinking.' Harry hoped he didn't. 'It's true Maggie is a lot more cynical now than she was in those days. And, I may as well admit it, she's a sight coarser as well. But there's a reason for it. Look, I'm going to tell you the whole story.'

Harry knew he didn't want to hear any more, but he stood rooted to the spot as Mel's torrent of confidences showed no sign of abating. The two men were now inches apart.

'Maggie became pregnant, and we got married as soon as we could. I've told you I had a good job. Well, now I had a good wife and a family – my first and only child was on the way. Everything in the garden looked rosy. Then things started to go wrong.

'First, it was my company. To cut a long story short it went bust... for financial reasons. It wasn't altogether my fault, but there was a police investigation. In the end there were no charges. Still, I couldn't get another job for love nor money. Nobody wants a finance manager, or even an accountant, whose stock had plummeted as swiftly and as low as mine.

'We even lost our house in Edinburgh. Then my aunt died, and fortunately – it was fortunate, believe me – left me her house in Great Malvern. It was only a small cottage, but it was heaven sent. Goodness knows what would have happened otherwise. So, the three of – our baby daughter Jasmine was eight weeks old by this time – moved back to my home town. After a few months I even managed to find a job as a bookkeeper with a small company. It looked as if things were slowly coming back together.

'That was when the real tragedy struck. Exactly one month from the day I started in my new job, Jasmine became very ill with meningitis. She died within the week. The poor child's life had hardly begun. I was heartbroken. It was so much worse for Maggie. She hardly ate and barely slept. God, she wouldn't even speak to me. She wouldn't so much as take a step outside the house. Four years went by in this way. I was at my wit's end, I can tell you.

'Then, quite suddenly, she started to go running again. It's something she used to do when she was a girl.' He smiled. 'You'd have to say she still is a girl compared with her old husband. I tell you, she comes in almost glowing after a run sometimes. Can you see why it's so important to me? That's the reason I'm so pleased to hear you'll be running with her. At first she had it in mind to run with Jeremy Smith, but the two of them didn't click for some reason. Then I suggested she had a word with young Lars, but he wasn't interested when she did.' Mel frowned. 'Oh, I hope you don't think I'm saying you were third choice.'

'Third choice?' Harry wondered if even Anthony Ferris had been asked – propositioned – before himself. 'Well, I suppose you might say I was third choice in a way,' he said, now warming to his role as a hypocrite. 'But I don't mind at all.

'By the way,' Harry continued. 'Your account of the six-wheeler and trailer on the Saturday night? I'm surprised Maggie didn't say anything to me about it. You say she was still out running at this time?'

'That's right. She was still outside somewhere. She didn't return to our cabin until a quarter-of-an-hour after the trailer had been driven off.'

'Outside? After two o'clock in the morning?'

'I'd say it was nearer to half-past-two by the time she came in,' said Mel pedantically. 'But it's not really unusual. Maggie doesn't sleep much either – doesn't seem to need it, that one. And in this country it's still not really dark by that time and it's safe as houses. At least we thought so until we heard… what had happened… it *was* as safe as houses. Maggie has been out running in the middle of the night a few times since we came to Greenland.'

'Did she say she'd seen anything outside?'

'No, she didn't. In fact she seemed a bit subdued – for Maggie that is – when she came in, so I asked if there was something bothering her.'

'And?' said Harry.

'She said "no". She didn't want to talk at all, really. I put it down to tiredness. She'd told me she was going to run all the way out to Kunmuit Rock that night. It's a fair way, I believe. Even Maggie has to have her limits.

'Well, I think I've told you everything, Harry. I've told you more than I intended. But I feel better for it. Thank you for listening.'

He couldn't avert his gaze from Mel's hunched figure as he watched him walking slowly back to his cabin. He seemed to have the world on his shoulders. Poor, deluded man. No wonder he was so grouchy. But what he'd said about Maggie alarmed him. She'd been outside around the time Essie died: was murdered, he corrected himself. And this was the woman Harry had made an assignation with for tomorrow morning.

5.3

Vonnie slipped her arm from the nook of Harry's elbow and patted his left buttock playfully. Harry couldn't help but be aware this was the exact spot where Maggie had pinched him not an hour before.

'Are you sure this holiday was the right choice for you, Harry? I'm not talking about what's happened. I'm talking about the country itself.'

To Harry, events since Sunday had taken on the quality of a nightmare. But the country itself? He wasn't able to separate Greenland from the murder as easily as Vonnie seemed to do, but tried to answer her question.

'Greenland? It's magnificent. I love the open air. There's plenty of it here. It would have been perfect. Why do you ask?'

'Because you don't seem to be relaxed in any way. Oh yes, I know it's been hard for all of us with the terrible thing happening to Essie Smith, but surely we should be able to start to put it behind us now. The big Inuit is safely locked up. We can try to appreciate what the country has to show us.'

Harry couldn't see this in the same neat way as Vonnie. But he tried to answer in a neutral way.

'I've said: it should have been a wonderful place. I've thought so from the day we landed. Big, open skies. To me it's even – spiritual, somehow.'

'Then why don't you take up Maggie's offer?'

Harry had started to go into a quiet reverie about the magnificence of Greenland, to put aside for a few precious moments the thoughts of Essie's murder now always haunting him. And Greenland was beautiful. The country was far more so than he'd been able to put into words. Now what Vonnie said brought him back to the present moment with a jolt.

'What? What did you say?'

'I was talking about her idea of getting you out on an early-morning run, of course. What did you think I meant, for goodness sake? Your mind's getting sluggish along with your body, my lad. A brisk jog would do you the world of good. I can't think why you turned down Maggie's suggestion. You took long enough about doing it. Seems to me you must have really wanted to go. Think about it again, Harry.'

They were walking some distance to the rear of the rest of the tour group, just as they had yesterday. The sky was a brilliantly clear blue and there was hardly any wind. Like the others had done a few minutes before, they'd turned their heads to look at the unusually-shaped and strangely dun-coloured Kunmuit Rock as they passed. The rock was supposed to mark the location of an outpost of a group of Norwegian settlers who were said to have been here in the tenth or eleventh century.

Lars had told Harry the name "Kunmuit" meant "river-dwellers", but now the only running water hereabouts was the gently gurgling stream they'd crossed via some flat stepping stones a half-mile back along the trail. Any river worthy of the name must have disappeared five or six hundred years ago along with the ancient settlers.

'I don't know Vonnie. I've neglected you more than enough on this holiday as it is.'

He'd told his wife about Maggie's approach, dressing it up as the harmless suggestion of a morning run. His thinking was that this would help him resist any temptation. At first it had seemed to work. The thought of any illicit liaison with Maggie had started to fade into the background of his mind. Harry had started to wonder how he should break the news about his change of heart to Maggie. Now it was Vonnie herself who'd returned the temptation to the centre stage of his mind. It was ironic she'd done so in perfect innocence.

'Don't be silly, love. You know there's nothing I like better in the mornings than to curl up with a good book for an hour of undisturbed reading. It'll be great to get you out of my hair for while. It'd be a change for me to have some peace instead of having you stomping around the cabin, especially in the way you've been doing for these last few days. Do you some good, too. You might lose an inch or two of flab around the middle. You've been putting on the pounds ever since you stopped work. Don't think I haven't noticed.'

'Oh, so that's it. You're trying to get rid of me now?'

Harry tried to make light of the way he said this, but the jest came out thinly. His thoughts were now focused on Maggie's blatant come-on. It sounded now as if he were being peevish. He could hardly blame Vonnie for misunderstanding him.

'Come on Harry. You know I was only joking about Jeremy Smith when I said that girlie stuff about him. I only thought of the man because he looks so much like you. Jeremy could be your kid brother if you weren't an only child. He's a younger, prettified, version of you, Mr Lanier.'

'Ah, so I see your plan. Trade me in for a newer, smarter model, would you?' This time the words came out lightly, as Harry intended.

'No I prefer the older version,' laughed Vonnie. 'More characterful. More lived in. You've been living in there for more than half-a-century. I'm used to you now, as infuriating as you can be sometimes.'

'I suppose I'd better take that as a compliment. It's the best I'm likely to get,' They linked arms again and walked on together. Each had a little more spring in their steps.

Harry smiled appreciatively at Vonnie. She was usually right about things. He'd thought hard about it and decided he couldn't keep his tryst in the morning. Now he reconsidered. Perhaps this might be the only opportunity he'd have to find out what Maggie was doing on Saturday night. Had she really run all the way to Kunmuit Rock? He'd meet her, but not for the sexual assignation she'd been plotting. He'd also have a chance to tell her what Dainty had said.

'You know, Vonnie. I think you may be right. A short run in the mornings might be the very thing I need. I've got my trainers with me, haven't I?'

'Yes, Harry. I made sure we packed them. You would never have thought of it, not if I know you. I brought your shorts as well. But you won't be needing any light clothing. It's cold here first thing in the morning. Besides, you wouldn't want to show yourself up running with Maggie, would you? She always runs in shorts. She's got a great pair of legs. I've seen them. They remind me of the way I looked twenty years ago.' She looked at Harry, obviously hoping for some sort of compliment but her husband didn't take the opportunity. He was thinking of Maggie. 'You wouldn't be distracted by those legs now, will you Harry?' she added, with some disappointment.

'I'll be too busy trying to keep up with her to think of her legs,' he managed to counter.

Harry tried to smile again. But he found it hard. He couldn't help forming in his mind images of Maggie with Terry, Jonno and – Nobby.

*

It was with reluctance that Harry approached Anthony Ferris. But Vonnie knew he'd offended the botanist in some undefined way – Harry had said as little as possible about the incident – and she was urging her husband to try to make amends. He wasn't sure he'd be able to do this, but was sure Vonnie would never forgive him if he didn't at least try to patch things up.

'Mr. Ferris? It's a fine morning we're having today, isn't it?'

Ferris ignored him.

'It's beautiful out here, wouldn't you say?'

'Yes,' said Ferris tersely.

'Look, I'm so sorry I said the wrong thing yesterday. I was tired after a long day. And this morning... honestly, I haven't been sleeping too well, that's the truth of it. I didn't know what I was saying.'

'Apology accepted.' Ferris kept on walking, not even turning his head to look at Harry.

'Did you see that rock we passed about half-an-hour ago? Kunmuit Rock?'

'Lars pointed it out to us,' said Ferris.

'It's supposed to mark the location of the village of some disappeared Norwegian settlers. The "River Dwellers" they called them. The rock itself is said to be of meteoric origin. To think about it: a few millions or billions of years ago it might've been somewhere else in the Universe. And a few hundred years ago it was an important landmark to a bunch of lost Norwegians. Quite a thought, eh?'

'Lars told us all that. Do you make a habit of repeating what's been said?'

Another error, Harry thought.

'Sorry, Mr Ferris. My wife and I were walking about thirty yards behind the main group.'

'Anyway,' said Ferris. 'I think you'd be more correct to call them "Northmen" or "Norsemen". Even "Vikings" would be better, although this really means "pirate raiders". Norway is the name of the modern state. The Scandinavian countries were united at various times and in various combinations over a period of twelve centuries or more. Independent Norway as we think of it today didn't exist until 1905.'

Harry realised he didn't know enough about modern Scandinavian history to dispute the point. Besides, the last thing he wanted to do now was to argue with Ferris about anything. He tried a different tack.

'I expect you get to see a lot of the countryside in your quest for flora and fauna,' he said. Even to himself it sounded strained, so he added, 'No doubt you keep your eyes open for other things when you're out. You must see a lot, eh?'

'I'm only interested in the flora, Mr Lanier. So, we want to play detectives again, do we? I wondered how soon we'd get round to that. It didn't take us long, did it? What's your next question? Where was I after ten o'clock on Saturday last? I was in bed, if you must know. Where you should've been, from what I hear.'

'That's unfair, Mr Ferris. I wasn't going to ask anything about Saturday. I was only trying to make some polite conversation.'

'In that case, Mr. Lanier, please be even more polite and don't try. I'd rather you didn't speak to me at all. I hoped you'd have taken the hint by now.'

Harry slowed his pace and Ferris quickened his own. His attempt at reconciliation had been an abject failure.

'Ferris gave you short shrift, did he?' came a voice from over his shoulder. It was Freddie Tanner, as Harry saw by glancing backwards. He was oddly different this morning. A bit slower and decidedly more subdued. 'He's a bit touchy, Ferris. Gave me an earful yesterday when I made a harmless joke about the bag he always carries. Well, so it does look like a handbag to me.'

'Never mind, Freddie.' Harry had to smile. It didn't take much to guess what Tanner had said to Ferris about the bag.

'So let's not you and I fall out, eh?' said Freddie. 'I really was doing no more than trying to help your wife with those binoculars of mine when we were at the Kemiligaq Cliffs. Honestly.'

Suddenly Harry realised what else was different about Freddie Tanner. His Lancashire accent had entirely gone. In its place were neutral tones, with a hint of London about them. And, somehow, this had added to the change in appearance, too. Gone was the fourth-rate Northern stand-up comic. In his place was a fattish, rather sad man of the London suburbs.

'As honest as your Lancashire accent, eh, Freddie?'

Freddie looked at him sheepishly. 'No,' he said. 'Like I told you, Dainty Clatworthy rumbled me only yesterday. A right telling off she gave me about pretending to be something I wasn't. You'll soon all know I'm really from London. You've probably guessed as much already. So, I decided to drop the Lancashire Jolly for the rest of this holiday. Probably afterwards too. I'm relieved about it, really.'

'Why should you try to fake a thing like that? It's going a bit far, don't you think?'

'It was more than a joke. I've told you about my wife? Well, she was from Lancashire. Aughton, a little place outside Ormskirk it was. I met her when I was working up North. Of course, I was only a teenager back then. Peggy was a lovely girl.' Tears were starting to fill Freddie's eyes as he stumbled along at Harry's side. Harry felt embarrassed by the man's readiness to show emotion. 'Her family were good to me, too. They were the only family I ever had. I never knew any of mine. Apart from my grandmother when I was small. She died before my seventh birthday.

'Then Peggy died after only fifteen years of our marriage. Now I try to talk like her father whenever I can because... because... Look Harry, can we finish this conversation another time? This evening maybe? I'm really sorry.'

'Freddie, I'm the one who should be saying sorry.'

As Harry touched Freddie's shoulder in farewell, he could see tears were starting to roll down his cheeks.

*

Vonnie caught up with him.

'Your attempts at peace and reconciliation haven't gone so well, have they?' she said. 'First I see Anthony Ferris stomping away with steam coming out of his ears. Then I swear I could see tears in Freddie Tanner's eyes just now.'

'Anthony Ferris is a real prickly pear. And Freddie's upset wasn't my fault, not really. Not at all, in fact.' He was resentful of Vonnie's criticism. This time, for once, he thought it to be unwarranted.

'You know Harry, you're not what anyone could call a people person, are you?'

'What do you mean? Folk always talk to me.'

'Maybe they do, but you so often get it wrong about what they tell you. Your – your instincts are all wrong. It's a wonder you were ever a policeman.'

Harry momentarily went rigid. Then, in quiet tones, he admitted something he had kept buried within himself for years.

'I never wanted to be one. Do you remember how, when I was a young man, I was always under a car bonnet?'

'You still are, when you get the chance.'

'Well, that was all I really ever I wanted to be: a motor mechanic. I'd have been as happy as a pig in muck if I'd been working in a garage and could do the competition shooting in my free time. But my mother saw everything differently. It was me being an only child. Her only real family, I suppose. She was always saying, "Your Uncle Horace has got himself a fine career with the police. You can't do better than follow his example. You don't want to be a grease monkey like Bert down the road." So, I became a police cadet and in time a policeman. But, in truth, that's exactly what I did want. All I wanted to be was a grease monkey like Bert Marshall.'

'You've never said one word to me about this before now, Harry. I always thought you liked being in the Force. Were cars the reason you spent all those years in the Traffic Division?'

'No. It was because I was no bloody good at being a policeman. No other bugger would have me once I was in the Traffics.'

5.4

Later, Vonnie was putting the things away in the lunch pack as Lars strolled up.

'Hello, stranger,' she said, glancing over her shoulder at their guide. 'We haven't seen much of you recently. You were with us all the time when we first landed in Greenland.'

Harry noticed the sharp, less than friendly, way in which Vonnie spoke. Her words about himself 'not being a people person' had stung him more than he liked to admit. Maybe they had more than a grain of truth in them. He should try to be more watchful. From now on he'd do his best to be more receptive to those about him.

'Trying to do the police work as well as looking after the party has been running me like a rag over these last few days, Madame Vonnie.'

'You mean it's been running you ragged,' Vonnie said. Harry noted his wife didn't give even the pretence of a quick laugh when saying this.

'Well, I feel just like a wet rag,' said Lars. 'Do you think I could have a private word, Harry? I won't keep you away from Madame Vonnie for long.'

Lars beckoned to Harry. Vonnie gave a slight but noticeable upward toss of her head and walked off without a word.

*

'What Vonnie said is true, Lars. You have been keeping your distance from us – from me – since Monday. OK, so now you don't want me to be involved in the official investigation. You've told me your enquiries are more or less complete but….'

Lars grimaced.

'You know how it is, Harry. There are still records to write up, interview notes to get into some sort of order, all that sort of thing. You'll remember it well enough from your own past experience. I wouldn't be at all surprised to find the Greenland police likes its paperwork even more than your Scotland Yard does.'

'I've told you Lars: I didn't work for Scotland Yard. I was in the Traffic Division of an ordinary County Constabulary. That's all: there was none of this glamour stuff for me. I can't say I'm sorry about it, either. What do you mean "interview notes", anyway? I didn't know you'd been doing any formal interviews, except with Nanoq of course.'

'I've briefly interviewed all the people from the Greenland Party, even Madam Vonnie. Hers was a very short one. It was more by way of a passing conversation, simply so I'd have something to put on the record. And I've formally spoken to Silumi and Ikateq as well as to a few of the other locals. For the sake of form I even had to go through the process of interviewing Olaf, although I knew well enough where he was on Saturday night. I've recorded a statement myself of where I was myself.'

Lars gave a wry smile.

'You can imagine that one raising a few eyebrows should somebody read it as they're filing away the paperwork in Nuuk in a few months' time. Knud Holm won't bother to read it, of course: I'll give him no more than an outline of what it says when I see him. But we like our paperwork in the police, as you know. For you and I, I've done no more than record summary details of the two of us finding the body on the Sunday morning. Holm will want a proper statement of events from both of us when he gets here, but this need only be a brief one.'

'I'm beginning to think that your "when" should be an "if".

Lars gave an impatient shrug of his shoulders in response to Harry's piece of cynicism. He said nothing.

'But you haven't spoken to me in any formal way since that Sunday morning in Qooroqilulissat,' Harry said. 'Surely I should be at least a key witness?'

'There was no need for me to seek a further interview. You only saw the same as I did in the valley. As for the rest, you'd already told me most of what I needed from you.' When Harry looked dumbly at him, Lars added mysteriously, 'Everything else I need to know I've been finding out by other means.'

'But I've hardly told you anything. As I've said, I'm sure Nanoq had to be working on the instructions of someone else when he disposed of the body. It has to be someone in our party. If only I could work out who might have a motive, we might understand a bit more. But everyone seems to be able to account for where they were. Except, that is, for Maggie Walters. She –'

Lars whole demeanour changed. Instead of a policeman going through the motions, he stiffened and assumed an air that Harry would have to describe as fury.

'Mrs Walters? So it's her you want to drag into this mess now? Please, Harry, please. No more. No more foolishness.'

'This isn't foolishness Lars. I've found out –'

'Harry, I've already drafted my report for Knud Holm. The final version will say Nanoq committed this crime alone. His motives were sexual. That's the way the murder will be recorded. Why isn't that good enough for you?'

Harry was puzzled. He wanted to ask about Henrik Rasmussen and other matters Lars seemed content to sweep under the counter. But something about Lars' blank-wall manner silenced him. Lars looked at Harry for a long moment before speaking again.

'Are you quite mad, Harry? Why do you persist? I've told you exactly what I'm going to say to Knud Holm. Why is this not enough for you? Do you not think I have done all I can?'

Mystified, Harry realised he'd have to change the subject. Lars was getting seriously angry. He'd seen a different side to the mild-mannered Dane over the last few days. And what on Earth was he talking about with his "*isn't that good enough for you*" and "*do you not think I have done all I can*"? He knew he couldn't ask the direct question. Nothing would be gained beyond Lars' furious disapproval.

'So when is Knud Holm coming?' he asked instead. It was a cop out and he knew it. 'He seems to be taking his time.'

'There are at present still thick fogs all down the East Coast, from the north of Mesters Vig right down to Augpilaqtoq. If Knud is unable to come by Thursday, they'll probably try to fly in somebody direct from Nuuk. They would have done it before now, especially since the victim was a visitor to our country, but I have told them this is a straightforward case and we already have the murderer under lock and key.'

'Lars, I don't think –'

'No more. I will not hear any more. This is not what I've come to talk to you about. What I wanted to tell you is that I've had a complaint from one of your fellow tour members about the way you're continuing to conduct yourself. It has to stop Harry.'

'Who? Who is it? What's this all about?'

'It is not for me to say who made the complaint.'

'Then how can I change my so-called attitude to that person? I could guess who it might be but I might be wrong. You have to tell me this much at least, Lars. We used to be friends, remember? Then I'll promise you I'll not say another word to that individual.'

'How can you say we are not still friends, Harry, after all I've done for you? After all I am still doing for you?'

He did not even begin to understand what Lars Erikssen was trying to say. Lars looked as bewildered as Harry felt. At last the Dane spoke again.

'Very well. I shall go along with you this far, but no further. It was Mr Anthony Ferris who complained to me about your approach to him this morning.'

'But I hardly said anything.' Harry was genuinely surprised. He'd guessed Ferris was the one who'd made the complaint, but he couldn't see any justification for it. 'I said no more than a few words. In fact, my whole idea was to make the peace after what I'd said to Ferris previously. I admit I overstepped the mark then. *He* was the one who was rude to *me* today, I'd have to say. It was the second time he'd rebuffed me.'

'Then your course of action is plainly written before you. However, I will spell it out so there can be no mistake in the future. I do not think you should speak to Mr Ferris again during the remainder of the time you are in Greenland. It would be best if you draw your mark a long way from him.'

'It will be a pleasure,' said Harry, himself growing angry now. 'What about you Lars? Should I also, as you put it, draw my mark a long way from you?'

'Now you are being stupid and petulant. Of course you know I do not want any such thing. When Knud Holm or the policemen from Nuuk have been and gone we can be friends as before. All of this unhappiness we can put behind us.'

'But not before then?'

Lars ignored the unstated question Harry was asking.

'Now, I want to say something to you to show you how much of a friend I still am. This morning I saw you talking to Mrs Walters. It was – what would you say? – an intimate conversation.'

'Oh, come on Lars. How can you possibly know what we were saying? You must have been in your own cabin. You'd have been too far away to hear a word.'

But, to himself, Harry was thinking "*if Lars saw us together how many others did as well?*" He did a quick reckoning and calculated with relief that only the windows in the cabins of Mel and Lars, plus that of Vonnie and himself would have been in the direct line of sight of the bench. He was sure Vonnie hadn't been watching them. Nor had Mel Walters, to judge by the way he'd acted afterward. Walters had almost – no, he *had* – taken Harry as his confidant a short time afterward.

'I know what Maggie was saying to you, Harry, because she'd said the same thing to me when we were in Aasiaat. She wants you to go running with her in the early mornings, am I right? Only she has made it very clear to you she has a different kind of exercise in mind. Am I correct in this?'

Harry did not answer. No words would come. He now knew he definitely wasn't Maggie's second choice; he was at least third in line. Instead of finding this piece of information insulting, he found it strangely arousing and exciting. But Lars' words as he walked away were:

'Remember Madame Vonnie in this, Harry. Remember her before you do anything you might regret. And remember me.'

*

'Well, you were a long time,' said Vonnie when he returned. 'What was all that about? I've never seen Lars so agitated.'

'Oh,' said Harry. He doesn't want me to talk to Ferris. The bloody man's gone and complained about me, would you believe? Well, it will be a pleasure not to have to say anything to him again. I wouldn't piss on him if he was on f –'

'Harry!'

'Sorry, love. The man really gets my goat.'

'If you're so happy to have no further contact with Mr. Ferris, then why should it have taken you so long to talk to Lars? It was plain to me that young man was getting really steamed up. There must have been something else.'

Harry didn't answer immediately. He could hardly tell her Lars had been warning him against Maggie Walters.

'Well Harry? I'm waiting.'

He made up his mind to tell his wife a sanitised version of the truth.

'Oh, he was telling me he'd seen me talking to one of the other women – Maggie Walters. He was saying you'd get jealous. Ridiculous, isn't it? I was only talking to Maggie about going running in the morning. I've already told you as much. I said you were too adult to get the wrong idea. Then he flew off the handle for no reason – well, you saw him.'

Vonnie looked at him doubtfully, as if she'd guessed Harry was telling her only part of the story. But what she said next took Harry by surprise.

'Hmmm. Yes, I did. I saw the way he was acting.' Vonnie looked thoughtful. 'But I'd have said young Lars was getting jealous on his own account, not on mine'.

5.5

In their cabin that evening, Vonnie was lazily yawning.

'Well, we've had a big dinner after another hard day of walking. It's an early night for me. I'll read a chapter or two of my novel and then I'll be more than ready to turn in. How about you, Harry love? You've had a long day yourself. And you were so restless again last night.'

'I'll be grateful for the chance of an early night, right enough. My sleep-levels are in serious need of topping-up. But I promised Freddie at dinner I'd meet him to have a word. I'll do that and then I'll be glad to call it a day.'

'It's good to see the two of you hitting it off at last. Freddie is as harmless as the day is long. Shame about Mr Ferris, though. You make sure you don't so much as look in his direction tomorrow. You know what you can be like. One thing will lead to another and then... well. Anyway, don't be too late chewing the fat with Freddie. Remember, you'll need to be in the best of condition for Maggie at seven o'clock. You don't want to let yourself down with a young woman like her. It'd be awful if you found yourself out of puff after a few minutes.'

Harry wished Vonnie had expressed it differently.

*

It was a lovely evening, the best they'd known since they'd been in Vatsaaq, or even at any other time in Greenland. It was hard to imagine weather conditions further south being so different. He wished Freddie hadn't suggested they should meet on this bench for a chat, the place Maggie had propositioned him so brazenly this morning.

Freddie was walking towards him, in his slow, waddling fashion. Guiltily, Harry realised his clumsy motion was one of the things that had made him take a dislike to the man. How unfair this had been. He saw now that the uneven gait was caused by a limp in Freddie's right leg. It appeared to be causing him a lot of pain, through which he was still trying to maintain the usual boyish eagerness on his face.

Harry felt ashamed. He'd been too ready to jump to conclusions about people during his time as a policeman. In private life he'd done no better. And on this holiday, he'd accumulated a negative score of staggering proportions. He made up his mind: he wouldn't make things any worse.

'Hello again Harry. I hope I haven't kept you waiting too long?' The smile on Freddie's flushed face was turned up a degree or two in magnitude.

'No, not at all. I've only been here for ten minutes or so. Anyway, I wanted to sit in the open for a while before we spoke. It's a lovely evening and I needed to do some quiet thinking on my own account. Is your leg causing you a lot of trouble? I've not noticed before that you had so much difficulty with it.'

'Four years ago I had an accident. I fell off a ladder, of all the stupid things to do. My fault entirely. I've made a more or less complete recovery, I'm pleased to say. The leg only really gives me gyp when I put too much weight on my right side for too long.' He patted his stomach. 'I know I'm carrying too much weight around the middle these days. And we've done miles of walking today.'

Harry nodded. 'I wouldn't have thought a holiday like this would've suited you. I'd have thought one of the popular resorts would be more your cup of tea. Entertainment laid on and all mod cons.'

'Why do you say a thing like that?' said Freddie, in a surprised tone. 'I wouldn't have missed Greenland for the world. The dome of blue sky, the open landscape, the fantastic emptiness, the cliffs and waterfalls. Even when it snowed it was wonderful. What do you take me for, some sort of Philistine?'

'No. Of course not,' Harry was lying. This was exactly what he'd been thinking.

'Still,' Freddie went on. 'I did hope to make a few chums here. It's been hard for me since I lost my Peggy. Seems I haven't done very well on the score of making friends and influencing people.'

'Nonsense Freddie. People do like you. They see you as a – character.'

Freddie gave a mournful half-smile.

'It's good of you to say so but I know very well what they think. Look, I didn't bring you out here so I could wallow in self-pity. We're here so I can tell someone the truth about the day in Gulfoss. I know what people are saying.'

Gulfoss? Harry sat up on the bench. Dainty's story? About Freddie fondling Essie's breasts?

To Freddie he said, 'Gulfoss? The huge falls in Iceland? They were really something to see. What happened there?'

'Don't try to humour me Harry. I expect better from you. You very well know what happened. Or what's supposed to have happened.'

'Sorry. I'd better shut up and let you do the talking. Go on.'

'It's true, I did touch Essie Smith's breasts. I'm not trying to deny it. But it didn't happen in the way you think. Not at all.'

Freddie cast his gaze downwards. Then he lifted his gaze and looked directly into Harry's eyes.

'Look, I'll tell you the whole story. My leg had started to play up – it does that sometimes near water – damp air, you see, and you'd have to say there's plenty of that around Gulfoss Falls. We were near enough to the torrent for there to be a tremendous number of water droplets in the atmosphere. There were far more than at the Puisialuk Falls today. But you'll remember Gulfoss.'

'Yes, I remember the air there. It was the best thing about the day. Of the whole week, in fact. You could see streams of light braiding through the air, rainbow after rainbow of them. It was fascinating. More than that – it was beautiful.'

'Not for me it wasn't, I'm afraid. It was bloody painful. Anyway, Essie Smith saw me limping and wincing. She said she'd help me down to the flat ground below. I thought it was very kind of her. The others hadn't been all that friendly since the night we landed in Keflavik Airport, even before we came to Greenland. People got talking while they were waiting for you to sort out that trouble with the suitcase – they tracked it down in Gothenburg or somewhere in Sweden in the end, didn't they? I thought then "this is going to be a friendly lot; I'm going to enjoy this holiday". But it didn't work out that way.' He sighed. 'Did you ever finally straighten out the suitcase nonsense, by the way?'

'Yes. It took me two whole days to retrieve the missing case, though. The only real difficulty was that my swimming trunks were in that case. It didn't much matter: Gudrun was able to borrow a pair for me in Selfoss, so in the end there was no problem.' Harry knew it did matter. It had been a real problem. It was then that things had started to go so badly wrong…

'Well,' Freddie continued, interrupting Harry's uncomfortable train of thought. 'Essie helped me down to the place where we were going to meet the bus. We sat on the seat for a while, waiting for the rest of you to come. Essie said "At least we've shaken Jeremy off. He follows me around like a shadow, that one. Let's go and have a look at that little forest over there. The others won't be down for a while yet".

'"Forest, you call it?",' I said. '"The tallest trees are no more than four feet high. You'd never get lost in that forest. If you did you'd only have to stand up." It made her laugh. You could say it set the tone for the rest of our conversation. I was only too ready to don the mask of Fun-loving Freddie, the Northern Comedian. I've done it so often before, so soon got myself into the swing of being the joker again. My leg was rested by this time. It wasn't so hard.

'So we walked over to this "forest" with me playing the fool and being the comic for all I was worth. Essie was shrieking like some little girl on a Sunday School outing. I'd got as far as my usual repertoire of jokes about my weight by the time we reached the trees. I'm more than a bit overweight, so I've got a good stock of them.'

Harry saw no reason to deny the fact of Freddie's excess flab.

'Then, all of a sudden, I saw that she'd unzipped her parka. She said "I've got a weight problem, too. Mine is mainly concentrated in this one place as you can see." Well, I didn't know what to say. She had a fantastic pair of –'

'Yes,' said Harry quickly. 'What happened then?'

'Well, I didn't know where to look. My eyes were on stalks, I can tell you. I'd always seen her in loose-fitting overclothes before that moment. I'm afraid what I said was something really daft. I tried to make a joke of it, as usual. I said, "Nay lass, tha's got a fine figure. Tha doesna get many o' them peaches to the pound". These last few nights when I've been alone in bed, I find those stupid words coming back to haunt me. Poor Essie. Poor, poor Essie. What I said was pure music-hall Lancashire, I know. You don't have to tell me. I act like that when I'm nervous.

'Anyway, she was delighted by what I said. She loved it. Then she says, bold as brass, "how would you like to have a little feel, then? You can weigh things up for yourself, sort of thing." I promise you Harry, I hadn't so much as looked at another woman since the day my Peggy passed away. But when it's set out before you like that – well, I am only human – so, I took her at her word.'

Freddie tried to grin. Instead, he looked desparatel sad.

'Naturally, I went to hold her properly instead of all this silly kids' stuff. That's when she jumped up, squealing with delight. Embarrassing, it was. It was then I saw Dainty Clatworthy. She'd come down early from the falls, too, only we hadn't noticed her. She must have been standing there watching us. Can you imagine how it must have looked? The old girl's mouth had dropped open, like you used to read about in the comic books. The two women stood looking at each other for a few moments, before Dainty stalked off. She really stomped away, as if she was disgusted. I suppose she was.

'Essie turned back to me, still chuckling away, very pleased with herself and then – do you know what she said? She said "well, nobody's going to want to squeeze her little titties, are they?" I didn't know where to put my face when she said that. I really didn't.'

Harry could see from Freddie's expression that he was re-living the moment. He could see his shame was genuine.

'I tried to speak to Essie later in the evening and again on the next day. I still thought maybe we could try to have a more adult relationship. After all, she'd made me more aware of my needs – she'd seen to that all right – and I thought she might have the same sort of feelings, too. But no, she didn't want to know about any of it. It was as if this playground stuff was all she wanted.

'That's it, I suppose. I've told you the whole story. Except that poor Essie was killed not much more than a week later. Poor girl. She might have had some very funny ideas about sex, but she wasn't a bad one. Never deserved what happened to her. Dainty must have told others in the party what she'd seen. I've overheard some of them whispering. You can't really blame the old girl, but my reputation was shot to pieces from that moment. I even thought some of them would be thinking it was me that killed her. Thank goodness I had a cast-iron alibi.'

'What alibi?' asked Harry, surprised.

'Well, I told Lars about it when he talked to all of us on Monday morning. Didn't he tell you? I thought the two of you were supposed to be working together?'

'What did you tell him?' said Harry, ignoring Freddie's question.

'I told him what had happened at the party. Nothing much, really. You know yourself. You were there. Well, you were there for most of the time. So was your wife. She was there all the time, fortunately for me. I was in the Great Hall with you and Vonnie until nearly two o'clock.' Freddie smiled ruefully. 'I remember I kept on asking you the way to Lambeth. Said I was going to walk all the way there. I was as drunk as a lord. Huh! If I'd have tried to walk anywhere I'd have falllen flat on my face.'

For a moment the grin of the Northern comic briefly lit Freddie's face. Then it quickly faded.

'Luckily for me, before you two left, Gudrun came in looking to see if I was still in the Hall. It was good of her to think of me. I thought she'd have been in the land of dreams by that time. I was swaying about, just inside the door. I was really pie-eyed . She helped me back to my cabin.

'Harry – don't you remember the part before Vonnie dragged you out? She was furious with you. No, I suppose you might not remember. You'd had even more to drink than me. You were really hitting the whisky bottle. And the local hooch into the bargain Anyway, none of it matters much now, does it?'

Freddie fell silent for a moment. Then he looked straight at Harry..

'There was the one awkward moment when Vonnie and I had to explain you'd gone off somewhere for half-an-hour or more.' He was silent again. Then he slowly said. 'Now they've got that big Inuit locked up for the crime. That's the end of the story. Thank goodness for that, eh?'

Harry didn't know what to think. Vonnie would've been able to vouch for Freddie, even though neither she nor Lars had said anything to him. But what about his own missing half-hour? Nobody could vouch for that time, least of all himself. All he had were a few half-memories of meeting Nanoq. They must have occurred, if they really did occur, during this time, He tried to put his blurred fragments of recollection together. Nanoq was supposed to have been the one who killed Essie, but he'd never quite been able to bring himself to believe that was what had really happened. What if...

‘Thanks Harry.’ Freddie’s words interrupted his thoughts. The images in his mind were moving down a deeply troubling path. ‘They say confession is good for the soul. Well, now I’ve proved it. Telling the story of the day at Gulfoss Falls is a great weight off my shoulders. Especially in the light of what happened afterwards to poor Essie, even though we know Nanoq was the murderer.’

‘Confession is good for the soul you say Freddie? Do you mind if I do some unloading on my own account?’

‘You? You can’t have any dark secrets, surely?’

‘I want to tell you about Essie.’

‘Isn’t ... isn’t this something you should be saying to Lars?’

Harry looked at Freddie. A flicker of doubt had entered Freddie’s eyes at the mention of Essie’s name. But Harry managed to control his emotions enough to tell the story that had been troubling him ever since the event.

‘It’s a story very much like yours. It’s something that happened only a few days before. In the pool at Selfoss this was; on the first day we went there. It was our second day in Iceland.’

Freddie visibly relaxed. Harry decided that Freddie would be unable to keep up any kind of pretence for long. Even his fake Northern accent, a fiction he’d apparently tried to maintain for years, had been blown away under Dainty’s scrutiny.

‘Well,’ said Harry. ‘I was wearing those borrowed swimming trunks Gudrun had got for me. They weren’t a very good fit, to be honest. Skimpy and at the same time a bit loose-fitting. I tell you, if I’d have tried to swim a length or two I’d have drawn the crowds all right.’

Freddie laughed.

'Anyway, it didn't matter too much because I didn't plan to swim any lengths. I'm not much of a swimmer at the best of times. All I wanted to do was to concentrate on keeping my shoulders under the water to protect them from the cold wind and bob about a bit. There was a fair breeze blowing across the pool. Makes you wonder why in Iceland they have so many of their swimming pools built in the open air. It must be freezing in the winter.'

'You're right there,' said Freddie.

'Quite soon, I'd decided I'd had enough of the cold wind. But I'd been sitting on the bottom of the pool in the shallow end and stood up a little too quickly. Of course, those damn' trunks slipped down a bit. It wouldn't have mattered normally – I'd have simply hitched them up, but, as I was about to do this, I heard a voice saying "Mr Lanier, you're not getting out because I'm getting in, surely?" It was Essie next to me.

'I hadn't heard her coming into the water. "Mrs Smith," I spluttered. I thought she was married then. "Why don't you call me Essie?" she said. "It's friendlier." I didn't say anything. She was wearing this two-piece swimming costume. How it ever stayed on, I'll never know. Like you were just saying, I'd always seen her in those loose jumpers and heavy coats before, but her – her figure – it was – it was…'

'I know,' said Freddie. 'Haven't I just told you about the day at the Gulfoss Falls?'

'I couldn't take my eyes off her,' said Harry. He'd hardly heard Freddie's words. He was lost in his memories of the day. 'All I could do was keep on staring at her. I couldn't help it. Of course, she saw me looking. She loved being looked at. She really loved it. Then she leaned forward so I could see even more of her. She did it on purpose.

'Then she looked down at me. I had – reacted – and those damned swimming trunks didn't cover anything, especially at half-mast as they were. She could see what had happened to me. I sat back down, double quick, let me tell you. She shrieked with laughter in that funny high-pitched laugh she has – had – as if she was delighted to see what she'd done. The squawking sound was almost the worst part. I can still hear it.'

Harry knew he should stop talking, but couldn't.

'And then – I still can't believe what she said as she looked down at me: "I never knew there were any wriggly fishies in here. This one's full grown by the look of him. He's a nice fat one, isn't he?" I tried to stammer something – something ludicrous about the way the wind was blowing across the pool – but she only laughed all the more before she turned around to swim.

'I'd have clambered out if I could, but this wasn't possible in my erect state. So, all I could do was sit low in the water and wait for the thing to die down. It took some time, with her still in the pool. Then, after she'd swum only one length, she climbed out. She waved and giggled and shook her bust at me. It was a few minutes more before I was able to get out myself.'

He stopped speaking as he remembered what happened next. Vonnie, unnoticed by him, had come to the side of the pool. She must have seen the whole thing, but waited until Essie had gone and Harry had climbed out before starting to question him. And it hadn't stopped there... He had no intention of mentioning this part of the story to Freddie.

'That's all there is to it, really. It's nothing much of a tale, but it's been on my mind ever since that day.'

Freddie looked questioningly at Harry. There was no trace of humour in his voice as he said, 'Harry. Do yourself a favour: don't tell that story to anyone else. Especially to Lars or to this Knud Hulm when he gets here. It might lead to more questions than you want to handle.'

Harry looked at him dumbly. Freddie had said, "confession is good for the soul". Well, it hadn't been good for his soul. He wished he'd said nothing.

*

He watched Freddie's back receding in the direction of the cabins, feeling the cold for the first time that night. Yet to go back to his cabin and face Vonnie with images of Selfoss newly-refreshed in his mind was something he knew he couldn't do now. He remained on the bench for a long time.

'Mr. Lanier? Do you mind if I join you for a moment?' The voice came from behind him.

'Miss Jonsdottir?' Harry turned. 'Or Mrs Jonsdottir? I'm sorry, I don't know what I should call you.'

'You should call me Gudrun, of course. And it's Gudrun Jonsdottir.' She laughed lightly as she took a seat next to Harry. 'We don't have quite the same traditions as you. I am married. My husband's name is Steingrimur Henrikssen. His father's name was Henrik, as the name of my own father is Jon. Do you see how it works? My husband is "Steingrimur, Henrik's son" and I am "Gudrun, Jon's daughter." It is all very simple and logical.'

The last thing Harry wanted was another conversation. Everything was still spinning around in his head. And Freddie had just told him Gudrun had been out after two o'clock on Sunday morning, the time Essie was killed. She was the last person he wanted to talk to at this moment. He decided to keep this as brief as possible.

'Where've you been, then. Out for a walk?' he asked, trying to sound more cheerful than he felt.

'Yes. Not far, though. I've been very busy for the last few days, writing up a report on the tragedy for the travel company. It's finished now. I find myself with time on my hands at last.'

Harry asked another question, even though he knew it was time to make his excuses and leave.

'Why should this be? Shouldn't you be with Lars, shepherding the sheep? If you don't mind me saying so, I've noticed you've hardly been out with us since we came to Greenland.'

'You're right. That's exactly what I should have been doing. But Lars said he could handle such a small party on his own – as he can of, course – and insisted I stayed behind. I did not mind at all.'

Harry was surprised. She was right in what she said, but wouldn't this make her surplus to requirements from the point of view of her employers? She'd put herself out of a job at this rate.

'Isn't that a bit risky?' he asked. 'I mean, the tour operater could see you as redundant if you're not doing much.'

'They could. But I do not mind. You see, I've already decided I will be leaving the company after this tour.'

'I understand. The murder was a terrible thing.'

'It was. But, in a way, you can look on this as no more than bad luck for me – I mean, to have such a thing happen on a tour you are responsible for is like being struck by forked lightning.'

Bad luck? What did she mean? What else was she going to say?

'No,' Gudrun continued. 'I cannot say it is because of the tragedy I am leaving. But, in a way, you could say it is because of your Essie Smith.'

Harry came to attention at the mention of Essie's name. He tensed, wondering what was coming next. She saw his reaction to her words.

'No, no. It is not to do with her sad death. You misunderstand. There is nothing relating to the crime in what I am going to say but it is a bit delicate. I hope you do not mind me talking directly in this way?'

Harry couldn't believe what he was hearing. Was he expected to be Father Confessor to an Icelander as well now? Who were next, the Inuit?'

To Gudrun he said, 'No, not at all'. She continued.

'Essie and I became friendly back in Iceland. I found her to be full of fun. You could say in many ways she was younger than me. At least she was in the way she sometimes looked at things. In fact, I am twenty-eight, and I know she was thirteen years older. I've seen the passports, you see.

'It was good to have somebody to laugh and share a joke with. These tours are pleasant enough but they wear you down sometimes. This one, especially. There were tensions within the company about running the tour so late in the year. They'd hoped to start in the spring, but they couldn't get all the arrangements in place.'

Gudrun took on a more serious expression.

'As I was saying, Essie became my friend. I enjoyed her company. Then she seemed to change. I saw another side of her. One that worried me.'

'Yes?' said Harry.

'Well, she started to show too much interest in – in a woman's life – for me to be comfortable with her. She knew I was married and kept asking me all sorts of questions about the – intimate side of married life. I thought, "why don't you go and find out for yourself? You don't have to be married to learn the things you always like to ask about." I became convinced she had no real experience of men.

'The truth, I am sure, was that she was frightened of any kind of physical intimacy. Still, I could say nothing. It would be for me to overstep the mark. Instead I tried to avoid her as often as I could. After she was killed I wished I had not done so. I did like her.'

Harry felt like shouting with relief after Gudrun's innocent "confession".

'I don't see why this should lead you to give up your job,' said Harry.

'Ah, you see, all of Essie's questions about the physical side of love made me realise how much I was missing my Steingrimur in Reykjavik. So, I decide I must go back to him. He has told me so many times he wants me to go back.' She smiled sweetly, and then told Harry the thing she'd really wanted to tell him. 'He will be very pleased to start our family, I know this well. It is romantic, do you not think?'

'Yes, it is,' said Harry without too much enthusiasm. But it was romantic. It made him feel all the more regretful about his base desires for Maggie. These were something he was still struggling to put aside.

'I know I shouldn't be telling you any of this. But soon I will be leaving Icesperience for ever and going back to my Steingrimur. And I know you are happily married. I can see this so well. Also, I've been told you were a policeman and will see no need to gossip unnecessarily. Thank you for listening to this not-very-good Tour Manager, Mr. Harry Lanier. And now I will say a good night to you.'

Gudrun turned and waved as she neared the cabins. She smiled and he tried to return her smile. She'd called herself a "not-very-good Tour Manager". He knew he'd been a not-very-good policeman. Would he also prove to be a not-very-good husband?

Chapter Six

Morning Tryst

Wednesday, 31st August, 1994, Vatsaaq, East Greenland

Harry had sneaked out of their cabin as stealthily as any cat burglar. He was anxious not to disturb the sleeping Vonnie. If she'd woken he knew he wouldn't be able to go through with this adventure. Gone was yesterday's pretence to himself that he was only intending to talk to Maggie. To ask her any questions about Saturday night was now the last thing on his mind.

It was shortly before ten minutes to seven on another bright, chilly morning. There was no sign of anyone. Still, seven o'clock was the time they'd set; another ten minutes away. He sauntered over to the bench, the rough wooden construction that had loomed so large in his consciousness recently. Although on the inside he was a tumble of emotions, to any observer – Harry desperately hoped there wouldn't be one – this would be a tranquil scene.

Thirty yards distant was the Great Hall. Harry realised, like Lars, he was now using this name quite naturally. There were three of the smallest buildings close to it. These were barely more than sheds.

Nanoq was still a prisoner in the most distant. The locals had soon given up any idea of mounting a permanent guard on its strong door. It seemed Lars must have acquiesced to this. The prisoner seemed at last to have accepted his fate quietly. He had ceased his hammering on the door and walls, to the accompaniment of an unending torrent of babble. The continual sound of this, rising and falling, had played badly on Harry's nerves when the Inuit was first locked up .

Beyond this group of buildings were the twelve cabins of the tourists. A number of these had remained empty when the party had taken possession. Harry was painfully aware that Essie's, the most distant of the smaller, single-occupancy cabins, had been empty since

Saturday night. Now he hoped Vonnie would be still asleep in their own, though felt a mixture of guilt and excitement when he thought what might be happening in the one shared by Maggie and Mel. She'd probably be pulling on her tight, brilliantly white, running shorts at this moment. He replayed the scene over and over in his imagination.

Separated from the tourist cabins by the best part of a mile or so was the settlement of Vatsaaq proper, a rag-tag collection comprising no more than twenty huts of various shapes and sizes. Most of the roofs were of turf construction. Every wall was crudely painted in a variety of flaking shades of khaki and green. In this they were unlike the neatly uniform cream-and-green of the tourist buildings.

The Danish brothers, Olaf and Christian Severen, in theory anyway, shared one of the brighter green-painted constructions in the Inuit settlement, Harry knew. Christian was nominally a resident of this, though probably spent more nights with his girlfriend. He wondered how much of a nominal resident Olaf was.

Harry could recognise the smallest, most ramshackle, cabin as being that of Nanoq. This was the only dwelling in the Inuit sector he'd been inside. The smell of rotting fish seemed like a physical presence in his nostrils when he merely looked at the exterior. He had no idea which of the cabins housed Silumi and Ikateq. He didn't even know the names of any of the other locals. He, like the other members of the Greenland Party, were an unwelcome intrusion into a pattern of life that had remained essentially unchanged for decades or even centuries.

He looked at his watch. A little surprised, he saw the time was already after five-past-seven. Had Maggie changed her mind? How would he feel if she had? Relieved? Slighted? Frustrated? All of them, certainly. But, while this thought was in his mind, a female voice called softly from behind him.

'Harry.'

Despite the morning chill, Maggie wore only a thin training vest and her white running shorts. She could have been out for a morning jog across the park in more temperate lands.

'Maggie – are you sure you're warm enough dressed like that?'

'I'll be warmed up soon enough. From our exercise, I mean,' she added, smiling mischievously. 'But not if you keep me here gossiping like an old fish-wife. Come on Harry. We've got a bit of proper running to do first. Someone might just be watching us. You'd better look good.'

'Are we going to run out to the Kungmuit Rock?' asked Harry. He remembered with some apprehension the long walk they'd made yesterday.

'Are you serious? The Kungmuit Rock? Running all that way on your first morning? You must be joking, man. I don't want you to have a heart attack on me now, do I? You'd be no use to me then. See the small outcrop about three-quarters of a mile due south? We're going there. Nobody will be able to see us once we get behind the rock. Do your best to keep up now.'

Even as she was saying this, she'd spun on her heel and was off, running at a fair pace. Harry awkwardly followed her. Quickly realising he had no chance of keeping up, or even coming close to it, he shortened and relaxed his stride. The space between them soon grew wider. Maggie glanced back at him, chuckling.

Whatever else she might have been, she was a fine athlete. A run out to Kungmuit Rock would have been nothing to her. Maggie could have made it in not much more than half-an-hour and... and. And what, exactly? What if he'd misunderstood her smutty sense of humour and they really were out here for nothing more than a run? No, not from what she'd said a moment ago they weren't...

Maggie reached the outcrop long before him. She turned about to face him. Her hands were comfortably on her hips and she was grinning in triumph.

'Ah, you're not really so bad for an old timer. You could have run a bit faster if you'd a mind. But I'll forgive you,' she said, as Harry panted up. 'You'll be saving yourself for the main event.'

'Phew!' puffed Harry. 'I'm all done in. I'm right out of condition, that's for sure. I need a rest.'

'You're being too hard on yourself. But you'll have your rest. I've been out here for half-an-hour already. Having a warm-up jog and preparing our nookie corner, that's what Maggie's been doing for you.'

Her last words removed the final ounce of doubt from Harry's mind. Now there could be no question about her intentions. He knew he shouldn't do it but let her link her arm through his, in exactly the way Vonnie had done the day before. She led him around to the back of the rocks.

'It's not de-luxe, but it's the best the staff could do at short notice,' she chuckled. 'Will this be alright for you Sir? The accommodation is basic, but we can promise you *every* service.'

'How can you get away with this?' Harry looked down at the blankets on the ground before them. 'Doesn't

Mel say anything? About the blankets I mean? How do you get them out of the cabin?'

Maggie laughed.

'Ah, my Mel's an angel. It's all a question of conditioning,' she laughed. 'Back home in the Malverns, I always take a couple of bitts of bedding packed in my rucksack. I tell him it's all for my training. Weight d'you see? The Lady with the Blankets, some of my boys call me. So, if I put a couple of warm things in my rucksack while I'm here, Mel thinks nothing of it. That's right,' she repeated, obviously very pleased with herself. 'The boys in the Malverns call me "The Lady with the Blankets". Well, it's what they say to my face, anyway. When I'm not there I know they give me another name. Nobby told me all about it. It rhymes with Maggie. Guess what it is?'

'What do you mean?' said Harry. He was still wondering what he was doing out here. But the feeling of excitement held him fast.

'Use that imagination of yours, Harry boy. Shaggy Maggie the boys call me.' She laughed loudly, plainly delighted with it all.

Harry didn't know what to say. He knew this was a mistake. His place was back in the cabin with Vonnie. But Maggie's careless wantonness was arousing him. He couldn't leave.

'Well, come on then. You're sweating like a pig, you are. If you stay out there yapping away like a puppy-dog you'll catch your death in this cold air. Me too.' Saying this she climbed in between the blankets, pulling up the top one around her chin. She met Harry's eyes and smiled wickedly.

'Come *on* Harry! I meant what I said about the cold.'

Trying to convince himself he was only doing it because of the chill wind blowing around the rocks and already raising goose pimples on his skin, Harry got in beside her.

'That's more like it. Now, keep warm and lie still. I can feel that old heart of yours hammering away.' She put a hand lightly on his chest. 'Is it through the running or because you're a teensy-weensy bit excited? You know what answer to give if you want your wicked way with Maggie.' She pressed her hand to him more firmly, allowing her fingers to play gently upon him. 'Fer Heaven's sake relax, will you man? Anyone would swear I'd got a cock virgin in here with me. What's a girl to do, eh?'

'Have these blankets had much use in Greenland?' asked Harry, surprising himself as much as Maggie. He was still feeling nervous and tried to postpone the moment his body was now demanding.

'Why, what a question to ask a fair young maiden,' she whispered inches from his ear. 'They're virgin blankets Harry. You can pretend I am too, if it's what turns you on.'

'Jeremy Smith? Has he been between these blankets?' Harry couldn't have said what made him ask this particular question.

'Jeremy?' Maggie was surprised, but gave an answer. 'He was a mistake. A bad mistake. I liked the look of him but he didn't want to play. Maybe he couldn't, if you know what I mean. Anyway, we don't want to talk about him or anyone else while we're here. It's you out here with me this morning, Harry. Don't play hard to get, now. You don't mind being second choice do you? I've been honest enough with you.'

'Lars Erikkssen?' Harry remembered what Lars had told him.

'What is this? The Third Degree?' snapped Maggie. Then she smiled. 'All right, Harry. I've met men like you before. Want to hear about the others, and all the things they like, do you? Turns some of you fellas on somehow. But I have to tell you, Lars was my second mistake on this holiday. I wasn't to know he swung the other way, was I now? My Mel would've had more chance with the little fairy.'

She smiled again and looked at Harry wickedly.

'And, before you ask, I hadn't even considered the other men in the group. Fat Freddie would have got out of breath at the thought of jogging inside Maggie's blankets. Tony is OK – I often stop for a chat with the lad in the mornings. But that's all it is – a chat. Anything else and he'd be forgetting what he was there for and whip out his magnifying glass to start examining bloody plants or whatever it is he's so keen on.'

In spite of everything, Harry had to laugh.

'We haven't got on to the Eskimos yet,' she said, winking at Harry. 'D'you know what I've heard about them?'

'Inuit.'

'What?'

'Inuit is their proper name. Nobody calls them Eskimos these days. An Eskimo is a "fish-eater". Inuit you should say.'

'Well, if we stay in this country another week we'll all be turning into bloody Eskimos. I've never seen so much fish. Cod. Cod. Cod. And then, just for a change, they give us haddock on Fridays.'

Harry laughed again. He'd hardly noticed that Maggie had quietly slipped her hand around his waist. But he noticed when the other was slipped confidently down to his groin.

'My, my. This is a fine piece o' handiwork you've got there. I shall have to start calling you Nobby the Second, that I will. You're a big lad. You know, there's nothing better than feeling a good man on top of you, and knowing he's satisfied himself. The few minutes afterward when he's given all he's got is the best time. You're going to show me the best you've got to give, aren't you Harry?'

Then all at once, it really hit him. Vonnie... She was lying there in her bed. In *their* bed. What had he been thinking? He turned.

'I can't do this,' he murmured.

'What?'

'Oh Essie. I'm sorry.'

'What did you call me?'

'Maggie. It's not –'

'No, you bloody well didn't call me Maggie. You bastard. You know what you called me. And too right you can't do this. What is it with you men? A pair of big udders and your bloody heads go. We'll get the key to the hut where she is now if you like and you can help yourself. She'll still be fresh.'

'Maggie, it was just –'

'Get off o' me. And get off my blanket. Bastard. Bastard. Bastard.'

Harry stood up and watched in dumb silence as Maggie, hands shaking, struggled to pack the blankets back into her rucksack. Then she set off at a shambling run in the direction of Kunmuit Rock. Not once did she look back. After some minutes he trudged off. Now he had neither the spirit nor the energy to run. As he was about to enter the cabin he shared with Vonnie, he caught a glimpse of Mel Walters peering anxiously through his side-window. He ducked out of sight as soon as he caught Harry's eye.

6.2

'Well, you must've had a good run. Look at the way you're sweating,' said Vonnie, as Harry came through the door. 'A bit too good a run if you ask me. You've overdone it, I'd say.'

'I think you're right Vonnie.' He knew now he'd never be cut out for this sort of thing. Running wasn't uppermost in his mind. 'It's not for me. No more of it.'

'You don't have to be so dramatic,' said Vonnie. 'You've only exercised too hard, that's all. I expected you to be out for a while yet. Where did you leave Maggie?'

'She ran on to the Kungmuit rock, I think.'

Vonnie looked at him.

'You *think*? You weren't much of a partner for her, were you? Well, I suppose she'll have plenty of time to make her way back from there. We're not leaving for two hours. Lars has changed his mind and re-jigged the itinerary again. We're off now to the place we'd originally planned to see yesterday.'

'What do you mean, Lars has changed his mind?' said Harry, raising his voice. 'He can't do that!'

'Don't get so excited, love. What's got into you? Of course he can change his mind.' Vonnie sounded surprised. 'Jeremy Smith had decided not to come with us after all. Tony Ferris was badgering Lars so he had to admit it would be a shame if we missed seeing this Ku- place and -'

'Qooroqilulissat,' corrected Harry.

'Anyway, he's been around to speak to us all.' Vonnie pointedly ignored her husband's careful pronunciation. 'Or at least he's spoken to most of us. You weren't here.'

'He shouldn't switch things around willy-nilly. Especially when it involves somewhere like Qooroqilulissat. Don't you know it's where he and I found –'

'Oh, don't argue Harry. You're like a big kid sometimes.'

'I'm not arguing.'

'Yes you are. Be sensible about it, please. We all know perfectly well where you both found the body on Sunday morning but, if Lars is willing to go back there, surely you should make the effort. The weather might make it impossible for us to go tomorrow. Besides, perhaps Jeremy Smith will be rejoining us then. It would be wrong to take *him* there.

'And then the full-time detective should be arriving in a day or two. There's no telling what that's going do to Lars' plans. So, far from deciding things "willy-nilly" as you call it, Lars has given the matter careful thought and talked to us about it. The Valley will look different today. Try to see it from the point of others, Harry.' She paused. 'Of course, you don't have to come with us if you don't want to. I'll understand.'

'I will come.' He said this too quickly. What Vonnie was saying made sense. Besides, it might be that he'd see something at Qooroqilulissat. Things might start to click in his confused mind.

'Well then. Don't have so much to say for yourself. Get in the shower and wash some of that sweat away. Then you can come and help me prepare our lunch. It's about time you did your share. And don't you dare say you're tired after all your running.'

*

'Haven't seen you in here before,' said Freddie. 'Had another row with the Missus?'

'No, I haven't,' said Harry. a little too shortly.

Freddie's jest had been too near the truth. When he'd emerged from the shower, Vonnie had continued her campaign of cutting remarks. All he could do in the face of her onslaught was to offer to come down and make their lunch unaided.

'Steady on Harry. I was only joking, you know.'

'Sorry Freddie. I didn't mean to snap. You caught me at a bad moment.'

'It's all right. This seems to be becoming man's work, anyway. Mel Waters has just left with that Ferris chap. You know, the one you get on with so famously?'

'Him! It's a good job I didn't come in twenty minutes earlier.'

Then Freddie Tanner looked more serious. It was clear he was going to say something else.

'I'm glad I've caught you alone. I wanted to tell you what I saw last night. There may be nothing to it, but you never know. It was when I was out for a walk.'

'On your own? Before or after you met me?' asked Harry. He was surprised Freddie had been out walking again. Hadn't he told him his leg was giving him trouble?

'Yes. I was by myself. What's so odd about that? It was about an hour-and-a half after I'd met you. I went out again for a short walk. I'd decided I ought to do more exercise. You never know; it might do me good. Nothing to earn me an Olympic medal, you understand. This is Freddie Tanner you're talking to, remember?'

'Sorry, Freddie. I was interrupting again.'

'It's OK. It might be nothing at all. Not sensational like the stories we told each other last night.' He laughed. 'No tits in this one.'

'Go on,' said Harry, thinking Freddie was being unnecessarily coarse. His levity about a dead woman was in poor taste.

'As I was saying,' said Freddie. 'I only went a short way. Only to that group of rocks back there.'

He pointed to the rock outcrop where he'd been with Maggie only a short while before. Uncomfortable thoughts raced through his mind. Had Freddie been watching them?

'Anyway, I reached the outcrop and only stayed for ten minutes. I stopped to have a blow. And then…'

'Go on, man.'

'Be patient, Harry. Surely you understand why I needed the rest? This old leg of mine?'

'Sorry again. I'm not letting you tell your story properly, am I?'

'It's not much of a story. It's getting a big build-up, but don't expect too much. Well, after I'd had a short rest, I started to walk back in the direction of our cabins. That was when I saw him.'

'Who?'

'I'll tell you if you gave me half a chance. One of those local fellows. The chap who'd been on guard duty before. He was standing by the store hut where that big one, Essie's murderer, is locked up. Right up against the door, the man was. When I got nearer – he was so intent on what he was doing he took not the slightest notice of me – I could see he was carrying on a conversation through the door.'

'Which of the Inuit was it?' asked Harry. 'Was it one of Lars'men, Silumi or Ikateq?'

'How the Devil should I know? They all look the same to me. Anyway, this is the important part. They were talking about the cabins – our cabins. I could see this because the one outside kept pointing back over his shoulder, even though the one locked in the shed couldn't see, of course. I watched carefully to see which one he was indicating. Whose cabin, I mean.'

'And?'

'It was yours Harry. I'm quite certain. There may be nothing to it but I'd make sure you lock your door tonight. Remember that. Lock your door.'

*

'OK, Ladies and Gentlemen,' said Lars. 'This is where we have to leave the trailer. We'll be walking for the rest of the way.'

There was a chorus of groans from the members of the party but it was good natured enough and they all stepped out of the vehicle. It was another bright day. The wind had chosen to be perfectly still. This gave the pleasant illusion they were much further south, on a fine day in late autumn. Most of them looked about eagerly. Lars had promised they'd be seeing the finest sights in the whole of Greenland this morning. They were ready for them.

The exception to this eager anticipation was Harry. The visit to the Valley of Qooroqilulissat was something he'd been dreading. The gritty black sand of Vatsaaq Bay had already provided him with a grim reminder of last Sunday morning. Despite his ferocious hangover, that day had started so well. It had ended in a waking nightmare. It was hard to believe it was just three days ago. So much had happened since.

'Come on Harry,' said Vonnie. 'You've got a face like thunder. You shouldn't have come with us if you knew you were going to be like this.'

Harry was painfully aware there was more to things than Vonnie knew. He'd almost been unfaithful to his wife. Thank heavens he could say "almost". If events had happened slightly differently, would he be able to say the same thing? No, he wouldn't. He owed it to Vonnie to make it up to her.

'I'm sorry, Vonnie. I've been thinking too much. All that's happened here ... It's getting to me. You're right: I shouldn't have come today.'

'I know Harry. You poor love. And I haven't been as understanding as I might have been. But you've been so ... so odd on this holiday. You've upset so many people. Anthony Ferris, Freddie Tanner – though thank heavens you seem to have patched up your differences with him. Even Lars is hardly speaking to you. And you must have upset Maggie Walters on your run this morning. What's wrong Harry?'

'Why do you say that about Maggie?' What did Vonnie know?

'Well, the way you suddenly left her to her own devices on the run. Then I noticed she didn't even acknowledge you when we got on that bus-thing this morning. She deliberately looked out of the window as you passed. She didn't so much as glance in my own direction. You must have done something to offend her, I'd say.'

'I found I couldn't run so far as I thought. The fact was, I was ashamed of myself. Maggie teased me about it, and I – I snapped.' Harry was alarmed at the ease with which the lies came to his lips.

'Oh, Harry!'

'I'll try not to get on the wrong side of anyone else. It must be something to do with this Northern climate. We'll go to Portugal again next year, shall we? Or, why not Bournemouth?'

He gave Vonnie's hand a squeeze.

'That's more like the Harry I know.' She leaned a little closer to him. It was far more than he deserved. 'But we'll talk about it next year, shall we?'

They trudged on, bearing to the north of the escarpment Harry and Lars had climbed on the Sunday morning. It was a longer way around but it did mean they'd avoid a taxing hike for Dainty. But, looking about him, Harry saw she was walking faster and seemingly more comfortably than Freddie Tanner. She looked in their direction and gave a bright wave.

*

'This is really something to see, Harry.' Vonnie's voice was hushed. 'The way those two blocks of ice are slowly circling each other in that pool. It's wonderful.'

Harry wanted to tell her that on Sunday there'd been three blocks, and Essie's corpse was horrifyingly attached to the largest. Neither Vonnie nor any other member of the party – perhaps not even Jeremy Smith – knew this was how Essie had been found. He and Lars had agreed to spare the others the gruesome details for as long as possible.

The two blocks were moving around with stately slowness. It was a peaceful, beautiful scene. He had to admit these were the right words, despite the grim associations. Looking at the tip of the glacier-finger, he could see that what was destined to become the next block of ice had already started to form. It was a natural process. This was one of nature's timepieces, one that had been beating a steady rhythm for hundreds, even thousands, of years. Perhaps Lars had been right – he'd been making too much of the temporary disruption to this rhythm. No wonder the Dane had looked at him oddly when he'd speculated so wildly on Sunday.

*

As they were walking back along the edge of the bay, Lars continually stared out to sea. Then he held up his hand to indicate they should halt.

'Ladies and Gentlemen,' he said. 'I think we shall have to cancel the second part of our journey. As you know, the idea was to walk a mile or so further west. Now I think we'd be wiser to return as soon as we can.'

'But why?' protested Mel. 'It's a grand day.'

'It will not remain so for much longer,' said Lars. 'You see that bank of rolling mist a mile or two out to sea? It's the harbinger of the storm fast heading inland. This is what they've been seeing in the south of the country for the last few days. Now it's our turn here in the east.'

Even as Lars spoke, they could see the storm bank was fast advancing. They quickened their pace, glad to see the six-wheeler speeding towards them. It arrived as the first raindrops started to fall from a rapidly darkening sky.

The brief shower Harry had seen on Sunday was as nothing compared with the heavy rain the shower quickly became. As soon as they'd taken their seats, weighty raindrops began bouncing off the roof of the vehicle. Water was soon cascading down its windows. The windscreen wipers, even at their fastest speed, seemed unable to clear the screen. Harry wondered how the driver, Ikateq, could see even the bare outlines of the way ahead. He noted, thankfully, that the Inuit was driving with extreme caution and slowness.

The engine made a straining, whining noise as the wheels turned slowly on the inadequate track, already turning into a quagmire. For a while Harry doubted they'd be able to make the short journey back to the settlement in safety. After what seemed an age, Ikateq applied the handbrake with a noisy crunch. Only then could Harry make out the shimmering shapes of buildings through the windows. They'd made it.

'We are here,' said Lars unnecessarily. 'I am afraid we are all going to get very wet as we run across, even though the rain is beginning to ease slightly. In one hour from now I shall arrange for the showing of a video in the Great Hall. I'm sorry we'll have to make do with a video, but you will learn much about the natural history of Greenland from this.'

*

Harry and Vonnie had been drenched by running the few yards. They disrobed and engulfed themselves in the huge white towels they'd grabbed as soon as they scrambled through their door. Until today, these had looked too big to be of practical use. Now it seemed as though they'd been made for this occasion.

'Well, that wasn't my idea of rain easing slightly,' Harry said. 'And we're going to get wet all over again when we go to see the video. What did he say it was about? Greenland's natural history?'

'We could always give it a miss,' said Vonnie.

'There's not much else to do here in the day, love. I've read all the leaflets and stuff. I don't really fancy reading one of your novels. One of your *ro*-mances. No, we might as well risk the rain.'

'Doesn't this big towel give you any better ideas Harry?'

'What do you mean?'

'We could always go to bed, couldn't we?'

Harry looked at Vonnie. It was the first time he'd really looked at her in months. She teasingly let her towel droop down a few inches.

'Vonnie...'

'Come to bed, Harry. No more talking.'

Saying this, Vonnie stepped forward and wrapped Harry around with her own towel, easing his to the ground until they were face-to-face with one king-size towel about them.

Harry was intensely aware of Vonnie's naked flesh against his own. She was still cool after the rainstorm, despite the towelling she had given herself. He shared her tremor of excitement.

'You're a bit on the cold side Vonnie.'

'Well then, perhaps you'd better do something about it.'

Chapter Seven
Manhunt

Thursday, 1st September, 1994, Vatsaaq, East Greenland

The sky was filled with swirling clouds. The morning was far colder. It seemed as if the icy grasp of the coming winter was already reaching out to claim Vatsaaq. All too soon the settlement would be firmly within the season's frozen grip. Now, thankfuly, the rain hammering on the metal roof of their cabin for hours past was falling as no more than a light shower, but the cold was already intense.

Harry glanced again at his watch and saw the time was exactly a quarter-to-seven. He'd spent a long time in bed with Vonnie. He'd come out early, hoping to catch Maggie to try to make some amends for slighting her yesterday. The likely response he'd meet with would be jeering abuse – he could picture her calling him "No-Nobby". This he was prepared for. Let her pour out her invective: it was no less than he deserved.

For the first night this week, Harry could say that eventually he'd slept soundly. It made the world look so much better, despite the puddles claiming the ground.

*

What Harry couldn't help thinking of as the "the towel sex" during the early part of his long hours in bed with Vonnie had enabled him to ease some of the turmoil planted in his mind by his ill-starred encounter with Maggie. But, far from being in any way exotic, he felt this was little more than the routine Friday-night lovemaking back in Reading. Vonnie said he'd been "only half-way there". She'd been right.

Part of the trouble was he'd been too conscious of Freddie's story of the Inuit pointing towards their door. Afterwards, he'd dozed no more than fitfully. He couldn't help continually stirring and straining his head from the pillow to see if he could make out the shadow of a would-be intruder outside. When they'd come back last night, he'd examined the lock. It didn't look like as if it would be capable of keeping anyone out.

Then, during one of his periods of fretful wakefulness, the idea had come to him of wedging the door with one of the cabin's heavy chairs, exactly as the hero might do in thriller films. The trouble was, this proved more difficult to achieve in life than on the screen. With his blundering efforts, he succeeded only in making a racket. Unsurprisingly, the noise had awoken Vonnie.

'What are you trying to do Harry?' Her voice made him start. 'I'm going to be barricaded in here with a mad sex-maniac, am I? Hmm; that sounds as if it might be an interesting experience.'

There was something different about her. This time, he'd slipped back into bed as if with a new and exciting woman. She *was* a new and exciting woman. For years their lovemaking had drifted into an event no more special than doing the gardening or the weekly shopping. Now she really wanted him. The clock had been turned back thirty years.

Their almost desperate lovemaking over, he'd drifted off into a deep, contented sleep. The chair was carelessly left where it was. Harry thought no more about Freddie's story of the Inuit pointing to their door.

The brief hours of semi-darkness were with them before Vonnie had risen from their bed and gone to make a sandwich from the few slices of bread and the scrap of salmon they were lucky enough to have in the cabin. This reminded Harry of the day when they were youngsters and found themselves alone in his uncle's house with the big goose feather-bed upstairs.

On that day, too, Vonnie had slipped out of bed to see what she could find to assuage their hunger. At the age of seventeen they'd also been satisfied with a roughly-made sandwich: Harry remembered his teenage pride that Vonnie couldn't bear to be parted from him long enough to prepare something more elaborate. Last night his mature pride had been exactly the same.

*

This morning, he'd torn himself from their bed to make some effort to put right at least one of the things he'd fouled up so badly this week.

Now he'd been out here for twenty minutes. There was no sign of Maggie or anyone else. It was as if there was no-one in the tourist cabins, or even in the Inuit settlement beyond. This did not trouble him; he was at peace with the dull ghostliness of the morning. He paced backwards and forwards, swishing his arms in an effort to keep warm.

It wouldn't matter in the least if Vonnie did look out and see him today. When they'd awoken together, he'd steeled himself to tell her the truth about the debacle of yesterday's tryst with Maggie.

'She threw herself at me, that Maggie,' he remembered saying. 'She really did. I must admit I was tempted, but then I thought of you…' This might be putting himself in a more favourable light but it was essentially true.

He'd been amazed at the generosity and understanding of Vonnie's reaction. If only he'd tried to speak to her properly before...

It had been Vonnie's idea that he should come out this morning to speak to Maggie. His wife had been wonderful. This was the only word for the way he felt about her. They'd talked for hours last night. They'd talked in a way they hadn't for years in between alternate dozing and petting. Later on, no more a matter of hours ago really, they'd made love again. This time it was gentle, even playful.

Another ten minutes, at the most. Then he'd be relieved to return to the warmth of their cabin and to his wife. Probably breakfast would be at the usual nine o'clock. That was two hours away yet, but Harry could already feel the first stirrings of his morning appetite. Lars would no doubt have to do some re-arrangement of the programme because of the weather but –

'*Wham!*'

Harry found himself face down on the wet ground with fragments of sharp and bitter-tasting gravel adhering to the sides of his lips. A pain seared across his shoulders. Some survival instinct told him to roll over onto his back and, through the pain, he managed to do so. Standing above him was an enraged Inuit. It was Nanoq, who'd felled him with one powerful punch between the shoulder blades.

'Kusanartoq Essie toquvoq! Tuluk ajorpoq!'

In Nanoq's enraged bellow Harry thought he recognised the same words spoken at the time of his arrest. But this was no time for speculation. Now the furious Inuit was scrambling on the ground for a large rock nearby. The man wanted to dash his brains out.

'Nanoq! Naaga!' Harry heard Lars running up to them.

Nanoq froze in his crouching position, his face a mask of anger. Harry could see he was wondering whether to continue his efforts to prise the heavy rock from the ground and make his assault. Harry knew he'd be defenceless if Nanoq levered the rock free. Already, it was loosening. It looked like the end for him.

'Nanoq! Naaga!' Lars called again, louder and more urgently.

With a snarl Nanoq jumped up and kicked Harry in the ribs, swiftly and violently. But this was no more than a parting gesture. Although he was winded, he'd not felt the full power of the Inuit's strength. Leaving Harry lying helplessly on the ground, Nanoq raced off in the direction of the Inuit settlement. He showed a surprising turn of speed for such a big man.

'Harry! Are you all right?' asked Lars, running up to him.

Harry hadn't been seriously hurt by the kick but the punch still pained him. He was shocked by the suddeness of the attack. At first he couldn't speak, but finally he did gasp out a few words.

'In one – piece. Am I glad to see you!'

'You'll be all right. Lie there quietly for a minute.'

Harry did as he was told. There wasn't much else he could do.

'Brave of you to run up like that, armed with only a pair of binoculars.' Harry tried to smile as he struggled painfully into a hunched position.

Lars looked down at the binoculars swinging around his neck, the strap now twisted together with his swinging knapsack.

'Not brave, Harry. I dashed over without thinking when I saw what was happening. Nanoq would have killed you for sure. What else could I do? You'd have done the same. Rest there a little longer, now.'

Harry wasn't sure he'd have had the nerve for the "you'd have done the same" bit. Nanoq had looked truly frightening as he'd towered above him.

'Well, you certainly came on the scene at the right time,' he said at last. 'He was ready make a real mess of me if you hadn't appeared when you did.'

'The timing was fortunate. Olaf and I had come out from our cabin to make the routine morning check of Nanoq's lock-up. We discovered he'd gone and the door was swinging open. I should have maintained the twenty-four hour guard on him, although this would probably have made no difference. It can only be that Silumi broke the lock from the outside. Of course he'll deny this when we put it to him. Silumi would have been part of the twenty-four hour guard.

'I grabbed these binoculars from my room and asked Olaf to get the hunting-rifles so he and I could track Nanoq. Then I looked around the area to see if there was any sign of him. I thought he'd have been long gone. The last thing I expected to see when I came around the corner of the Great Hall was The Bear standing over you, shouting his head off.'

At that moment Olaf came into sight, carrying two large guns. Harry could see these weren't the BSA Martinis. They were larger and clearly more powerful weapons, even being fitted with telescopic sights. He sauntered up towards them, not displaying any degree of urgency. Harry could see that Lars' expression was set, but neither of the Danes said anything. When Olaf reached them, he unceremoniously dumped the rifles at Lars' feet. He looked contemptuously at Harry, still half-squatting on the ground. Then he said in a loud tones, clearly partly meant for Harry's ears, although he could not understand the words:

'*Jeg vil ikke have mit hoved skudt af for syvhundrede og halvtreds kroner om måneden*!'

He said nothing further, nor did he wait for Lars' reply. Instead, he turned and stamped away, fists clenched by his side.

'What was it he said?' said Harry.

'He said, "I'm not going to get my head blown off for seven-hundred-and-fifty kroner a month". And who can blame him, if you think of it like that?'

Harry didn't see it as charitably, but thought it wisest not to say so. 'What are you going to do now, Lars?' he asked.

'I have to go after Nanoq. If I don't he'll be sure to be back with his own hunting-rifle. There's no telling what he'll do then. And you'd be first on his list.'

'His own gun? You mean you haven't already got his weapon safely under lock and key?' asked Harry incredulously.

'Ikateq was going to pick up the rifle yesterday. Nanoq keeps it with his boat about four or five kilometres west along the coast. But the storm made us change our plans. Ikateq was going back for it today.'

'And instead Nanoq is going to get it. It's going to be dangerous for you to go after him when he gets his gun.'

'You might say that.'

Lars regarded Harry silently. His expression was almost one of anger.

'Well, what else can I say?'

Lars didn't answer straight away. Then he fixed Harry firmly in the eye.

'Harry, I want you to come with me. You're a better marksman than either of us – Nanoq as well as me – from what you've told me of your rifle club. Nanoq will take the short-cut over the rocks and we'll have to take the long way around with the land-rover, but if we go now we'll at least have more chance of seeing Nanoq before he sees us.'

Harry couldn't believe what he was hearing. He had indeed boasted to Lars about his expert marksmanship. But it was one thing to fire at paper targets at the local rifle-range and quite another to go on an armed man-hunt. First of all Lars had asked for his help in this case. Then he'd snubbed it. Now he was asking for aid again. He was demanding it. This was surely the most dangerous phase of all. What was going on? He struggled to his feet.

'You don't know what you're asking, Lars.'

'I know exactly what I'm asking. And you know you owe this to me.'

What was Lars talking about? Yes, the Dane had saved him from serious injury, even death, by appearing on the scene when he did. But now he was asking for repayment with something more than interest.

'This is professional police work,' said Harry. We should wait until Knud Holm is here. We've done more than our bit. We both have.'

'Still pretending, Harry? said Lars. 'Very well. You pretend. Then I will have to go after Nanoq myself. If you want to be the hunted and not the hunter, it will be up to you. You'll be the first one in the sights of Nanoq's rifle if I fail to track him down or if he gets the better of me while I'm alone and returns to Vatsaaq. He surely would do this, you know.'

Saying this, Lars picked up the two telescopic rifles, fixed Harry with a look of contempt, then turned on his heel to walk towards the Land Rover.

'Wait,' Harry called as he struggled to stand. He managed to scramble up after the Dane, catching him by the elbow.

'Wait, Lars,' he repeated. 'I will come with you,'

Harry was thinking of Vonnie, still lying in their marital bed with no knowledge of what had happened. He wanted to retract his reckless promise as soon as he uttered the words, but a dark fear made him hold his tongue. What Lars had said prevented him. The image of Nanoq returning with his rifle was horrifying. Lars said he'd be the first in Nanoq's rifle sights. Would Vonnie be the second?

Lars didn't respond. Instead, he continued to stride in the direction of the vehicle. Harry limped along after him.

'What was Nanoq shouting? I know that *"Naaga"* means "no". But what was the other thing he was saying, *"Kusanartoq Essie* something"? I'm sure it was the same thing he said when we arrested him on Sunday. Something about Essie.'

Lars stopped and looked hard at him for a moment. Then he replied:

'I don't know what he was so angry about if you say you don't, Harry. I've told you before: Nanoq speaks nonsense most of the time.'

'How the Devil should I know?' shouted Harry, becoming exasperated at Lars' obtuseness. 'Come on – tell me. You know I don't speak Greenlandic. You must have understood what Nanoq was trying to say.'

Lars made no reply. He continued to march purposefully towards the Land Rover. Harry fell into stride with him, puzzled as to what was going on. Just before they reached the vehicle, Lars stopped and looked steadily at Harry.

'Do you really want to come with me?'

'Yes. I've said as much.'

'Then stop this sham. Here; take the gun.'

Lars thrust one of the heavy telescopic rifles into his arms. Then he went around to open the driver's door of the Land Rover. Harry was perplexed. What sham? What pretence? But, when Lars opened the door on the passenger side for him, he climbed stiffly into the seat, saying nothing.

7.2

The journey for its first part was the same as the one they'd made yesterday in the tourist bus but it was very different in mood. Lars gave no sign of wanting to talk. Instead he sat, grim-faced, behind the wheel. Harry obliged him. Instead of trying to say or ask something to fill the silence, as he once would have, he contented himself with examining the heavy gun he'd been given and was now nursing on his knees.

From its distinctive angular shape he recognised it was a Norwegian Vapensmia NM149s. It had clearly not seen much use. Only within the last few years had this powerful telescopic rifle been adopted by the Norwegian Army. Harry had read a few articles about it in his magazines at home but had never before seen, let alone held, one.

The gun must have been especially imported. It surely couldn't be standard police issue, particularly in a tiny outpost like this. He was fairly sure he'd read that it was in service with the Nowegian rather than Danish Police. Harry was surprised at the number of rifles Lars seemed to have at his disposal, though dared not venture a question in his companions's grim mood.

At around twelve pounds, the Vapensmia was a weighty object. No one could have called it graceful or elegant, but its hard lines and beech-laminated stock gave Harry real aesthetic pleasure. It was a true killing machine. He tried to push aside any thought of how this gun had found its way into his hands. A more practical consideration came to him. He wanted to ask Lars how the telescopic sights had been adjusted, though was still reluctant to break the silence in the cab of the Land Rover. The young Dane's mouth was set in a firm, uncompromising line.

What was wrong with Lars? Harry, nothing more than a tourist in this country, now found himself on a dangerous man-hunt. Lars was almost acting – he *was* acting – as if Harry had a *duty* to accompany him. True, the Dane had appeared in time to save him from Lord knows what fate at the hands of the enraged Nanoq. It was also true enough he'd told Lars, with some justification, about his expert markmanship. But surely there was a limit to what he should be asked to do?

His instinct was to make Lars stop the Land Rover, get out and walk back to Vonnie. Only Lars' stark warning about Nanoq's armed return restrained him. There was also the reminder of the ache across his shoulders, the result of the Inuit's attack. Even so, he kept asking himself what he was doing on this dangerous police mission.

Lars was driving far more recklessly than Ikateq had done yesterday. As the coast came into sight, Lars turned west instead of east and the track immediately became bumpier. They trampolined along the ragged and increasingly obscure way for what Harry guessed to be not much more than a mile.

Instead of going further around to reach the coast, they drove straight toward some ugly, jagged rocks. As they reached them, Lars slowed the vehicle. He switched off the engine and noisily applied the hand-brake. Silently, he leaned back to pick up his own rifle, from the rear seat. This was a Vapensmia NM149s identical to Harry's own. Absently, he smoothed his palm along the barrel. There was distaste in the way he looked at the weapon.

At last he knitted his brows and spoke for the first time since they'd left Vatsaaq.

'This is it. We can drive no further. The rest of the way must be on foot. I thought Nanoq would have left us behind by now. We'll have to go after him.'

They stepped out of vehicle into the stillness around them.

Lars' remark had been superfluous. It was clear they couldn't have driven any further. Indeed, as Harry looked up at the overhanging rocks, they seemed to present an impassable barrier to them on foot. He tried to inject some levity into the dark mood of the moment.

'I suppose we'll be able to stop for lunch half-way across?'

'This is not one of your picnics,' said Lars, taking him literally. 'Anyway, I've brought no food. I fear we will be regretting my oversight before this day is done.' Harry was made keenly aware of the fact that he'd had nothing to eat since yesterday, beyond Vonnie's night-time sandwich. 'Thank goodness I always keep a flask of water in this knapsack,' added Lars

Seeing Harry's worried look at the pillars of stone before them, Lars spoke again.

'There is a way through ahead. It is not as difficult as it looks. You will have to do a little scrambling, maybe. No more.'

Saying this, and without waiting or explaining further, Lars made for a narrow gap between two of the rocks, a tiny opening Harry hadn't before noticed. Lars squeezed himself through without much difficulty. Harry followed. Although he was far taller and broader than Lars, he managed to struggle through. He found himself entering an enclosed passage, almost a tunnel. When his eyes became accustomed to the semi-darkness, he was surprised to see Lars halfway up a step-like formation at the far end of the passageway, following shafts of light shining down from above.

'Wait for me!'

Lars looked back but said nothing. He didn't stop, merely slowed his pace to allow Harry to catch up. They'd emerged into full daylight again before he was able to reach the Dane. He was sweating profusely in spite of the cold. His breath was forming clouds of steam before his eyes. It gave visible proof of how much colder it was this morning.

'That was the easy bit,' said Lars. 'You wait until you see what lies ahead of us. But from now on, may I ask you please do not shout so much. We do not want to give Nanoq warning of our approach.'

This annoyed Harry. He'd hardly said anything. He'd been too much out of breath. But at least Lars' frostiness seemed to be thawing.

'Can we rest a bit? That climb was hard work.'

'If you wish. Not for too long. We still have some distance to go and every minute we waste will give an advantage to Nanoq.'

'Is Nanoq likely to be far ahead?' asked Harry, anxiously. The memory of the Inuit towering above him was still strong.

'We won't see him for another kilometre or two, I should think'. Lars was clearly doing some mental arithmetic. 'That is, if he is where I think we will find him. He'll have headed straight for his boat, if I know The Bear. We call the place he keeps it, "*Najugaq Nanoq*" – "Nanoq's place". No-one else goes there. Nanoq doesn't like people near when he's hunting.'

Harry was pleased to see Lars had begun to relax. It felt at last as if they were working together.

'But we're going to this Nanoq's place, aren't we?' he said.

'Of course. The idea will be for us to see him before he sees us. This is why I don't want you to announce our arrival. Besides, I might be wrong in my supposition. If he has really hurried, he may already have reached *Najugaq Nanoq*. Even now he could be heading back our way with his rifle. I do not think this will be so, but we should be prepared. He will not have gone so fast, not if I know the ways of Nanoq. He is truly like a hunting bear that one, moving steadily over the land. And we are in his territory now. This is not my København or your Reading.'

Harry nervously looked ahead along the smooth path of rock stretching before them, and decided they should be safe here for a while at least. Now that Lars was finally holding something like a proper conversation with him, he was feeling slightly more comfortable. He cast about for ways to prolong their discussion. Although he'd regained his breath, he was in no hurry to press on into danger. He felt an odd gratitude for the chance to speak to Lars again in almost the way he had before Sunday morning. Before? This had only been a few days ago. Absently, he ran his thumb and forefinger along the smooth barrel of the rifle.

'How is it there are so many guns you can put your hands on? You have these two Norwegian telescopic weapons and six of the smaller-bore rifles. It seems a real arsenal for a small police outpost like this.'

'You can put it down to some classic bumbling in Nuuk,' said Lars, smiling grimly. 'We are supposed to have only two BSA Martinis in Vatsaaq. When I was posted here I telephoned them to ask for a better supply of ammunition. They sent me the ammunition *and* two more rifles. When I phoned again to tell them of their error they sent me two more. So then I gave up and kept quiet about it.'

'And the Valpensmias? They can't be standard police issue, surely?'

'They are mine. I ordered them from Norway. And, before you ask, no, I don't like rifles. I bought them because of Olaf; he's the fan of guns here. Like you are Harry.'

A shadow passed across Lars' face as he mentioned Olaf's name. Harry thought he should change the subject.

'What's all this about "Nanoq's Place"? I thought Nanoq had a cabin in Vatsaaq?'

'So he does, but in the summer – that's for only a couple of months, as you know – he spends most of his time in *Najugaq Nanoq*. Even in the dark winter months he comes out here quite often.'

'Nanoq knows the country well, then?'

'Yes. He knows it far better than anyone else. This is what makes our hunt today so dangerous. But you know what we are up against already. Now, I think it is time for us to move on.' Lars smiled as he said this, but the smile was quickly replaced by a troubled look.

The stone pathway opened up once more as they ascended, though more gradually this time. They were soon at least two or three hundred feet above sea-level. Harry could see this through the increasing frequency of openings in the rocks. There were numbers of skuas, guillemots and gyrfalcons; far more than Harry had seen at the nearby Kumilgaq Cliffs. Once, he even thought he glimpsed some sort of eagle through the mists. Lars took no notice of their surroundings and kept up a brisk pace.

'Lars, can I speak?' whispered Harry. 'If I do it quietly?'

'If you do it quietly *and* quickly. We are getting nearer to *Najugaq Nanoq*. Anyway, it sounds as if you're going to talk, whatever I say.'

'It's only that it occurred to me – why isn't this walk included in our tour itinerary? The view is really wonderful. The only steep ascent is at the start of the track and I'm sure his could be avoided. Here, the walking underfoot is so smooth that the path might have been man-made. Today, the mist is hiding the surface of the sea but on a morning like yesterday, it would have been shimmering and sparkling below us. It would be beautiful.'

'You are a poet, Harry. But the man from Icesperience who came last year to inspect the places we'd planned for the tour was no poet. He was only worried about his tourists stepping off this path into thin air and the sea below. Insurance and lawyers were on his mind, I am sorry to say. Did he wish us to install a safety-rail? His real worry lies around the bend ahead of us. I told you that the worst was yet to come, didn't I? Well, there's a narrow rock bridge. I wouldn't cross it myself if stout ropes hadn't been strung across to give us a hand-hold.'

The pathway became more uneven in its approach to the the bend. But when he rounded it, Harry gasped. The steep walls on either side suddenly plummeted away. The only way to progress was across the rock bridge Lars had mentioned. After this, the path widened again and the walls once more returned to provide some sort of sanity, but the crossing was frighteningly narrow and crumbling in the middle.

'I can't go over this! Where are the ropes you were talking about?"

'The ropes...,' said Lars. 'They've gone!'

As they edged closer, what had happened became clear. Someone had cut the ropes from the other side. They now dangled vertiginously down the sides of the chasm. Harry felt nauseous simply peering over the side.

'Nanoq!' he said.

'It must be Nanoq's work,' said Lars. 'Of this much we can be sure. But what was his thinking? I suppose he cut the hand ropes as a quick way of disabling the bridge. It would have taken him too long to bring the rock down. Yes, that must be the way he saw it.'

'Whatever he was thinking, I can't cross this without a rope to hold onto.'

Lars said nothing, but continued to look thoughtful.

'Well? What do we do now?' said Harry, when Lars maintained his silence.

'A mile back along our path there is another way down, said Lars, finally. 'From there, we could take a long arc around to Nanoq's place. But it seems to me that Nanoq will have planned for us to do exactly this. He'll be expecting us to retrace our steps and go the long way around. It is a much less direct route. It will be dangerous underfoot all the way down.'

Harry sensed that Lars was going to add something else. He was right.

'Should we try to cross here anyway? I have a short length of cord in my rucksack. Here'. Lars showed him a thin piece of string. 'It may help us, though it can't be a substitute for the long ropes Nanoq has cut.'

Harry could hardly believe what Lars was saying. How could this flimsy thing help? Did he think it would give him confidence in some mysterious way? The sight of it was having the opposite effect.

'The other thing we could do is go around the longer way and risk whatever Nanoq has planned for us. He'll surely have decided to lay a trap. Well, what do you want to do Harry? We have a straight choice.'

Harry really wanted to say he thought they should turn back and return to the settlement without trying to reach *Najugaq Nanoq*. This narrow bridge of rock spanning a drop of three hundred or so feet was truly frightening, But the 'other way' sounded equally alarming. Now Lars' warnings about Nanoq's intentions once he'd reclaimed his gun made him hold his tongue. He didn't know how to reply.

'Shouldn't we turn back instead of doing either thing?' he muttered, despairingly.

'If you want to turn back, you can turn back. But go quickly. Nanoq will also head back after he has dealt with me. He will not be far behind you.'

7.3

This was anything but a good idea. Harry could understand Lars had no real choice but...

It wouldn't have been sensible for them to descend the dangerous slope in the way Nanoq had so obviously planned. Even now, he'd probably be calmly aiming his rifle at his chosen spot, preparing to take leisured pot-shots at them as they scrambled downwards. Harry had visions of the scene. From what Lars had told him, they'd have needed their hands as well as their legs to cling on. They wouldn't be able to return fire, even if they were able to make out the Inuit's hiding-place.

The fifteen-foot length of string – it could hardly even be dignified with the name of cord – binding them to each other by means of a loop knotted around their waists was the worst thing. Lars clearly entertained some vague notion that this would give Harry more confidence. It was laughable to think it would, but he didn't feel like laughing. Harry wished Lars hadn't found it coiled at the bottom of his small knapsack. It would almost certainly break if put to the test of their weights. If it didn't, it would mean both of of them plunging to their deaths. He'd said nothing. The Dane was trying to give him confidence. Now they were about to use the string in earnest, it was having the exactly opposite effect.

'Are you ready Harry?'

'Will I ever be? Are you sure you want us to do this, Lars?'

'Look, we've been through this a hundred times. If we try to go down the slope back there, Nanoq will be sure to be waiting to pick us off with his rifle. If we turn back to the settlement to get a better length of rope, Nanoq will certainly come after us. I wouldn't like him behind us with a gun, bad shot as he is. He'd easily outpace us.'

This all sounded logical enough, until Harry looked again at the narrowness of the bridge formation they'd be crossing – more likely falling from – in a few minutes. At its narrowest point halfway across it was barely three feet wide. Lars, too, didn't look nearly as bold as he was trying to sound.

'What if we simply wait here for him?' asked Harry.

'I had thought of that,' said Lars. 'It seemed a reasonable alternative to me at first, but you mustn't forget there is more than one way up the slope. If we don't appear, Nanoq can climb up and reach the path where we've already walked. Then he'd be able to get back to Vatsaaq without us knowing. I wouldn't want to be responsible for letting a wild man loose on the settlement. Neither would you, Harry. Madam Vonnie is there.

'Look, we can't kneel here all day debating the point, my friend. Up to now Nanoq won't have had time to do much more than collect his rifle. Every minute that we waste will give him more alternatives. Are you ready to cross?'

'I'm ready,' said Harry, with a resolve he did not feel.

A guillemot, hotly pursued by a gyrfalcon, dived past. The pair of birds flew close to Harry. He felt horribly exposed in this awkwardly crouched position. The birds reminded him of the respective roles of Nanoq and themselves. Lars and he were supposed to be the hunters and Nanoq the hunted. It didn't feel like that now.

Lars crawled forwards, slowly but steadily. They'd agreed he should lead the way, a few feet at a time, with Harry crossing in stages after him. He prayed Lars wouldn't lose his grip. The only emergency plan they'd agreed – "brace yourself" – sounded ludicrous.

All too soon the slack of the thin cord was taken up. This was the signal for Harry to edge himself forward to allow Lars to shuffle onward a few more feet. When he didn't move straight away, Lars nodded back at him anxiously. Harry crept forward gingerly, trying not to look at the dizzying drop to each side of him. They'd agreed it would be wiser if only one of them tried to move at any time. Lars remained perfectly still. Already the rock formation was becoming narrower. Harry became even more aware of the alarming drop below.

Their forward shuffling movements seemed to take an age. Harry's mouth was dry. His arms felt weak and shaky. His knees were sore with crawling over the rough rock. He could hear the sounds of his own strained breathing and the wild hammering of his heart. Trying to calm his nerves, he grunted at Lars. Once more it was time for the Dane to edge forward. They were coming to the narrowest part of the crossing.

Lars made a choking sound in reply, then slid his left knee forwards by no more than a few inches, then did the same thing with his right. He was moving more slowly than previously. Even from several feet behind, Harry could tell that the Dane's breathing was becoming irregular and laboured.

Shortly before Lars reached the halfway point, where the jutting rock would have made their crossing relatively comfortable if they'd had a proper length of rope to loop around it, he stopped altogether. The young man was trembling uncontrollably.

'What's wrong?' Harry managed to gasp. The words were superfluous; he could see exactly what was wrong. His companion's nerve had deserted him.

Lars didn't answer. He turned his head and moved his lips silently. Harry was reminded of a fish in a tank. He knew that somehow he'd have to keep talking to Lars, despite the dryness of his own throat.

'Now, relax. I'll catch up with you soon. Try to take deep breaths. Move slowly when you move.' Lars wasn't moving at all and gave no sign that he ever would.

He gave not the slightest sign of having heard Harry. He was visibly shaking. The wind, which had momentarily dropped to almost a light breeze, blew more sharply with an eerie warning whistle.

'Stay still for a moment if it's easier.' Lars held his rigid crouch, still shaking.

Harry edged forward. Soon he was close enough to touch Lars, but didn't dare do so. He was himself afraid to lift his arm. Instead, he tried to soothe him with words.

'It's all right, my friend. We'll do this. We'll do it together.'

'I – I can't move Harry.'

'No need to move yet. Keep still.' Harry was saying the opposite of what he was thinking. The wind was gaining in strength all the time. He was finding it difficult to ignore or to cope with its icy blast. The whistling was fast rising to an animal-like howl.

At last, Lars' left foot trembled. He did manage to edge it forward by no more than a fraction of an inch. After what seemed like another five minutes, he slid his right foot forward an equal tiny distance. Soon he was moving more regularly again. The string between them tightened once more. He nodded back to Harry, even managing something like a foolish grin.

Now it was Harry's turn to move once more. Although he still felt the need to move forward ultra-cautiously, he found his progress to be fractionally easier this time, even though he was now crossing the narrowest part of the rock. Maybe, he thought, this was because they were at last working together on their task. Perhaps, too, it had helped when Lars had allowed frailty in himself to show for the first time.

There was little sign of weakness when Lars made his final motion across. Harry, too, was given confidence by the fact that the ledge was now widening, although he still felt the need to move gingerly.

After what seemed like an eternity, they'd both made it. He gratefully felt the solid ground beneath him. Both of them rose slowly from their awkward crouching position. Harry gripped Lars' hand spontaneously.

'We've done it together!' he almost shouted.

'Yes. Now our troubles will really begin,' Lars murmured. Harry's elation evaporated at his companion's tones. 'We took too long with our crossing. Nanoq will have realised we didn't go down the slope after all. He may be on his way here already. We have no time to lose.'

'How long did the crossing take?' asked Harry, glancing at his watch, pointlessly. He realised he had not the slightest idea whether their ordeal had been accomplished in ten minutes or two hours.

'A lifetime.'

*

The path became less of a natural walkway on the other side. Sometimes the way ahead was far less clear. The going underfoot was harder through the irregular large patches of scree. Harry was all the more aware of this because the efforts they'd so far made had caused the searing pain in his shoulders to return. It was spreading to his buttocks. Fortunately, they were now steadily but unmistakably descending.

After a half kilometre their route became comparatively featureless. Harry felt he could have been out mountain walking in some isolated spot in Wales or Scotland. Lars, subdued by the fact that his nerve had betrayed him, showed no inclination to talk, even in whispers. Harry maintained his own silence.

The only variation to Lars' steady walking pace came when he frequently halted their progress with a signal from his hand. At these brief breaks in their journey he remained quite still, watching and listening. Whenever he could, he would scour the track ahead with his binoculars.

Halts were longer when they approached a bend, or some other spot where Nanoq might have decided to conceal himself. There were many of these, and Harry was uncomfortably aware the Inuit could pick and choose where to lie in wait with his gun.

Lars held up his hand again. This time he spoke.

'Harry, ahead of us is real peril. We've had to be cautious up to now, but it does seem to me that Nanoq must have gone back to *Najugaq Nanoq*. By this time, we'd have run into him for sure if he'd decided to return to look for us. Soon, we'll certainly be within his sight and the range of his rifle. The rocks ahead are brilliantly white and we'll be neatly silhouetted. I'm going to go forward to see what there is to see.'

Lars knew the lie of the land much better than he ever could. Harry didn't waste time by suggesting he should be the one to volunteer. Again he asked himself what he was doing here. Was it because Lars trusted his marksmanship and wanted him to come along? No – there had to be more to it. Lars had almost seemed to *expect* him to be here. Why? He had no answer.

It wasn't long before Lars was back.

'Come, he said, beckoning. 'I want you to see this. Make sure you crouch down as you come, although I think you should be safe enough.'

Almost on all fours again, Harry scrambled over to the spot where Lars stood. It hurt his back and legs to move so awkwardly. All the time he could imagine Nanoq's bullets zinging into the white rock behind him.

'Look through these in that direction,' said Lars, handing over his binoculars. 'There – follow my arm. What do you see?'.

Harry held the eyepieces to his eyes. They were moist from Lars' use. He wondered why he was doing it.

'I see nothing much. Wait – let me adjust the focus. What am I supposed to be looking for?'

'Do you see that archway of rock? That is *Najugaq Nanoq*. Do you see what is beneath it?'

'Let me fiddle with this – ah, I see it now. It's a boat, isn't it?'

'Look inside the boat, at its rear end. What do you see?'

'Is this a sight test?' said Harry. 'There's something dark green in there. I can't make out what it is.'

'Neither can I, properly. We can have a better look when we get lower down. But I'm almost sure we can see Nanoq's rifle-case in the boat. I'd say it looks as if the rifle is still inside. It can only mean that, for whatever reason, Nanoq isn't here.'

7.4

Surely this couldn't be wise? Why did Lars want to delay doing the obvious thing. Why didn't he head straight back to Vatsaaq?

When they reached an easier part of the descent, Harry tried again to voice his concerns.

'We shouldn't be wasting time on this,' he said. 'It would have been far more sensible if we'd headed straight back to the settlement as soon as we realised Nanoq wasn't here.'

'I know what we must do.' This was Lars' only response.

'But he could be anywhere along the trail by now. My fear is that he'll have tricked us and doubled back to the settlement. They're all unprotected in Vatsaaq. He's a dangerous man, even without his gun. I've seen that for myself.'

Despite what he was saying about them *all* being unprotected in Vatsaaq, the thought of Vonnie as he'd last seen her was on his mind. He pictured her still lying contentedly in their bed, blissfully unaware of any danger.

'You are not thinking, Harry. We certainly want to get to Nanoq's gun before he does so himself. This has to be our number one priority. Besides, Olaf should be still in Vatsaaq. He'll look after things there.'

'*Yes, in the way he should be looking after them here*,' Harry wanted to say, but thought better of it. He doubted that Olaf would have remained in Vatsaaq. Instead he said, 'Aren't you going to take another look through those before we go further down?'

'If it will make you happy,' said Lars. 'But I'm sure of what I saw when I looked before.' He briefly raised the binoculars to his eyes. 'Yes; his gun is there in the rifle case safely enough. Come on.'

'Wait a minute. Let me take a look. If I'm going down there with you I should at least see what I'm going for.'

Harry took the binoculars Lars impatiently proffered to him and scanned the boat. The rifle-case was undeniably there. It certainly seemed to contain a rifle, to judge by the way it was propped up stiffly against the keel of the boat. He spent more time than necessary surveying the scene.

'Come on Harry, please. We don't have a moment to waste. The sooner Nanoq's rifle is safe in my hands, the happier I'll be.'

'OK. We'll go all the way down. But I don't understand why Nanoq should have left his rifle in the boat.'

'Neither do I,' said Lars. 'But one thing at a time, eh?'

*

Lars and Harry approached the strange formation called *Najugaq Nanoq*. The outcrop provided good cover and they made full use of it in their descent. But Harry couldn't help wishing he knew exactly from what they were taking cover, or even from which direction danger might threaten. *Najugaq Nanoq* was a natural shelter. Harry guessed it would have kept the boat – and the rifle – mainly dry, even from the wild storms they'd seen yesterday.

When they were fewer than ten yards from the boat, Lars halted and crouched lower behind the final jag of rock that might give them protection from the unexpected . He stared at *Najugaq Nanoq* doubtfully.

'You know Harry, I still can't understand why Nanoq hasn't been back here for his rifle. Where is he? It worries me.'

'It's what I've been saying all along. Well, there's the rifle, sitting up nicely at the back of his boat. Aren't you going to fetch the thing after bringing us all the way down?'

In answer Lars grimaced, rose to his feet and, in contrast to his earlier extreme caution, ambled over to the boat as if he were going to pick up a plant in a garden centre. He grinned back at Harry, then reached for the gun-case. As he picked it up, his expression changed immediately. Something was wrong...

As if in slow-motion, Harry watched two zinging impacts on the ground in front of the boat's prow and saw a plume of fine dust spiraling upwards. Lars simply stood there, immobile. Someone was firing at him from some way off...

'Down Lars! Get down!'

Harry flung himself forward and rugby-tackled Lars. They both came down heavily behind the boat. Lars came to his senses.

'Quick Harry! Behind that rock!'

The two men scrambled the short distance and crouched down. Three more shots cracked behind them as they ran. They looked at each other, Lars still holding the gun-case he'd picked up from the boat. He unzipped it. A few stones and two iron bars fell out.

'Nanoq has tricked us,' he said. 'We shouldn't – I shouldn't – have underestimated him. Thank Heavens he's not a better shot. He fooled us well. All he did was stuff stones and bars into the gun-case. His idea was to make us think he hadn't yet collected his rifle. All the time he was somewhere up there taking aim at the boat.'

'Where is he? Did you see where the shots came from?'

Lars poked the gun-case above their shelter, expecting a rifle shot to ring out and betray Nanoq's position. There wasn't one. Their surroundings were deathly quiet.

'He's near enough to see that was the rifle-case and not us. Damn!'

'And we've left our own rifles over there,' said Harry. 'We can't even shoot back. What do we do now?'

'Nanoq will soon be sure we don't have our own guns. Then he'll come down from wherever he is. Even he won't miss from point blank range. I have to get to those rifles of ours. It's our only chance.'

'Wait, Lars. He might pick you off if you stick your head up now. We'll wait five minutes and then we'll make a run together. If the two of us go for it at the same time it might confuse him.'

'He might kill only one of us then, eh? I think he might shoot both of us, knowing our luck today.'

Lars clenched his teeth.

'Do you have any better ideas?'

Lars' scowl told Harry he hadn't. The next few minutes passed in silence and very slowly. The image of Olaf only hours before kept coming back to him. What was it Lars said his angry words meant? *"I'm not going to get my head blown off for seven-hundred-and-fifty kroner a month"*? Well, that was fine then. Harry was doing it free of charge.

'We can't wait any longer, Harry. Nanoq will be edging his way down here before we know it. He's probably on his way already.'

'OK then, Lars. You count to ten. We'll both make a run for it at exactly the same time. I'll head for the right hand side of our guns and you go for the left. The last thing we want to do is collide with each other like a pair of ninnies. We'll be a pair of dead ninnies if we do.'

'1 - 2 - 3 - 4 -5,' the Dane counted.

This was crazy. He was going to get killed. He was supposed to be on holiday.

'6 - 7 - 8 - 9 - NOW!'

They scrambled toward the rock, Harry a fraction behind Lars because he'd expected the Dane to actually count the '10'. Three more shots rang out in quick succession as they tumbled back with their weapons. What do they say? If you hear the shots they haven't hit you? Both men fell behind the rock, panting with relief. Nanoq must indeed be a poor shot, or else his eyesight was failing badly.

'I'll fire in his direction. This will let him know we've got our own guns and won't present sitting targets for him.'

Lars did this, although he could be no more than roughly aware of the direction in which to shoot. The Vapensmia barked ominously. It made an echoing report, almost like a small cannon. The sound was magnified by the enclosure of the surrounding rocks.

'What happens now? We're hardly better off than we were a moment ago, except we can fire back if he comes nearer. It's stalemate.'

'I don't think it is Harry. Nanoq is sure to find a better place to advance. He's on the hunt now. Look, there he goes!'

Harry caught a quick sight of Nanoq's light-coloured coat disappearing between two prominent rocks. The glimpse was much too fleeting for him to even think of levelling his own rifle.

'What's he doing?' he said.

'Working his way down to us,' Lars said. 'He won't come directly. That's not what the hunter does. You see the track over to our left? That's the route he'll take, I should think. It'll give him shelter. When he gets further down he'll be able to take a clear shot without us being properly able to fire back. Quick Harry!'

Once again Harry found himself in the open, this time being half-dragged by his smaller companion. This time, he felt even more exposed to Nanoq's shots, but none came. Nanoq must be on the move himself. They reached a small depression and flung themselves into it, Lars helping him on his way.

'What was all that about?' Harry demanded angrily from from his now-prone position. 'If I'm going to get my head blown off for no kroner at all, you might at least tell me what we're trying to do.'

'Sorry. That was our one chance, while Nanoq was concentrating on moving to our left. I didn't have time to explain.'

'Then explain now!'

'You see that tall column? From there it will be possible for us to climb, while keeping out of Nanoq's sight. We can get above him. It has to be our best chance. It's probably our only chance.'

'Climb? You must be joking. After all we've done? I can hardly walk.'

'You have to climb. That's all there is to it. If you don't you may as well walk into the open with a "shoot me now, please" sign around your neck. In ten minutes' time, if we remain here, Nanoq will be able to pick us off at his leisure, bad shot as he is. Come on, Harry. The way up's not so hard.'

The climb, or scramble, would have been more than difficult enough in normal circumstances. Harry was now troubled by his aching limbs. Several times the lighter Lars had to exert all of his own wiry strength to give him a hand up. At last they reached a relatively smooth surface. From this high vantage point they could look down dizzily.

Harry would have collapsed in a heap if he could. But there wasn't room on the small platform.

'The rock-edge will provide us with enough cover if we do not move to present Nanoq with a target. We can stay here.

'And then what?' asked Harry. 'I'm all in.'

Lars looked at him, clearly making a judgement as to how far he could rely on Harry's remaining strength.

'We wait,' said Lars. 'We aim our rifles very carefully in the direction we've come from, and we wait. Let's hope I was right about Nanoq's plans. If not, then I don't know what's going to happen.'

*

Harry was achingly aware of the sharp pain that had begun in his calves and buttocks and had now made a home for itself in the small of his back

'I feel sick,' he said.

Lars had responded to these few words with an angry glare and a finger to his lips. Harry was so tired that his head was nodding forward. The ledge on which they could at best half-stand was fragile and crumbling. It already seemed as if they'd been waiting in this cramped position for hours.

Lars nudged him violently in the ribs. Nanoq was coming. He hadn't seen them. Harry offered up a silent prayer of thanks.

The Greenlander was creeping forwards, arched toward the ground as if he were hunting a weaker animal. Only now he wasn't aware his intended objects of prey were thirty feet above him, looking down at him with guns in their hands. Harry watched, fascinated, as the Inuit silently approached the place where they'd been concealed a short time before. If they'd remained there, his advance would have been invisible to them. It was a cruel irony: Nanoq thought he was out of their sight and all the time he was only too visible to them. Soon, he would discover that once more their roles had been reversed. The hunted had again become the hunters.

'Take aim Harry. Aim your rifle,' Lars whispered urgently.

Harry dutifully looked through his telescopic sight as he lined up the barrel at the unsuspecting Nanoq. He was expecting Lars to do the same; in fact he was thinking his own shot, even if it were required, would be no more than a back-up to the one from Lars' gun. But he shouldn't have to think of pulling his own trigger: Nanoq would make an easy target for Lars at this range.

'Why aren't you aiming your rifle, Lars?'

'I can't. Don't ask me. Anyway, I'm a poor shot.'

Harry was amazed by this answer. He turned to his companion.

'Aim, Lars. This has to be down to you.'

'You owe me this one at least Harry. It should be your bullet that kills The Bear. Do you want Nanoq to go back to Vatsaaq with his gun? Do you want him to go looking for Madam Vonnie?'

'This is insane,' shouted Harry. 'You're supposed to be the policeman. Shoot! For Heaven's sake shoot, man!'

Their shouting caused Nanoq to look up in surprise. He quickly started to raise and aim his own rifle. Harry reacted instinctively. Nanoq was unmissable at this short range, as would have been he and Lars, even to Nanoq. He closed his finger around the trigger, firing a single shot a second before Nanoq was about to let fly.

Framed in the telescopic sight, the Inuit's look of surprise as a neat red hole appeared in his forehead would be an image to haunt Harry for the rest of his life. As if in slow-motion, Nanoq's eyebrows shot up momentarily, in a grim echo of those of the young Inuit boy in Vatsaaq. His expression held the same question, '*why are you here*?' Now Harry felt even less capable of answering.

Nanoq, The Bear, slumped forward heavily. Harry could see the gaping red wound his bullet had made on its exit. When his heavy body fell face downward, he felt he could count the fragments of shattered bone at the back of the Inuit's skull. The Vapensmia was a powerful weapon.

He forced himself to keep looking, despite his feeling of horror at what he'd done.

Still Lars had not raised his own weapon.

'What's happening?' Harry demanded. 'You left me with no choice but to shoot. You made me do it. It was him or us. For all I know, I might have shot an innocent man.'

'You did shoot an innocent man.'

'What are you talking about,? Tell me, Lars: if Nanoq didn't kill Essie then who did?

'You did, Harry. You did.'

7.5

'What do mean, Lars?' Harry persisted. 'Are you mad? Is this your idea of a joke? Answer me – what are you saying?'

Lars ignored him, maintaining a silence until they reached Nanoq's inert form.

'He's dead all right,' he said. 'We'll put the body under the boat to give it some shelter. I'll have it picked up later'

Fortunately, the craft proved to be light enough for the two of them to manhandle it into position. Harry was grateful not to have to touch the corpse. He started to repeat the questions he'd put to Lars during their descent. Still the Dane wouldn't answer, putting a finger to his lips and frowning each time Harry spoke. Harry took this to mean they should concentrate on the business in hand.

When they'd finished their gruesome task of covering Nanoq's lifeless form, Lars still refused to answer any of the questions Harry threw at him. Instead, he turned, as if he intended to lead the way back to Vatsaaq in silence. It was too much for Harry.

'Why won't you talk to me, you bloody man?' Saying this, he spun Lars around by the shoulder, almost causing him to lose balance.

'You still want to carry on with your game of make-believe, do you Harry? Even now you persist in continuing this act of yours? Why? We are the only ones out here, the only ones beside a few Greenlanders who know the truth. They won't talk. Well, I'm not going to pretend with you any longer. Your secret died with Nanoq. You needn't worry: I shan't say anything to Knud Holm or to anyone else. If I were going to tell the story of what happened last

Saturday night, don't you think I'd have done it before now?'

What Lars was saying baffled Harry, although his words were chilling. *What if...?* The Dane angrily turned on his heel, making as if to ascend the slope. After he'd gone a dozen paces, Harry ran after him and again grabbed him, this time by both shoulders. He twisted him around sharply. Their faces were inches apart.

'Look, I honestly do not know what you're talking about.' Harry spat out the words.

'I can't see why I should do this.' Lars shrugged off Harry's hands and sighed deeply. 'Haven't I done enough for you already? Now you still want me to cater for your charades. The time for pretence between us, if there ever should have been such a time, is over.'

'Indulge me,' said Harry, not knowing why he was saying it. 'I promise not to ask you anything else. Tell me once what on Earth you're talking about and then we'll head back to Vatsaaq without another word passing my lips. How can you say I was the one who killed Essie? All along you were saying to me as well as to everyone else Nanoq was the killer. What's going on?'

'You should know, This was part of your strange game and I was going along with it. For you, Harry. For you. Nanoq was the one who told me you killed Essie. He even accused you in front of me.'

'What do you mean? I don't know what the Devil you're trying to say. I really don't.'

Lars looked hard at him, giving every appearance of being as confused as Harry was feeling.

'Very well. I will say it. Do you remember him shouting *"Kusanartoq Essie toquvoq! Tuluk ajorpoq!"*

when he attacked you back in Vatsaaq? Nanoq gets his words mixed up sometimes but, when I thought about it, his meaning was clear enough.'

'And exactly what does that mean? You know I can't speak Greenlandic.'

'It means something like *"Essie the beautiful one! Wicked Englishman!"* He said much the same thing when we brought him in. Do you remember that?'

'Yes.'

Harry did remember Nanoq's outbursts but couldn't begin to understand what Lars was trying to say now.

'I thought it strange when we first arrested him,' said Lars. 'But later, when I questioned him privately, I got the whole story out of him, bit by bit. It was then I made him promise not to tell anyone else what he'd said to me. But it seems he told Silumi everything through the storehouse door. This was why Silumi broke the door open to let Nanoq escape.'

'What story? I had too much to drink on Saturday night, I know I did. I had a crazy, drunken conversation with Nanoq. Then I helped him back to his cabin. That's all I can remember.'

'Look, I'm going to tell you the whole thing from start to finish only once and then it'll be time for you to drop this pantomime. There'll be no need for you to stick to your elaborate fairy tale for a moment longer. You tried to fool me on that Sunday morning in Qooroqilulissat and you've been trying to do the same ever since. Do you take me for an idiot? As far as Knud Holm is concerned, Nanoq will be the one who killed Essie on Saturday night. Today, you shot him in our self-defence. The story we'll give will fit all the facts Knud Holm will be able to uncover. Are we agreed on that?'

'Agreed,' said Harry. He knew he'd have to say this to keep Lars talking. In reality, he could agree nothing. There were a thousand questions crowding in on his mind but he knew the only way he was going to get any of them answered was to be patient and let the Dane speak.

'Do you remember the things Olaf said? About Essie doing a dance – if we can call it a dance – with Nanoq on the Saturday night?'

'Yes. I was in the other room. I didn't see any of it. The first I heard about it was that evening when Olaf told us the story.' How could he forget Olaf's lurid description of Nanoq with Essie?

'If you still want to say so, Harry. But you did see some of it, didn't you?'

Harry was certain he hadn't. He was sure he'd only heard about it from the lips of Olaf. But he knew if he tried to deny it any further, Lars would say nothing more.

'Go on, Lars,' he said.

'Well, Nanoq told me you came in from somewhere and saw him dancing with Essie Smith. You looked furious, he said, although you didn't actually do or even say anything. Then you went back into the other room.

'After the dance, as Olaf and others have told us, Nanoq left with Essie. He took her back to his cabin. From what he says it seemed she wasn't exactly keen to go with him. At first he thought she was simply being coy. Then, when he managed to get her inside, she behaved even more strangely. This is what he told me. I believe him, Harry. He is like a child in so many ways. The woman was crying and trembling. Nanoq couldn't understand. It didn't fit in with the way she'd been behaving towards him in the Great Hall. Anyway, to cut Nanoq's story short, he became frightened by her outburst. He let her go and she ran off.'

'And you are ready to believe what you were told?'

'Yes I am. You did not know Nanoq. I did. Ms Smith would certainly have alarmed and confused him with tears and hysterics. He'd have let her go, exactly as he said.'

Lars looked at Harry with puzzlement, clearly wondering why he needed to tell him this story.

'Anyway, Nanoq told me that afterwards he stayed in his cabin for a short while and then made his way back towards the Great Hall. Outside, on the bench, exactly as you told me, he saw you. Do you remember telling me this? Or do you want to invent something else now?'

'He saw me on the bench,' said Harry, not trusting himself to say more.

'You and he had some sort of drunken exchange. Then you helped him back to his cabin. Again it's what you told me. Right?'

Harry raised a finger.

'But you told me Nanoq said this didn't happen.'

'I wanted to see what you'd say. My idea was to see if you'd tell me the whole truth. But you didn't. You persisted with your lies.'

'I could only tell you what I remembered,' said Harry.

Lars regarded him with scorn.

'After you left his cabin, Nanoq lay on his bed,' went on Lars, ignoring Harry's attempt at interjection. 'But then he said that no more than minutes afterward you came back into his cabin. You were shaking, so he told me. You pressed a big wad of Danish kroner and Icelandic kronur into his hands and more or less dragged him outside. We found the money in his cabin, as I told you on Sunday evening. Where would Nanoq get Icelandic notes if not from a member of your party? And don't you dare say from Gudrun.'

Lars glared at Harry, challenging him to deny what he was saying. Harry knew it would be better to say nothing. Besides, he couldn't think of anything to say in the face of the certainties the Dane was expressing. Exactly what did happen on Saturday night?

'Well, outside you showed him Ms Smith's body on the ground,' went on Lars. 'You'd killed her.'

Harry tried to interject.

'Don't interrupt or I won't say anything else. I am only telling you what you already know. You, Harry Lanier, had killed her. He then told me the next thing you did was to get him to help you strip the clothes from her corpse. Why you did this, I'll never know, unless you had some drunken theory that this action would make the body harder to identify.

'Then, you must have put the clothes in a pile on the ground, where later you came back to set fire to them. Olaf and I discovered the charred heap still there when I went back to Vatsaaq on Sunday morning, after you and I found the body. What I wasn't aware of until later was that you knew the corpse would be out there somewhere. You were simply surprised it was found in the pool so quickly, and by you and I.

Lars stopped and looked hard into Harry's eyes.

'When you'd stripped her you signed to Nanoq you wanted him to get rid of the body for you. So, for some reason known only to himself, he took her to Qooroqilulissat. This was where you and I found the corpse next morning. I'm sure you were as surprised as I was to find her locked to that block of ice. You hadn't known how and where Nanoq had disposed of the body. It must have seemed to you like an incredible piece of bad luck that we should have been the ones to find the corpse. Something about your reaction by the pool raised doubts in me. I started to wonder even then if you really knew far more than you were telling me.'

'This is all so crazy –'

'Quiet Harry. I've heard enough of your lies. Let me speak. I'm not going through all this again. Don't you think I've done enough for you?' Lars looked at him with distaste before continuing. 'When I saw you scrabbling around the glacier and coming up with those harebrained theories my suspicions grew. After we arrested Nanoq, he told me a little of what had happened. Then, piece by piece, I managed to get him to tell me the whole story.'

Lars' voice dropped in volume.

'All I wanted to do from that moment on was to keep an eye on you until Knud Holm arrived. At that time, I hadn't finally decided whether to tell him all Nanoq had said. Then, The Bear broke free and forced my decision. We know now he escaped with the help of Silumi. More than likely with the help of Ikateq as well. I knew I couldn't have this madman on the loose with a gun. He'd have killed you for sure. Almost certainly he'd have killed others.'

Lars looked at him again, as if daring him to speak. Harry maintained his silence, aghast at what he was hearing.

'I knew you could handle a gun better than any of us, Lars continued. 'This was one of the reasons I wanted you to come with me to hunt Nanoq. You knew you were the one who had to do it, in spite of the act you went through before coming along. I'm only glad you were the one who pulled the trigger on Nanoq. I could never have killed an innocent man, mad or not.

'Yes; Nanoq was blameless, except for helping you with the body. Anyway, after all I'd done to protect you, the least you could do was go after Nanoq with me. This was only right: you were content to let him take the blame for the murder, so you should be the one to make sure your secret died with him.'

This was a nightmare. Harry couldn't remember anything from Saturday night after helping Nanoq back to his cabin. Surely he'd have some kind of recollection of killing Essie? He dredged his memory, but it was as blank as before. Lars seemed utterly convinced of his guilt. And, Nanoq had been certain of what he'd seen, that was clear.

'Listen,' he heard a quaver in his own voice. 'Why should I have killed Essie? What motive would I have had?'

'I don't know. Sexual probably. Frustrated desire, from what I've been able to piece together. Why should I even need to think about it? It doesn't matter much now, does it?. As far as the criminal records go, it will be Nanoq who has killed Essie.'

'Sexual? How can this be? You told me yourself Pesut said Essie was still a virgin.'

'Look, Harry. None of this matters now. Please stop pretending to me. I've had enough. Nanoq will be the one to take the blame for the death of Ms Smith, even if we both know he didn't do it.'

'So, not only does he have to lose his life, but he's to be labelled a murderer into the bargain?'

Lars regarded Harry with surprise.

'Why this sudden attack of conscience?' said the Dane. 'You've been happy enough to let Nanoq take the blame for your crime up until now. It was you who shot him.'

'I told you before, I am not Essie's killer.' He paused, then spoke the words he knew to be inevitable. 'When Knud Holm arrives, I'm going to tell him everything I can. Everything I knew before and the things you've told me now. It's not right to let Nanoq take the blame. If I really killed her, I should answer for it. But I still don't see that –'

'Suit yourself, Harry, suit yourself,' Lars interrupted. 'I've done all I can for you. Much more than I should have, even as a friend.'

Then he paused. For a second his whole demeanour changed. His mask slipped.

'Harry, I did it for you. Don't you see that?'

'But I don't understand...'

'Perhaps you never will, truly.'

Lars held his gaze for a long moment and then slipped the mask back on. Now he was the efficient tour-guide and part-time policeman again.

'You won't have long to wait before you speak to Knud,' he continued. 'I heard from Ammassalik shortly before we came away. The weather is at last clearing enough for them to fly a helicopter out. He's expected in Vatsaaq some time this evening. So, come on. Let's get back. We've wasted enough time talking, in feeding this ridiculous charade of yours. We want to be at the settlement before Holm arrives. We can get *him* picked up later.' Lars indicated Nanoq's corpse with a tilt of his head. 'He's served your purpose.'

Harry looked back at the boat covering Nanoq's body. Whatever the truth of Saturday night, there could be no denying he was responsible for this death.

Lars turned and started climbing the slope back towards the path. It was all Harry could do to keep pace with him over the rough ground. One painful question kept echoing around his head. It was a question to which he could find no answer: what if he *had* murdered Essie in his drunken state during the early hours of Sunday morning?

7.6

They eased themselves down the step-like formation into darkness. Before long they'd reach the gap in the rocks. Waiting there would be the Land Rover to take them back to Vatsaaq and something like a normal world. One where, if he didn't confess to Knud Holm that was, he might continue to be thought of as an ex-policeman on holiday, not as a murderer. Or should that be as a double-murderer?

The pain in Harry's legs had long since given way to a dead numbness. He knew he couldn't walk much further and wasn't ready to face the others, especially Vonnie. An enervating despair came upon him.

'Lars,' he called. 'Ten minutes. Let me rest for ten minutes before we get into the Land Rover. I'm all in.'

'Ten minutes? OK. For old times sake.' Lars laughed mirthlessly. 'For the sake of the few days before Sunday morning when we were friends with no questions asked.'

They sat down on the rock steps. It was a long time before either spoke.

'I wish we were still friends,' Harry said at last.

'Like Olaf is my friend? It might not be to your taste.'

'No, I didn't mean it in that way. Just friends.' For a moment Harry wondered what he'd really meant when he said "just friends". This was a question he knew it wouldn't be wise to consider further.

'We are still friends Harry.' Lars's voice was not much above a whisper. 'Do you think I'd be doing all this for you if we weren't friends?'

'Will you get into trouble for withholding what you believed to be the truth? If I came clean with Knud Holm, I mean.' Harry was alarmed to find himself talking as if he were Essie's murderer. What was the truth? It might be exactly this.

'There will be some trouble, maybe. But, if you think about it, perhaps there will be not too much. You killed Nanoq in our self-defence; this is the truth and nobody will be able to argue with it. Olaf and others will be ready to swear they saw Nanoq with Ms Smith on Saturday night. We can be sure he was the one who disposed of the body. I can tell Knud Holm that only when we were out hunting Nanoq did I become suspicious of you.' He looked hard at Harry. 'Look, my friend – I still call you my friend – are you quite sure you do not want Nanoq to take the blame? He is dead now; it will be all the same to him.'

'Not if he didn't do it. It won't be all the same at all,' said Harry. Nanoq was lying back there with a hole in his skull because of this mess. Wasn't that bad enough? Did the Inuit's name have to be forever blackened as well? He wanted to tell Lars he had no reason to doubt himself, but he was weary of protesting his innocence. Anyway, could he now be sure of anything? The blank in his memory from the time he'd staggered drunkenly with Nanoq back to his cabin had become a frighteningly solid object in his mind.

'Shall we go Harry?' said Lars.

'Another five minutes. Please. I need to get more of my strength back.' A thought occurred to him. 'Lars, aren't you afraid to leave a gun in the hands of a killer?' he said, brandishing the Vapensmia.

'What am I supposed to do? Take it off you? You're bigger and stronger than me. And you're better with guns. Besides, what would you gain by killing me? What would you do then – hide out in Tanu? The winter will be upon us in a matter of weeks. The weather would kill you even if Olaf and Knud didn't do it first.' He chuckled. 'No, Harry. Don't be silly. I know you won't kill me. Come, let's go.'

Harry smiled grimly. He didn't want to tell the Dane he had been seriously considering using the gun. Not on Lars, but on himself.

*

Vatsaaq appeared to be deserted when they arrived in the Land Rover. Even the Inuit settlement was devoid of people. For a moment, Harry wondered, with a pounding heart, whether Nanoq had somehow contrived to double-back to the unsuspecting Greenland Party before he and Lars had managed to catch up with him. As Harry was thinking this they saw, to his great relief, the whole tourist group trooping out of the Great Hall in a line to meet them. Gudrun was at its head. She had a determined look on her face and had almost comically slung one of the BSA rifles across her shoulder.

'Have you found Nanoq?' she asked, as soon as they approached near enough.

'Yes, we found him. He won't be bothering anyone now,' Lars said. Harry was grateful the Dane hadn't been more explicit. 'Where's Olaf?' Lars asked Gudrun.

'Gone,' she said. 'He and his brother left soon after you did. We don't know where they went. They spoke to nobody after telling me, almost as an afterthought, that Nanoq was on the loose.'

She glanced anxiously at Harry.

'Christian told me Nanoq had already attacked Mr Lanier. I feared for the rest of us after I heard this.'

Lars looked shocked at the news about Olaf. For his own part, Harry wasn't in the least surprised to learn that the blond Dane had taken flight, nor that his brother had gone with him.

'Have you heard anything further from Ammassalik?' Lars asked.

'Yes we have. Knud Holm will be here in about two hours, at around six o'clock. He and his team will be taking Ms Smith's body back with them to Ammassalik. They might be doing this as soon as tomorrow, from what I've been told. Then they'll be taking it onward – either to Nuuk or Kaupmannahöfn – there's some dispute as to which, I believe – for the full post-mortem.' Harry couldn't help noticing she used the Icelandic name for the capital city of Denmark; not the Danish 'København'.

'Then I suggest we all go back to our own cabins and get some rest before Knud arrives and – Madam Vonnie –'

'Yes?' she said. It was the first word Vonnie had uttered since their return.

'Harry has endured a harder day than any of us. Be kind to him. Unfortunately, Knud Holm will need to speak to him this evening, straight after I have made my own report. But until that time ... spoil him. He hasn't had anything to eat all day. And Harry,' he added. 'Don't think too hard about what you're going to say to Knud. Get some rest and have something to eat. You know what else you should do. I won't say more.'

Lars gently touched Harry on the back. Vonnie came forward and warmly put her arms around him.

'My husband is wonderful,' she said. 'Gudrun told us he must have volunteered to go with Lars. She saw them drive off together. So brave!'

Harry shook his head, saying nothing. He didn't feel one bit like a hero.

*

A half-hour later Harry had still spoken hardly a word to Vonnie. Despite the fact that he'd had next to nothing to eat in the last twenty-four hours, the sick feeling in the pit of his stomach prevented him from doing more than toy with the food Vonnie prepared.

'Why don't you try to sleep for an hour before you have to see that Danish detective? Lars suggested as much,' she said. 'You must be dog tired.'

Harry was exhausted. Did dogs get this tired? His limbs were aching and sore. But his mind was still swirling with endless questions. What was he going to say to Knud Holm? The truth? What was the truth? He'd certainly killed Nanoq. Had he killed Essie, too?

'Vonnie,' he murmured. 'I killed a man today.'

She looked at him, concern etched on her features.

'I guessed as much, Harry. But I'm sure you and Lars wouldn't have done it unless you'd been in real danger. Don't think too much about it. You can talk later. You need to rest now.'

Would there ever be a time when he'd be able to tell Vonnie what had happened? Even now, he couldn't bring himself to tell her it had been a bullet fired from the gun he'd carried that ended Nanoq's life. Lars hadn't even put a finger on the trigger of his own gun, let alone fired it. Still less could he tell her that he might be the one who'd killed Essie.

Lars and Nanoq had been certain he was the murderer. He suddenly realised the Vapensmia was still leaning against his chair. Had Lars left it with him deliberately? What had the Dane meant when he'd said "*you know what else you should do. I won't say more*"? Did he expect Harry to end his own life? Should this be the way for this awful week to end? There would be some poetic justice to it. Three deaths. In desperation he cast about for something – anything – to say to Vonnie to steer his thoughts away from this idea.

'Tell me about your day, Vonnie.'

'My day? I've spent the most boring day of my life. You really don't want to hear about it.'

'Tell me anyway. It might send me to sleep.'

'There's so little to say. When you, Lars and Olaf went off, Gudrun panicked a bit. We can hardly blame her. She realised all at once we were alone in Vatsaaq, with Nanoq on the loose. We couldn't even trust Silumi and Ikateq.

'So, she herded us all into the Great Hall and went to get a rifle from Lars' cabin. She had to break into the chest to get it. Poor Gudrun – she was more scared than any of us. But I'll say this for her – she kind of "stood guard" all day long. Every so often she even went outside, alone, to scout around. That took guts when she was so frightened herself.'

Harry pictured Gudrun marching up and down with the BSA Martini across her shoulder. Despite the way he felt he laughed gently. Vonnie looked at him questioningly, but said nothing.

'It doesn't sound such a bad time you've had, Vonnie,' he managed at last to say.

'Well, you try it for a whole day and see if you like it. There wasn't much in the way of food in the Great Hall. Plenty of it, yes, but there was nothing but black bread and slices of salmon. We've all got so sick of salmon and cod on this holiday. Gudrun wouldn't hear of it when Jeremy and Freddie offered to fetch some other stuff from the stores. She wouldn't go herself, either – said she didn't want to go away and leave us more than she had to in case Nanoq was watching from somewhere nearby. But he couldn't have been, could he?'

Harry said nothing. He wasn't going to tell Vonnie the full story of Nanoq's death. Not today. If he'd ever be able do it.

'So, what did you do all day in between the black bread and salmon sandwiches?' he asked, more to change the subject than because he wanted to know.

'We talked. It was funny really. There was a kind of segregation of the sexes. Freddie, Jeremy, Anthony and Mel were at one end of the hall, near the door. I felt really sorry for Jeremy. I could see he was barely joining in the conversations with the other three. You could hardly blame him.

'Dainty, Maggie and I sat at the other end, with Gudrun putting in an appearance when she thought her guard duties could spare her. This wasn't often, I'll say that for her. I tell you, Harry, I wished Gudrun had brought another gun so I could have joined in on her patrols. Or I might have pointed it at Dainty and Maggie and told them to shut up.'

Harry smiled thinly. 'Dainty and Maggie aren't that bad, are they?'

'Well, I may be exaggerating. But Dainty can get very wearing after a few hours. I didn't really want to talk. After all, my husband was outside on some crazy adventure, you know.' She gripped his elbow and shook his arm. They both tried to smile. 'And Maggie didn't seem to want to talk at all. Now and again she'd interject with one of her sarky remarks. You know her. But most of the time she seemed happy to let Dainty and me to make all the running. Oh – that reminds me. She did say one thing I remember. It would've made you sit up and pay attention a few days ago. I was pretty taken aback myself, I can tell you.'

'And what was that?' Harry prompted her.

'Maggie mentioned, quite casually, she'd been out in the small hours of Sunday morning. She'd been running at about two o'clock, would you believe?'

Two o'clock. Harry hadn't followed up the earlier revelation from Mel. So much had happened since.

'She hadn't been by herself, either, from all the broad hints she was giving,' continued Vonnie. 'Two o'clock was around the time poor Essie Smith… Harry, where do you think you're going? And what are you doing with the gun?'

7.7

Harry's fist pounded on the Walters' cabin door. Vonnie ran up behind him.

'What do you think you're up to, Harry? Have you lost your senses?'

He ignored his wife and hammered again. It was a few moments before the door was opened by a dishevelled Mel Walters. His shirt-sleeves were undone, his hair unkempt and his eyes puffy. He'd clearly been asleep.

'What the Devil's going on here?' he said. He looked down. 'That's a gun you've got!'

'Yes it is. It's a Norwegian Army rifle. And I know exactly how to use it. Don't worry; I don't plan to fire it – yet. I want to talk to Maggie.'

'Well, you can't.' Mel was white and shaking, but stood his ground. 'Not while you're holding a gun. Maggie's having a nap right now.'

'Harry, please. Why won't you tell me what's going on?' said Vonnie from behind him. 'This is insane.'

'I can't explain yet, love. I will very soon.' He raised the rifle and looked at Mel. 'Look, I haven't got time to waste. Get me Maggie.'

At that moment, Maggie appeared in the doorway, peering over Mel's shoulder. At first her eyes opened wide with alarm when she saw the Vapensmia, but her expression changed to one of wry amusement

'Well, what's this variety performance about?' she said.

'Maggie, tell all of us about last Saturday night,' demanded Harry.

'So you're back to that "where were you on the night of the twenty-eighth of August" stuff again, eh? I thought we'd all had enough of that. Even you must be tired of it by now.'

'Shut up Maggie,' said Mel. 'Can't you see he means business? Whatever that business is...'

'Aye, you're damn stupid, Harry Lanier. At least stop waving that bloody weapon around on our doorstep and get yourself in here.' She looked dismissively down at the rifle. Then, quite calmly, she turned around and walked back into the interior.

Maggie had recovered her composure very quickly. She assumed charge of the situation, leading the other three into the main room of the cabin as if she were hosting a social evening. Harry was beginning to feel foolish about his dramatic outburst. But he wanted some answers.

'Tell everyone about your night-time run on Saturday, Maggie,' he said, as soon as they'd entered the room.

'Now, Harry,' she said. 'You'll give us a chance to settle ourselves down before you start, won't you? There are only three seats, so I'll perch myself on this table. You OK with this chair, Vonnie? And stop waving that damn' gun around, man. We're not going anywhere.'

She made elaborate play of seeing everyone was sitting comfortably. To judge by their expressions, Mel and Vonnie were perplexed by the scene unfolding before them. Harry was itching to speak, although now was less sure of what he wanted to say. He put the gun down carefully.

'Right. That's a bit more civilised,' said Maggie. 'Well, Harry, you already know most of this already. Mel and I left you drunken oafs in the Great Hall at about ten o'clock. We came back to our cabin for some sanity. I was reading one of my running magazines and Mel was reading a novel or something dull like that. I fell asleep in that chair – the one you're sitting in now, Harry – quite soon afterward. The trouble was, when we turned in about an hour later, I couldn't sleep. I've already told you I'm not a very good sleeper. So, after a while, I decided to go outside for a spot of running. There's nothing unusual in that – I've been out late many other times on this holiday. I ran all the way out to the Kungmuit Rock. Then I ran back. That's it. End of story.'

'And what time was this?' asked Harry.

'I don't wear a watch when I'm running. Sometimes I take my stop watch with me. But not on Saturday night. I didn't bother.'

'It was around half-past-two when you came back, Maggie,' said Harry.

'Well, what difference does it make? Were you boys following me? Running after the little Lady with the Blankets? Or what's the other name they call her? Wanted a lie down and some comfort did you? Well, Harry, you'd have been too drunk to be of any use to me.'

'No. Mel told me where you'd been,' said Harry, dismissing her provocation and trying not to look in Vonnie's direction.

Maggie shot a hostile glance at her husband. She curled her lip as she spoke again.

'Ah, so you boys have been talking about Maggie's doings, have you?'

'Maggie, did you see anyone else outside?' asked Harry, trying to sound more patient than he was feeling.

'You seem to know all there is to know already. You tell me.'

Vonnie was looking anxiously from one face to the other as if she wanted to say something, but didn't know what.

'Look, Harry.' Mel could keep silent no longer.'Don't you think this business has gone far enough?' said Mel. 'That big Eskimo killed poor Essie Smith. Why can't we leave it there now? All this raking things over is getting us nowhere and making us bad friends.'

'Mel, we can't "leave it there now" because "that big Eskimo" is lying dead under his boat. And I killed him.' The three others in the room looked in surprise at Harry. 'That's right, Vonnie. Me. Your Harry. Not Lars and I. It was me. My bullet shattered his skull. Lars didn't even pull the trigger of his own gun. He didn't even bloody well take aim. I think I might be able live with the knowledge of what I've done if I knew the truth. But I'm no nearer to it now than I was on Sunday morning. In fact I seem to be further away. I haven't got a clue who killed Essie Smith. It might have been me.'

'Oh, love. Don't say that,' said Vonnie.

'I'm saying it with good reason. Lars thinks it was me. And so did Nanoq. Now, are you going to tell us what you know, Maggie? Help me find a way out of this torment, please. I'm begging you.'

Maggie looked down without speaking. She remained silent for a long moment. The stares of the others were all upon her.

'If you know anything that might help Harry you should tell him, Maggie,' said Mel. 'Tell him everything.'

'Everything? Right. I'll tell all of you everything.'

She looked at the worried faces of Vonnie and Mel. She didn't meet Harry's eyes.

'I saw someone. A friend of mine.' Her expression remained defiant but there was a tremor in her voice as she continued. 'That's right. A male friend. I've got a few of those, haven't I Harry? Ah, don't you pretend to look so shocked, Mel. You've known it too well for years.'

Mel blinked hard but said nothing.

'Anyway, there I was running back from the Kungmuit Rock when I saw him. Sitting there on the ground he was with his head in his hands. So I thought I'd cheer him up by giving him some special attention. But the daft bugger didn't want to know again. What kind of man is that?'

'Who was it?' said Harry. 'Say his name.'

'You know very well who it was. It was Jeremy Smith.'

'Jeremy Smith? Essie's brother?' said Vonnie.

'Ah, he's not her brother. That's what he told that nosey old bat Dainty Clatworthy to shut her up. Then she told all of you, and you believed it, like the daft sods you are. Jeremy never mentioned being her brother again but he told me the truth. He probably told Lars, too, for all I know. If he knows what's good for him, he'll surely have to tell the full-time policeman when he gets here. Jeremy had the same surname as Miss Big Boobies. That's all there is to it. The man was no more than what you'd call "an admirer" of the fat cow. "An admirer". Huh. He'd been following her around like a panting dog for years. What sort o' man is that?'

'Maggie,' said Mel. 'Don't say such things. Essie Smith is dead.'

Maggie sneered.

'Well, it's true. Our Jeremy has been following her around the world for the last six years. All she's given him in return is a feel of those big groodies. He didn't even get so much as that on this holiday. They had some sort of row back in Iceland and that was the end of the sports for our boy. I offered to be nice to him – he'd have had more than a quick feel of my titties, I can tell you – but he didn't want to know. Bastard. Bastard. The things some o' you men will do for a pair of fat udders, eh, Harry?' She tried to smile defiantly, but couldn't prevent her lower lip from trembling.

Harry noticed the desperate look on the face of Mel Waters. But he had no time to be sympathetic. He rose to his feet, picking up the Vapensmia NM149s.

'Where do you think you're off to with that gun?' said Vonnie.

'You know very well where I'm going. I'm going to see Jeremy Smith.'

'I thought so,' she said. 'And I'm going with you.'

7.8

This time it was Vonnie's fist pounding on a cabin door.

She stopped her hammering for a moment and turned to her husband. 'For God's sake put that damned rifle down, Harry. Go and lean it against the side of the cabin or something.'

'This is an expensive weapon, Vonnie. I shouldn't simply leave it lying around.'

'Look, you're in enough trouble as it is. Do it. Let me handle this.' Harry did as he was instructed and Vonnie resumed her impatient thumping. Eventually, the door was peeped opened a fraction. One of Jeremy's eyes was visible in the interior gloom.

'Yes?' he said.

'We need to talk to you Mr Smith,' said Vonnie. She said it in a way that meant she didn't intend to be contradicted.

'Can't it wait? Now is not the most convenient time for me. Perhaps you could come back tomorrow?'

'No, it can't wait. We need to talk to you this minute.' Her voice was calm and level, but Harry could sense the steely determination lying behind it. Jeremy Smith would be aware of this, too.

Grudgingly, the door was eased open a few more inches. Harry could see that Jeremy had set his mouth in a firm line that would have deterred most people.

'Yes? I really do hope this won't take long,' he said.

'We hope not, too, Mr Smith. It would be better if we could come into your cabin to talk properly. There are some things that shouldn't be spoken about on the front doorstep.'

'I was about to take a shower. It would be better if we did this tomorrow, you know.'

Vonnie's voice remained calm and steady. She could have been in a shop, dealing with a tiresome customer.

'We need to talk to you about Essie, Mr Smith,' said Vonnie. 'Please don't waste our time. Open the door properly and let us in.'

'My sister? I'm sorry. I don't want to talk about her with comparative strangers. It's still distressing to me. You must understand this. I'm sorry.'

'She wasn't your sister, Mr Smith. We know that all too well.' His face dropped at those words. The carefully-assumed veneer of a reasonable man disturbed and annoyed by an unwanted caller disappeared in an instant. But he regained enough of his composure to reply.

'Look. I have no reason to talk to you. You're not a member of the police. Neither is your husband, no matter what he seems to think. I've already spoken to Mr Erikssen and I'll be speaking briefly to the full-time policeman when he gets here. I understand he'll be here shortly. So, go away. Go away now.'

Vonnie turned to Harry. 'Mr Smith wants us to go. I thought he'd be more sensible. It seems your way is going to be the right way, after all. Get the gun Harry.' Harry looked at his wife in astonishment. 'Yes. Get the gun I said.'

The rifle was not far away. Harry had only leaned it against the side wall. He returned quickly with the weapon slung under his arm, pointing it squarely at Jeremy's chest.

'Now you're being ridiculous,' Jeremy Smith said. But he was shaking as he said it.

'I've already killed one person,' said Harry quietly, taking his cue from Vonnie. 'Some people think it's two. I could easily make it two . I'm sick of all this. I'm at the end of my tether. Now, are you going to let us in? Or do I have to fire this thing? A gun like this will make a big hole in you at close range.' He advanced a pace. Jeremy stepped back.

'I honestly don't know what this is all about,' Smith blustered. 'You'd better come in and I'll talk to you for no more than one minute.' He stepped back into the cabin and looked at Vonnie. 'I must say I've found your husband's psychology more than a little strange but, really, I am most surprised at you Mrs Lanier. Isn't this indulging his whims a bit too far?'

Vonnie winked at Harry as they followed Jeremy inside. She seemed to be enjoying this moment.

'You'd best sit down,' said Jeremy Smith, indicating the soft chairs and taking an awkward seat on the wooden one. He was still trying, unsuccessfully, to maintain some sort of dignity. 'Please stop pointing the rifle in my direction, Mr Lanier. It might go off if you're not careful.'

'You keep it pointed exactly where it is, Harry. I don't trust this man,' said Vonnie, still standing. 'Mr Smith, I'm not going to ask you where you were on Saturday night. We know exactly where you were. Maggie and Mel Walters have already told us everything.'

'Maggie Walters? That Scottish tart? She was out running on Saturday night. That's what she told me, at least. What did Mel Walters have to say?'

'I told you. Everything. He saw everything' said Vonnie confidently. 'He didn't want to say anything to Lars

Erikssen because he didn't want to get his wife – the Scottish tart, remember? – into trouble. What we still don't know is, why did you kill Essie? And why did you let that innocent Inuit take the blame? My husband – my poor husband – has been through Hell on Earth this week. And I've had to stand by and watch him walking through the flames.'

Harry looked anxiously at Vonnie. Was she pushing this bluff too far? Mel Walters hadn't told them anything. He hadn't been able to tell them anything – he'd seen nothing apart from a person, some heavily-built man, he'd said, carrying what could only have been Essie's body into the trailer. That was probably Nanoq, not Jeremy Smith. And Mel had less than brilliant eyesight. He couldn't be absolutely sure of what he'd seen.

All they really had to go on was what Maggie had said. They knew Jeremy was there at the crucial time. But so, too, was Nanoq. Jeremy Smith's face was impassive, giving nothing away.

'All right Vonnie. I can see we're wasting our time here,' Harry said. 'Mr Smith will deny everything even in the face of what Mel and Maggie have told us.'

Harry watched Vonnie's eyes widening at his bluff, but pressed on.

' He'll even try to deny it when the full-time policeman reads him the confession Nanoq made to Lars and me this afternoon.'

Harry's anxiety level rose another notch. He was desperately fighting off the exhaustion, now really grinding him down after the longest day of his life. Had his own bluff made things worse? Surely Jeremy would demand to know why Lars wasn't the one asking these questions. Why should Vonnie and Harry be doing it?

His invention on the spur of the moment had no more foundation than Vonnie's. Far from listening to Nanoq's supposed confession, Lars had been only too keen to see the Inuit take the blame. In Lars' case this had been motivated by a misguided attempt to protect Harry. There was a long silence, then Jeremy looked down on the floor. His expression changed.

'All right Harry.' Smith seemed to crumple . 'The last thing I wanted was for you to get mixed up in this mess. But you insisted on letting yourself get dragged in.' He sighed. 'You don't know what it's been like since I met Essie, following her about the world, hoping things would somehow change and we could at last have an adult relationship.

'But you can hardly say Nanoq was an innocent party. When I found that Essie had... had casually given herself to him after me wasting years of my life for nothing, my blood boiled over. I waited for her to come back from the cabin so I could tackle her and...' He shuddered. 'There were rocks on the ground and I didn't know what I was doing. I only wanted to have it out with her.'

Smith was white and shaking. He looked to be barely aware of the others in the room.

'Something snapped. Next thing I saw her lying on the ground before me. That's the way it was, I swear. I still can't believe I did it.'

Now he'd begun to talk, it seemed he couldn't stop.

'Then I had the idea of getting Nanoq to dispose of the body. So I rushed back to my own cabin to get all the cash I could put my hands on, then went to his own. The door was half open. I didn't even have to knock.'

They could see he was reliving that night.

'He was asleep face down on the bed but I shook him awake. I thought he was going to tear me apart until he saw the money I was offering. It was probably more than he'd ever seen in his life.

'I managed to get him outside and make him understand what I wanted. As soon as he got the message, he picked up Essie's body to carry it to the vehicle. Then I thought of something else.'

He lowered his head and was silent for a second.

'I stopped him… made him wait. I wanted to get her clothes off. Then I burnt them.

'Why?' Harry stared at Jeremy. 'Why?'

'I can't really say why. Except... she was wearing that red coat. She knew I liked it. It was the one I bought for her fortieth birthday. Now I hated it. Hated it. I tore it off. Soon, I was in a kind of frenzy, grabbing, tearing. I couldn't stop until she was naked.'

Vonnie sat down heavily in the chair behind her,

'It felt like a cleansing, burning her clothes. There was some poetic justice, the fire and seeing her corpse being carried off by the Inuit who'd violated her. I was surprised when he ran back to his cabin to get a piece of sacking to wrap her body in. This after he'd drunkenly enjoyed her!'

Jeremy stopped speaking. He took a deep breath. Harry could see he was back there in his mind.

'I didn't see what happened after he carried her away.' Smith raised his head and looked at them. 'I know it sounds callous but I went back to bed. You see, I thought it would be better if I left the scene. You must understand...'

He spread his hands in mute appeal. Neither Harry nor Vonnie said anything but Harry lowered the Vapensmia slightly. After a moment, Smith started to speak again.

'It was only later I found out Nanoq had been blamed for Essie's death. I didn't plan it that way. I didn't plan anything at all but,

when I thought about it, it did seem right after what he'd done.'

He sighed.

'That's it; that's the whole story. Or it would've been if Nanoq hadn't then got you and me confused. What's that joke – we all look the same to them? Ha bloody ha. He was convinced you were me.'

'*Do we really look that alike?*' thought Harry. He was going to speak but Smith rushed on.

'And then you and Lars found Essie's body next morning. That's a twist of fate if there ever was one. I'm sorry Harry. I'm really sorry. In a way I'm relieved it's all over now. But if you've been through Hell for the last five days, let me tell you I've been living in the place for what seems a lifetime.'

'It's Essie you should be saying sorry to,' said Harry, quietly. 'She didn't "give herself to that Inuit". She died a virgin. And you should think of Nanoq. He also died because of you. There are two deaths on your hands. And I've got a gun right here in my own hands, right now.'

He raised the rifle again and pointed it steadily at Jeremy Smith's head.

'Harry! No!' Vonnie sprang from her chair.

Harry kept it for a long minute. Then he lowered it again.

'It's all right, love. I wasn't going to shoot. I'm no murderer, or at least I didn't mean to be one. But I wanted to see one sweat.'

At that moment there was a series of loud thumps on the door. Lars burst in, a frown creasing his brow.

'Madam Vonnie? Harry? What is going on? Mrs Walters ran over to my cabin to tell me you were in some kind of confrontation with Mr Smith. She told me I should get over here. She also said I should bring my rifle. But I didn't want to carry a gun. So, what's wrong? What's happening?'

'Nothing. Nothing at all,' said Vonnie. 'It's all over. Lars, Mr Smith has some things he wants to tell you.'

7.9

Harry and Vonnie were late for the six-thirty meeting Lars' had called with the party. They'd almost decided not to come at all. Approaching the Great Hall, they met the Dane. He'd obviously planned to be the last to arrive. His face fell briefly when he saw them coming toward him but he quickly rearranged his features. For the first time that day his faced showed fatigue.

'Harry, Madame Vonnie. I didn't get the chance before. I'm so pleased to have this opportunity to thank –'

'Gratitude is not something we want,' interrupted Harry. 'It's thanks to me that Nanoq is lying out there now. Have you brought his body back?'

'Silumi and Ikateq will be going out for him as soon as I relieve them of guard duty on the winter storeroom. I'll do that when I finish here.' He looked hard at Harry. 'We'd never have found the real killer without –'

'Shall we just get on with it?' said Vonnie. 'What do you plan to do, anyway?'

'Only to make a short statement to the others,' said Lars. 'I think Icesperience owes them that much. They're planning some sort of compensation package for you all, I understand. Gudrun should have the full details tomorrow.'

'By the way,' Harry said. 'This is yours.' He took from his pocket the small silver flask.

'No. No.' Lars shook his head. 'You keep it, Harry. You keep it as a gift from me.'

'I think not,' Harry said, placing it firmly into the Dane's hand. Then he guided Vonnie purposefully towards the door of the Great Hall, leaving Lars where he stood.

*

Inside, there was a hushed stillness. Mel had his arm around Maggie, who seemed uncharacteristically subdued. Dainty perched on the edge of her seat, eyes darting about. Anthony Ferris sat stiffly, staring ahead. Freddie was crumpled in a heap, looking ready to burst into tears. Harry and Vonnie found two chairs and sat close together, their shoulders touching.

It was some minutes before Lars entered. Gudrun, looking anxious, rose to her feet as soon as she saw him and waved him over.

Lars stood before the tourists and spoke swiftly and quietly. His tones were flat, nothing like his performance on Monday.

'Ladies and gentlemen,' he said. 'Thank you for coming together at such short notice. I felt I owed it to you to say something this evening. As you will have learned, the true killer of Ms Smith has been found. Mr Jeremy Smith has signed a confession and is safely under lock and key. Mr Knud Holm will be here very shortly and will take charge. There is no more to say, except that I would like to –'

Harry's chair scraped noisily on the floor as he pushed it back, stood and walked quickly towards the door. No-one said anything.

*

Vonnie joined Harry outside.

'Where did you go?' she asked.

'Nowhere. Nothing. Nothing important. What did he say after I left?'

'Lars? Not much. Said he'd need to go back with Knud Holm, so sorry about our holiday but we'd be in Gudrun's capable hands. Then he suddenly sat down. I'm sure he intended to say more. Gudrun was expecting him to say something else, that's for sure. Anyway, she stood up and started to talk as best she could about what was going to happen to the holiday and something about this compensation package they're dreaming11 up. She's still talking in there now.'

'Look,' said Harry, pointing at the sky. 'There, to the south, in the distance. It must be Knud Holm's helicopter.'

Vonnie shielded her eyes and squinted upwards.

'Well,' she said. 'He's a bit late. It will be good to see what the mysterious Mr Holm looks like, if nothing else.'

'Perhaps he'll be taking Jeremy back with him this evening,' said Harry.

'There's no reason why not. After all, other people have been doing his job for him over the last few days.'

Harry looked at Vonnie.

'Bournemouth next year, then?

'Let's wait and see,' she said.

Recently by Tom East:

The Eve of St Eligius

Coming Soon:

Tommy's War: July 1914

Printed in Great Britain
by Amazon

11871646R00176